Picara

Pat MacEnulty

To Craig & Heather! Great writers — Enjoy your life together. Lots of love, Pat MacEnulty 12-20-09

Livingston Press
The University of West Alabama

Typesetting and page layout: Joe Taylor
Proofreading: Margaret Walburn, Emily Mills, Valisha Fincher,
Heather Love, Connie James, Jill Harris
Cover design and layout: Jennifer Brown
Cover photo: Lily Schorr, (Model: Megan Ruckman)

This is a work of fiction.
Surely you know the rest: any resemblance
to persons living or dead is coincidental.

Livingston Press is part of The University of West Alabama,
and thereby has non-profit status.
Donations are tax-deductible:
brothers and sisters, we need 'em.

first edition
6 5 4 3 3 2 1

The stream we gazed on then, rolled by;
Its waves are unreturning;
  But we yet stand
  In a lone land,
Like tombs to mark the memory
Of hopes and fears, which fade and flee
  In the light of life's dim morning.

- Percy Bysshe Shelley

***

From *Webster's New Universal Unabridged Dictionary*—
Picara: n. a female picaro.
Picaro: n. a rogue or vagabond.

In memory of my Godmother,
Elise Hallowes,
who exemplified grace and elegance
in everything she did

and
for Celina

Picara

1

Mattie, my grandfather's second wife, spirited me away from my alcoholic mother before I was two years old. The story Mattie told me was that Marguerite (my mother) was living in a two-bedroom trailer on the outskirts of town and that she, Mattie that is, stopped by one day to check up on me after my dad and my mom had split up. Mattie found my mother sprawled on the couch wearing high heels and a black slip with an empty Jack Daniels bottle tucked in the crook of her arm, and me trapped and crying in a playpen, wearing nothing but a dirty diaper. Mattie took me away that day, and then sometime after that—the details get fuzzy—my mother got on a Greyhound bus and never came back. My dad, like some sort of pioneer, lit out for the West shortly after she left. Grandaddy died of a stroke when I was five so that left me and Mattie and Miz Johnny, a maid whose family had been interlinked with mine since the days of slavery—not one of us related by blood but bound together nonetheless—in a big brick house in Augusta, Georgia, a few blocks from the Savannah River.

My dad, Willie Burnes, never made it as far as the West Coast. He settled in a town called Webster Groves, Missouri, and became a DJ in St. Louis. He came to visit us for Christmas and sometimes during the summer. Eventually he brought pregnant Cleo with him and they were married. But we never saw or heard from my mother; they assumed she had died. Neither Mattie nor Miz Johnny ever mentioned her. And who was I to miss a person I couldn't remember? Especially when I had Mattie and Miz Johnny to take care of me. Mattie spoiled me, and Miz Johnny disciplined me when she could catch me.

After Grandaddy died, Mattie devoted her life to two things: me and the Southern Opera Guild, the old theater downtown that Grandaddy had given to Mattie in order to entice her in to marrying him. While other kids were home at night watching *Bonanza*, I was at the Southern Opera Guild. For hours I played dress up in elaborate costumes or had swordfights with imaginary enemies in the rehearsal room. During performances I would turn pages for the pianist or sit in the lighting booth and read cues for the spotlight man. When rehearsals ran late, I would sleep backstage on the spare sets while the sound of arias shrouded me like a dream.

When we weren't at the opera, I had free reign to come and go. I rode the streets of Augusta on my bike and imagined I was a gunslinger on a stallion that no one but me could ride. I didn't have many friends, but I didn't need them. I peopled my world with characters from my imagination. And it always felt as though Mattie's friends were my friends. I considered myself a small adult, and I think they considered themselves large children so I guess we met somewhere in between. Our house was the central location for evening parties where they sang around the Steinway that Carl played with a cigarette in his mouth, a highball glass on a stack of sheet music. I usually stretched out underneath the piano with my marbles or plastic horses and created stories till I fell asleep.

Then when I was twelve I met a girl named Gretchen, who had miraculously moved from half-way across the world with her German father and American mother. Gretchen had an older sister named Lana, who brought all things bad with her, and an older brother named Wolfgang, an aloof philosophical boy with shaggy hair and bushy eyebrows, a boy who made me go mad with love the first time I saw him.

Beyond the borders of our small town, all kinds of things were going on. Rock music had conquered the world, guys in puffy white suits were jumping on the moon, a crazy man shot down Bobby

Kennedy and another loonie gunned down Martin Luther King, Jr. After both killings the house on The Hill went into mourning, though I didn't understand why we cried over the deaths of men we had never met. There were riots and revolutions and hippies and Woodstock and all kinds of things the good citizens of Augusta, Georgia, tried to ignore, but the world would not be ignored. It was slouching toward us inexorably and arrived in a rain of smoke and ash in May, 1970. But it was not the brutal race riot that ended my perfect childhood. My perfect childhood dissolved a few months earlier when something growing inside Mattie suddenly emerged and stole the life out of her. I was fourteen years old.

***

As I stood shrouded in the darkness backstage, watching Mattie sink to her knees in the bright spotlight and collapse in a pile of pink silk, I was not thinking of death or even of opera. Around her the singers mourned and the tenor bellowed "Mimi" in a crescendo of notes. But my mind easily transposed the scene and instead of Mimi and her Bohemian friends, I was the one sinking to the ground, gazing into the greenish-brown eyes of Wolfgang, who had finally realized how much he loved me. He was bending down ever so slowly to kiss me.

At that moment the curtain closed for the final time and the performers came rushing off stage, and Fallene, the contralto, was saying to Mattie, "No one dies as brilliantly as you do, Mathilda."

Then Mattie stood in front of me, her eyes sparkling full of spotlights, her hands clasping mine.

"How did you like the performance, precious?" As if the applause wasn't enough. It never was. She always needed my approval. I always gave it. I may have become a teenager without either of us expecting it, but still I adored her.

"Brilliant," I said, stealing Fallene's word because I hadn't fully collected myself back out of Wolfgang's arms. Then as reality came into focus, I added my favorite word of the moment, "Phenomenal."

Mattie smiled with relief as if she'd feared I might suddenly say that she was awful and she should never show her face on a stage again. She kissed the air beside my ear as her cheek brushed against mine. "Come help me out of this straightjacket."

Just like that I was once again Mattie's little helper. I followed her back to the dressing room where the other women were already stripping out of their long dresses and holding the hair off the backs of their necks, standing in front of a large revolving fan. "Jesus, it's hot out there," one of them said.

We weaved through the other women to Mattie's dressing table in the back. Lightbulbs shone from the sides and top of the mirror, and Mattie sat down to wipe off her pancake make-up with a tissue smeared with cold cream. I helped her take off the blond cascading wig and then placed it on the styrofoam head with its crayoned blue eyes. When I was little, I grew quite attached to that head and named her Dilly. For one solid year when I was six, I dragged Dilly around with me and explained to people that she was a queen and I was her butler.

The women's voices in the dressing room climbed over each other in that after-show mix of hilarity, exhaustion and yearning for it not to end quite yet. The thing they felt was almost palpable. And I knew they'd all head somewhere to unwind. Usually, the unwinding happened at our house where Miz Johnny would have left plates full of little sandwiches and the bar would be stocked, the Steinway freshly tuned, its ivory keys waiting for Carl to sit down and dance his fingers over them.

"You know I could never play Mimi in New York at my age," Mattie said to no one in particular, "and yet I don't think I've ever done her better."

"It just goes to show you," Fallene called from her vanity nearby. "Age gives us the experience to bring depth to a role."

"You're right," Mattie said, wiping the tissue across her eyelids.

"But I don't need to grow another second older, thank you. I've got enough bloody experience."

Fallene laughed. When they were together, they obsessed about their ages. Mattie swore she'd go home and jump off the London Bridge if she had to grow old and feeble with her hips breaking and her skin sagging to the ground the way her grandmother had. Mattie had left England at the age of nineteen, but it was still "home" to her and she made a point of keeping her fancy-sounding accent intact.

Louise came trundling over. She and her husband Max, a postman, were in all of Mattie's operas. Louise usually played some minor role, and Max, an enormously fat man, always played the lead tenor in spite of his bulk because he had as good a voice as you could find on the entire continent, Mattie always said, perpetually astounded that Max was just a postman in Augusta, Georgia. *Who would have dreamed?*

"Are we going to your house, Mathilda?" Louise asked.

"Of course," Mattie said. "Too bad there aren't any good pubs in this town."

"It depends what you mean by good," Fallene said.

"A classy piano bar like we had in New York is what I mean," Mattie said.

She stood up and tried to unzip herself. I took the zipper from her fingers and pulled down.

"Thank you, precious," she said. She pulled the dress from her shoulders and I started to turn away to go outside and buy a bottle of coke from the machine in the hallway with the nickel in my pocket. Even then a drink for a nickel was a novelty. But as I was turning, Mattie bent forward sharply. She gasped, and a wave of terror washed over me.

"Mattie?" I asked, wheeling back toward her. "Are you all right?"

She looked up and our eyes met in the mirror. I noticed sweat against her hairline. Her gray eyes looked startled.

"What is it?" I asked.

She held onto the chair in front of her and grimaced.

"I just had the worst pain."

"Is it gas?" Fallene asked.

Mattie straightened up slowly and let the dress fall to the floor. She was wearing a bra underneath and a half-slip.

"And look how fat I am," she muttered. "I couldn't even put on a girdle earlier."

Fallene stood up. We both stared at Mattie's abdomen bulging beneath her white nylon slip.

"I think you should see a doctor," Fallene said.

Mattie went to the doctor on Monday while I was at school. Usually, I would bike over to the park after school with Gretchen and we would go to our favorite hideout—a bridge over the canal that we could hide under and try French inhaling Winston cigarettes stolen from Gretchen's mother. Later we would go buy a grape Nehi and some bubble gum and we'd run the younger kids off the jungle gym so we could climb on top of the bars and watch the boys doing whatever stupid things they had thought of doing that day.

But on that Monday I went straight home. We lived in a big two-storey brick house with dormer windows and a large porch. The lawn was wild and weedy because Mattie didn't care about such things. She said what happened inside a house was more important than how it looked outside. So the screen door needed painting, and one of the shutters on the living room window hung by one hinge. Miz Johnny did all she could to keep the spider webs off the porch, but otherwise the exterior of our house was left to its own devices.

I leapt up the stone steps and went inside. I'd been worried earlier that day, but sometime during lunch when I had gone off to the restroom by myself, as I sat in the stall taking a small moment of privacy, I seemed to hear a voice inside my head. A voice in your head should say something good. It should be an angel's voice telling you that everything is going to be fine, but this voice was not angelic. The only thing I can say for sure is that it had no doubts. It said simply,

"This is it. Curtain call." And a strange certainty filled me that left no room for fear or worry. I knew that whatever was wrong with Mattie was deadly serious. It's an odd thing, this knowing. It seems to seep into your skin, sinking down through your fat, your muscles, your minuscule nerves, your blood tunnels and into the marrow of your bones. I'd never felt anything like it before.

Mattie was sitting in the sun room with a cup of tea, reading the newspaper when I walked in. She looked up at me. Her pale eyebrows rose and fell. She seemed to be mustering up a comforting lie, but then she didn't have the heart to tell it. Instead she let her eyes fall; her shoulders hunched forward as if she were hiding something. I pulled a wicker chair up next to her, took her hand and nestled my face against her body.

We stayed like that until Miz Johnny called us in for dinner.

Spring came. The azaleas had a brawl of color in our yard. The dogwood turned snowy white, and forsythia wands of gold waved their spells. While the earth obliviously burst forth in a fountain of color, the news on our old black & white TV set was mostly bad: Some anti-war activists blew themselves to pieces in New York City, The Beatles broke up, and four college students were killed in Ohio by National Guardsmen. Each of these events occasioned a call from my father, whose life seemed to revolve around such atrocities. We never said a word about what Mattie had or how long she had to live. I kept going to school, and Mattie planned next year's opera season, and Miz Johnny cleaned and cooked and tried her damnedest not to show undue tenderness to Mattie.

2

I knew Mattie was dying but I knew it in a clinical sort of way. Not in the heart-crushing, hot-coal-in-the-belly way I would later feel when it actually happened, a feeling that drove me away from everything I had known, including my own father.

As I lay in my bed night after night, I began to wonder what would happen to me after Mattie's death. Since my dad had new children, I wasn't sure if he wanted me. Whenever he came to visit us, he was always affectionate with me but sometimes I felt as if he were playing a role that he didn't quite fit, like happened sometimes in Mattie's operas when Max, the fat postman with the amazing voice, had to play a handsome young lover.

In my room on my antique dresser I kept a "treasure box," an old cigar box that I decorated in the fourth grade with rhinestones and paint. This box had things I thought I should keep forever: some silver spoons with a great-grandmother's initials, a little gold cross Miz Johnny had given me, a pencil once owned by Wolfgang, an old daguerrotype of some ancestor from before the Civil War, a few of my favorite marbles from childhood and the only picture I had of my mother, Marguerite. The photo was a black and white picture of her and my dad, standing by a long sleek car. I was not born when this picture was taken. My mother was not smiling in the picture. I could see that her hair was dark and thick. But I could not, of course, see the color of her eyes. My father—a younger version of him than the one I had last seen—stared at her in the picture and she stared at the camera.

I always thought she was looking at the future, looking at me.

One night I pulled out the picture to stare at it. What had happened to her, I wondered. What if she wasn't dead? Would she, I wondered, take me in? What if I showed up at her door, if she had a door, and said, "Hi, I'm your kid."

No one ever spoke about my mother, and I felt that somehow it would hurt Mattie if I asked about her, that it would make Mattie feel I wasn't happy or that I didn't love her.

The only mention of my mother that I could remember had happened when I was around nine or ten at one of Mattie's parties.

"Go get dressed," Miz Johnny said after I had set the table. The smell of ham studded with cloves filled the whole house and caused my stomach to whine.

I put on a dress for the dinner party because Mattie always insisted that I look "elegant" as if that were even possible. My dress for tonight was black velvet and had white pearls sewn onto the neckline. They weren't real pearls, not like the ones Mattie wore, the ones she had promised she would give me when I turned eighteen. I didn't mind getting dressed up for the annual end-of-the-opera-season dinner party—a party for just the select few who worked with her all year round to produce the operas and keep the Southern Opera Guild running. Mattie's regular parties were larger and did not involve dinner. Instead Miz Johnny made platters of finger foods that would be gobbled by the guests in between songs. But tonight we would have a full course meal, and then her friends would sing their favorite arias and be their own audience.

The first guests rang the bell; I opened the door for Edward and Lawrence, two of Mattie's "dearest" friends who were invited to our house for almost any occasion. Edward produced most of Mattie's operas. Lawrence played first violin in the orchestra. They lived together in a house with red paintings of nude men on the walls, and fake leopard-skin furniture. Edward was tall and black-eyed and not particularly nice to me, which never bothered me. Lawrence was soft and pudgy and I loved the way he would stop and smile and really see me every time he came over. And he would always say something that I didn't quite understand but which sounded like a compliment.

Tonight when he came in, he stopped and stared at the purple bruise on my face that I'd gotten from a fight earlier with a kid named Marvin.

"Oh, my goodness, have you been roustabouting? Are you trying to get a match with Cassius Clay?" he asked.

I didn't know much about boxing, but even I knew who Cassius Clay was.

"No," I answered. "I'm satisfied kicking asses around here."

Lawrence burst out laughing. Just then Mattie stood at the top of the stairs. She wore a red dress and black high heels and her hair was pinned in a French twist.

"Oh, you're here," Mattie called out as if they were the two most important people who had ever lived.

"Ravishing!" Lawrence said. "You are ravishing."

Mattie floated down the stairs and asked, "What are you drinking?"

"Martinis as dry as the desert," black-eyed Edward answered, stopping to kiss her on the cheek.

She led them into the living room where there was a bar and the Steinway and the chandelier that Mattie loved. It was where the party would move after dinner, where they would sing songs and laugh and drink though hardly anyone ever got drunk, except Mattie's friend Fallene who got "tipsy." Mattie said you couldn't make good music if you were drunk.

Then the doorbell rang and I answered it again. Carl stood at the door, holding some flowers. They weren't roses. They looked like something he had picked from the side of the road.

He handed them to me and said, "Good evening, Eli."

"What are these?" I asked. "They look like poison weeds to me."

Carl grinned but Lawrence, who had come back into the foyer, grabbed Carl's arm and said to him, "Careful, she's got a killer right hook."

"Does she?" Carl asked and turned to look at me.

I stuck out my tongue and went to the kitchen with the flowers.

"Edward, Lawrence and Carl are here," I announced to Miz Johnny. Miz Johnny wiped her forehead and scrunched her face.

"Well, one man outta three ain't a bad start," she muttered. I had only just learned about "queers," but I had known Edward and Lawrence since before memory so they seemed about as normal as anyone else to me.

"Who else's coming?" she asked. "She said to cook for eight."

I shrugged. The doorbell rang again.

By dinnertime, which was eight o'clock, everyone had arrived. In addition to Carl, Mattie's accompanist, and Lawrence and Edward, Max and Louise had arrived. Last came Fallene, who had been married four times and laughed a lot and cried a lot and drank a lot.

"I wish I had a little girl," Fallene said to me whenever she'd had a couple of drinks. "But I got boys. Two boys and they both hate me. I hate them, too." Which was a lie. She managed to bring up their wondrous accomplishments regularly enough, and I heard her tell Louise that she didn't like girls because girls were sneaky.

Miz Johnny served the dinner, which was ham, broccoli, potatoes au gratin, fresh rolls and green-bean salad.

"Good heavens, look at the copious amounts of food on this table," Lawrence said with wide eyes. "Miz Johnny, you are a veritable culinary genius."

Miz Johnny said thank you, but didn't waste time reveling in their compliments. She would hustle back to the kitchen to make sure the lemon meringue pie wasn't burning.

When we needed something, more water or some dishes taken away, Mattie would push the little buzzer under the Oriental rug with her foot, and Miz Johnny would miraculously appear. Miz Johnny never bossed us around during the dinner parties, but if she noticed Fallene going for the wine decanter a third or fourth time, she simply whisked it off the table and said the coffee was ready.

Before the pie arrived, Louise turned to me. She had bright bottle-red hair and was wide-bodied with thick lips and several chins.

"You know, you have an odd name, Eli. Isn't that a boy's name? Shouldn't it be Ellie?"

There was no better way to get me in a rage than to call me Ellie, but since technically she hadn't called me Ellie, I couldn't do much.

"But that's very Southern, to give a girl some family name that sounds like a man's," Fallene said. "My name has been in the family for six generations. It's a way to subvert the patriarchy."

"Her name is Elisa, but she's always been called Eli," Mattie said, "which is a pity because Elisa is a beautiful name. However, Will Junior wanted her called Eli, and so that's what we call her."

That night after the lemon meringue pie and the coffee, of which I was allowed my own demitasse with lots of cream and sugar, the guests all went to the living room. I helped Miz Johnny clear off the table. Then she was left to clean the kitchen, and I felt bad for her, but would not stay to help. I wanted to be in the big room where they were singing and telling stories. Besides, Miz Johnny said I got underfoot like a calico cat.

When I came in, Lawrence poured me a glass of sherry, which I hated but which I pretended to drink. Soon Carl was at the piano and Mattie was crooning "Summertime." Carl had a trim little beard and serious brown eyes. He was Mattie's pet and had gotten involved in the opera when he was a piano student at the local university. Now he was a teacher during the day at the same university and a musician by night—sometimes for Mattie's operas; other times he might play jazz at one of the hotel bars. He came over almost every Friday and Saturday night after the opera rehearsals or after one of his "gigs" and sat in the big living room with Mattie and talked till the dream hours of the morning. Occasionally he'd show up with some other musicians and the house would shiver with sound.

After a while, I fell asleep under the piano on some cushions. I could sleep through anything. Usually Carl would pick me up and carry me to bed before he left.

But this night I woke up before he had left. I don't know what woke me up, maybe it was a crick in my neck from sleeping on the floor or maybe it was the fact that no one was singing. Instead I heard the murmur of voices. I cracked my eyes open and recognized Carl's black shoes and brown pants legs. I saw Mattie's black heels, one leg crossed over the other. I could smell Carl's cigarette, and Fallene's red shoes were on the floor empty, so she must have *had her feet curled up on the couch underneath her.*

"What's bothering you, Mathilda?"

"Someone apparently called Eli's mother a quote nigger-loving whore. I wish she didn't have to hear things like that. It's distasteful."

"That's why she was fighting," Lawrence said, perceptively enough.

"A whore?" Carl asked.

"Well, she was a tramp," Mattie said.

"But a pretty one," Fallene interrupted.

"Yes, she was attractive, enough so that she got men into trouble," Mattie said. "Including my stepson."

"And you never got men in trouble?" Fallene asked.

"Not like that." Mattie's foot kicked out. "All three of them could have been killed."

Killed? Did she mean me, too, I wondered.

"Do you ever hear anything from her?" Fallene asked.

"Of course not," Mattie said. "She's probably dead. Otherwise, we would have heard something. A request for money if nothing else."

Probably dead, Mattie had said. Not definitely dead. Maybe alive. Maybe sober. But who could I ask? There was no one willing to talk to me about it.

To our complete surprise, one day we received a call from Willie. He was coming through Augusta on his way to Washington for a protest against the Vietnam War. He hadn't been to see us the previous Christmas. One of his kids was sick, and Cleo was tired, and he didn't have any money. Those were his excuses. I pretended not to be disappointed. I wasn't even sure whether or not he knew Mattie was sick.

He was dropped off at the house by a couple of guys who drove away in a black Chevy. I stood shyly on the porch as he came up the walkway. His hair had gotten even longer than it was the last time I saw him, and now in addition to the mustache, he had a copper colored beard. When he saw me, he picked me up and tried to twirl me around the way he did when I was little, but I pulled out of his arms. I wasn't a little kid anymore.

"You're too heavy to pick up," he said, covering up his embarrassment.

"I'm fourteen," I said. "Almost fifteen."

"Yeah, I know, but it's surprising, that's all," he answered.

When we went inside, Mattie's eyebrows arched.

"You look like one of those young people on TV who are always marching on Washington for one reason or another," Mattie said.

Willie nodded. "That would be me. We'll keep it peaceful though. Not like Chicago. This war has got to stop, Mattie."

"I quite agree," she said. Mattie and my dad were always oddly formal with each other. "But don't march in Augusta, please, Willie. They aren't very open minded around here."

"Don't worry. I'm just here to visit with you and Eli for the night," Willie said.

Miz Johnny made a steak in Willie's honor, and we ate in the dining room with her hovering over him. He kept glancing over at me. I had gotten taller. I felt ungainly and ugly and wished I could have remained a kid for my whole life. Willie didn't say much. He seemed to be trying to get used to the teenage me. Without the boys and Cleo around to distract him, he had to figure out who I was.

"How about we go bowling tonight?" he asked.

I shrugged. When I was little, bowling was a ritual part of each visit, and I had loved it. It didn't seem to matter so much anymore. But an hour later we were at the bowling alley with the sound of the heavy balls rolling along the smooth floor and clattering against pins a constant background noise. A group of high school guys kept looking at us. I could tell they were trying to think of something to say about Willie's long hair and the Rolling Stones t-shirt he was wearing. We had a few "freaks" in Augusta, but you didn't seem them in bowling alleys. Then the guy who owned the bowling alley came over and gave Willie a bear hug.

"Willie! You look like a damn hippie!" he said with a laugh. He glanced in my direction and apologized. Personally, I liked the look my dad had acquired, and I envied him for being out in "the world" while I stagnated in Augusta, an old maid of town if there ever was one. The high school boys lost interest in my dad after it was evident he had an ally in the alley.

I was a terrible bowler, and my balls gravitated to the gutter as soon as they left my fingers. I lost both games.

After we left the bowling alley, we drove back into town and took the road along the river. Willlie pulled into a little park and we got out of the car. On nearly every visit we tried to take a walk along the river. This time we found a spot on the concrete bank and let our feet dangle inches over the water.

"You can never step in the same river twice," Willie said. He had a can of beer that he'd bought at the bowling alley and he took a final sip before crushing the can.

That made no sense to me and I said so.

"The water is always changing," he explained. "Look at it running past you. It's never the same river."

"Oh," I said and thought that perhaps after the water had gone to the ocean or the gulf or wherever it went and evaporated and then became clouds which could be blown back over the source of the river where they would rain and become river again and if you stepped in it at the exact time it was coming past . . . but I knew he was right. Those waters would have dispersed and mixed with other waters. Even in the clouds they'd get mixed up. It was never the same river.

I looked up at the stars twinkling above like so many cheap rhinestones.

"Maybe some time you can come stay with me and Cleo and the boys," Willie said.

"Maybe," I said with a shrug. Did he know that Mattie was sick? We weren't telling anyone. I don't know why Mattie was keeping it such a secret, but if she hadn't told him, I wasn't going to.

"Hey, Eli, has Mattie talked to you about sex?" Willie asked suddenly as if just realizing some parental duty he had neglected in his annual visits. I wasn't about to tell him I hadn't even started having periods yet.

"Damn, Willie," I answered. "I've grown up on opera. And it's all about sex. And whatever they left out, Gretchen's older sister explained to us in gory details two years ago."

"Oh. Well, I just don't want you to make a mistake," he said. The water rustled around restlessly below us and the sky felt like heavy wool.

"Like you did? I was a mistake, wasn't I?"

He shrugged and then cleared his throat, before saying, "We didn't expect you, no. But I'm not sorry you were born, baby. Some mistakes are good." He had turned to face me, his head tilted as if maybe he could slide his words into my brain and I would believe them.

I didn't ask him why had he left me. I didn't want it to seem like I was unhappy. Things were what they were. He put his hand over mine on the cracked concrete. It felt warm and big.

"Willie, where is my mother?" I asked. "Is she dead?"

He lifted his hand off mine and tugged at a piece of grass behind him.

"I don't know where she is, Eli," he said. "I don't want to know. And you don't want to know either."

The next morning I found Willie in the kitchen boiling some water.

"What are you doing?"

"We're gonna pierce your ears," he said.

I immediately clapped my hands to my ear lobes.

"Does it hurt?" I asked.

"Not much," he said. He took a metal ice cube tray from the freezer, pulled up the handle, cracking the cubes free, and dumped them into the sink. Taking one of the cubes, he told me to hold it to my ear.

"But it's cold," I said, placing it to my ear. I sat down on the wooden stool by the green linoleum counter. The sunlight was searching the room like it always did in the morning. I smelled coffee and the pine cleaner that Miz Johnny used on the counters and the floor. "Have you ever done this before?"

"No, but I watched Cleo do it at a festival," he said. "It's easy."

After my earlobe was frozen, he poked a hole through it with a needle he had sterilized in the boiling water. He was right, it didn't hurt. The freezing hurt much worse. Then we did the other ear.

"Better put these earrings in now, and you've got to get some hydrogen peroxide to keep them clean." He pulled a little box out of pocket and opened it. Inside was a pair of cameo earrings. I thought they were beautiful.

A car horn honked outside. Willie kissed my forehead and said "I'll see you later."

"Willie," I said. I was about to tell him about Mattie. Then the horn honked again.

"What, baby?"

"Nothing. I'll see you later," I said.

The house had felt different with my dad in it. Now he was gone again. I kept touching my earlobes with the cameo earrings in them. At least he left me something.

3

Miz Johnny had never worked for us on Sundays. Over the years if Mattie had a Saturday night party, Mattie and I cleaned up the house when we got up on Sunday. Then on Monday Miz Johnny would criticize everything we had done, in spite of the fact she was happy not to have to dump out all those lead crystal ashtrays filled with smelly cigarette butts or wash out the gin and the bourbon from the tumblers scattered on coasters in the living room.

But things had changed with Mattie's illness. Since *La Boheme* closed, even the small gatherings had ceased. Carl or Fallene would often come over at night and recline in the living room, smoking cigarettes and talking away, pretending nothing was wrong, until Mattie would finally say, "Dear, it's getting late. Hadn't you better go home and get your beauty rest?"

It used to be that Mattie would stay up till 2 or 3 in the morning. Now she rarely let them stay past 10:30 or 11. They never said a word about her being ill. But they never left without kissing her cheek.

Even though Miz Johnny didn't have to be at the house with us on weekends, she came by on Saturdays and Sundays to make sure Mattie was eating something. On the Sunday after the four college students were shot to death in Ohio, Miz Johnny came over to the house still wearing her Sunday church dress. It was a bright yellow dress with a matching pillbox hat and a little half veil over her eyes and a patent leather handbag dangling from her arm. She looked as pretty as a canary to me, and I told her so.

"Hush," she said, dropping her purse on the kitchen table where I was sitting, drinking a cup of coffee. She took off her hat and said, "Come upstairs. I need to talk to you and Miz Mattie. She up?"

"Yes ma'am," I said. "I was just fixing to bring her a cup of coffee."

"Well, come on," Miz Johnny said, climbing the steps slowly to Mattie's room. When we got in the room, Mattie smiled at Miz Johnny. She seemed to be feeling stronger today as she sat up in bed.

"Have you come to visit me, Miz Johnny?" Mattie said, teasing, but then she noticed the distracted way that Miz Johnny plunked herself into the armchair by the window. Outside I'd hung a birdfeeder so that Mattie could watch the birds if she woke up while I was at school. A cardinal was outside the window tossing seeds everywhere.

"Miz Johnny, is everything all right?"

"No'm," Miz Johnny said. "It's not."

I set the cup and saucer down on the table by Mattie's bed and scooted onto the end of the bed. We waited for Miz Johnny to say what was on her mind, and a feeling of dread mixed with curiosity sat heavy on my tongue.

"You know that boy that died in jail last week? That boy Charles Oatman?"

"Yes," Mattie said. "It was in the paper."

Miz Johnny nodded. "His grandma is a good friend of mine. We been knowing each other since we were little girls."

Then she sighed and looked out the window.

"What about him, Miz Johnny?" Mattie asked softly.

"They took the body to Cary's funeral home to fix him for the viewing."

Miz Johnny stopped talking again. She seemed to be trying to collect herself, but it wasn't easy. We waited silently. Mattie's hands were clasped and her forehead furrowed. Outside the window a mockingbird and a blue jay squabbled over the bird feeder.

"Somebody beat that boy to death. Somebody burned him with

cigarettes on his buttocks. Somebody burned him with cigarettes on his arms and legs and his back. They stabbed him with forks and lashed him across his back. Charles was slow. He wasn't quite right in the head. And he was a little thing, not more than a hundred pounds soaking wet. Don't know what he was doing in that jail with grown men," Miz Johnny said, shaking her head. Then she looked at us and her eyes were dark as the bottom of the river. "First the sheriff said he fell out the bunk and hit his head. Then they say that the other men in the jailhouse killed him over a card game."

"Oh, how awful," Mattie said. "How awful."

My heart beat like a little tin drum. A boy, a black boy, had been tortured in my town and beaten to death.

Miz Johnny looked at me.

"There's going to be a demonstration tomorrow, so you can't go to school. Matter fact, I don't want you leaving this house till I say so, you understand me?"

I nodded. She rose from the chair where she had been sitting. If she had once been our maid, she was now the pillar of our small family. Her mouth was set in a tight grimace, and the gray hairs in the neat braids that circled her head gleamed like a silver crown.

***

When I woke up on Monday morning, Miz Johnny was already at the house. I had just come out of the bathroom when I saw her coming up the steps. She reached the top of the steps and stood for a moment, framed by the window at the back of the house. She opened the window to the fresh morning air. A breeze wafted in and shafts of light poked through the forest of trees in the backyard. Birds clamored for attention.

Miz Johnny opened the door to Mattie's room and went inside. I followed her. She gently shook Mattie. Mattie woke up easily and sat up in her bed.

"Miz Mattie, I can't stay today," she said.

"That's all right, Miz Johnny," she said. "You take care of your business. We'll be fine. I feel good this morning."

"Okay. I made those English biscuits you like and tea and there's plenty soup in the fridge," Miz Johnny said. "I don't want either of you going out today, hear?"

"We hear you," Mattie said.

Miz Johnny gave me one of her famous looks that said, you better do what I tell you if you know what's good for you, and patted Mattie on the hand before she left the room.

I caught up with her in the kitchen as she was gathering her purse. Miz Johnny was distracted. I knew she was worried about the demonstration. But in spite of all the bad things in the news, it was impossible for me to imagine our little town in danger.

"Miz Johnny, what's going to happen today?" I asked.

"People're going downtown to try to find out what happened to that boy," she said. "They're mad as hornets."

"Is it only because of what happened to Charles?" I asked.

"That's part of it. But not all. These young people today want to be treated better. They want to be treated like white people."

"But," I said, confused. "Colored kids have been coming to white schools and theaters and restaurants now for a few years. Augusta is integrated, Miz Johnny. I don't understand why they're mad."

"You wouldn't," she said, turning to face me. "When my boys were growing up, they went to Miz Lucy Laney's school. Haines Academy. They got a good education there. Not just book learning, she taught them to be young men. They learned about respect and dignity. Miz Laney cared about them children. And they are both successful men." She shook her head angrily. "You can keep your integration if this is all the good it's gonna do. It's taken away our pride. Now we aren't separate and we're not equal either."

I wanted to say, "Miz Johnny, it's not my fault." But I couldn't help feeling that somehow it was. And I guess I knew what she meant about the schools. I saw how the black kids in my classes sat to themselves and the teachers hardly ever called on them. And no one crossed those invisible lines that said who could live where in our town. Everyone knew their place and kept to it. Maybe folks were tired of keeping to their places.

After Miz Johnny left, Mattie came downstairs and had breakfast with me.

"I'm feeling much better today," she said.

Mattie settled down with a book in the sun room, which was just off the living room at the back of the house. I, on the other hand, felt restless. I wondered if I was the only kid who didn't go to school that day. I wandered around the big quiet house. When I came by the sun room, I saw that Mattie had fallen asleep and her book was resting on her lap.

Finally about noon the phone rang and I grabbed it quickly.

"Eli, want to go see what's happening?" Gretchen asked.

"I can't leave," I said.

"You can. Just tell Mattie you're coming over here to my house," she said. "Wolfgang has got the keys to my mom's car. We can go see what's going on." She had said the magic word: Wolfgang. I couldn't say no.

***

Fifteen minutes later I was waiting on the corner of our deserted street when Wolfgang and Gretchen appeared in their mom's Falcon. I dove into the back seat and Wolfgang headed toward Broad Street.

"Wolfie knows a guy who lives down there by Green's."

Green's was the department store on Broad Street. It was where black people had staged a sit-in a few years back. That was when there were still restrooms and water fountains that were marked "colored only" but I could barely remember that time. As we drove down those ordinary streets, I noticed the white flowered dogwoods waving their spindly branches. We didn't see much in the way of human activity until we got near the municipal building and we looked down a side street. Then we saw what looked like thousands of black folks converging on Greene Street. None of us said a word.

Wolfgang parked the car, and the three of us got out and started cautiously walking toward the crowd. It was like a magnet pulling us. We were three white kids. Maybe they wouldn't want us at their demonstration, but that didn't stop us from wandering along the side street to where they had gathered.

"Holy shit," Gretchen whispered when we got to the back of the crowd. A thin young woman with the heels of her shoes crumpled under her feet turned and looked at us suspiciously but most folks directed their attention toward the building where a tall man stood on the steps and talked to the crowd through a bullhorn. It was hard to understand what he was saying.

"They better get out here and tell us something real," a guy with a thick 'fro said in a disgusted voice.

I glanced above the crowd. Policemen stood at the windows of the building pointing guns down at the speaker and at people in the crowd. Why did they need guns? Couldn't they just let the people talk? Then the state flag started to flop in the air. A group of people at the bottom of the flagpole were ripping it down. I couldn't see what happened to it, but smoke trailed above the spot and I wondered if they were burning it. Wolfgang tapped me on the shoulder. His thick eyebrows were tight over his eyes.

"We got to get outta here," he said quietly.

I followed him and Gretchen back down the side street. Behind us we heard people shouting, and something loud hit a wall. I turned around to see a garbage can rolling into the street, spilling its contents of papers, cans and chicken bones onto the black tar.

The guy Wolfgang knew lived just a block away right on Broad Street in an upstairs apartment. We walked fast and scared.

"Did you see those pigs with guns?" Gretchen asked as we stepped into the hallway behind Wolfgang. "They want to shoot those people."

"They're just trying to scare them," I said. "You can't shoot unarmed people."

Gretchen looked at me like I was stupid, and I knew it was a stupid thing to say. Four college kids had just been killed. But still, it couldn't happen again. Not here. This was Augusta, city of gentility, famous for Woodrow Wilson and golf courses.

We climbed up the narrow steps to Wolfgang's friend's apartment. I had never been in one of the apartments over the businesses downtown. It belonged to a guy named Pete, who had already graduated from high school. The apartment smelled like fresh paint. The only furniture in the living room was a big unfinished spool table, a couple of bean bag chairs and an RCA color console television squatting on four legs in the corner of the room.

Pete had three beers in his refrigerator. I didn't care for the taste of beer, but today seemed like a good day for beer if I were ever going to drink it, so Gretchen and I said we'd split one.

I had just taken a sip of the harsh yellow brew when we heard a loud crash and then yelling outside in the street. We crowded around the window. Down below people were throwing rocks at plate glass windows and at cars. Garbage cans flew like drunk pigeons and careened off the tops of cars. I couldn't help feeling like I was watching one of Mattie's operas on a very big stage. I expected someone to stop and sing an aria at any moment.

Wolfgang's body next to mine was warm and smelled like cigarettes. Gretchen giggled nervously and turned to me with bug-eyes.

"Do you believe this shit?" she asked.

I shook my head and turned my gaze back to the throngs of people running in all directions, zigzagging along Broad Street. Some of them carried bricks. Others just picked up whatever happened to be available. I watched a boy in blue jeans and a black t-shirt. He looked to be about twelve or thirteen. His arms were wiry and he buzzed around crazily. He had a piece of charred red cloth draped over his chest like a Miss America banner.

"The flag," Wolfgang said.

"What?" I asked.

"He's wearing a piece of the flag," he said.

"I thought they burned it," Gretchen said.

"Not all of it, I guess," I chimed in. The Georgia flag didn't mean a whole lot to me. Mattie and her friends said that our governor, Lester Maddox, was a bonafide bigot.

"The mayor got on the TV last week and said we didn't have no race problems," Pete said with a laugh. "I guess he's eating some roast crow about now."

The boy with the piece of flag looked up, and for a second I glimpsed his face. His eyes were lit with an inward fire. There was something joyous in it.

"Oh shit," Pete said and pointed down the street.

A swarm of people had surrounded a car and began to shake it.

"Is someone inside?" Gretchen asked. We couldn't tell.

"Dang, man, they're going to tump it over," Pete said.

And they did. They tumped that car on its top and it looked like a rolled over bug. I felt a nervous thrill. The excitement of the crowd gripped us. I took a swig of the nasty-tasting beer to try to steady my sizzling nerves. Gretchen pried the can from my hand and drank also.

"Don't get drunk," Wolfgang warned us.

"On one can?" Gretchen scoffed.

I wasn't worried about getting drunk. I felt as if I were in a shower of emotions, each one rushing after the other. I was scared, happy, appalled, worried and ashamed to name just a few. In the corner Pete's television was on with no sound. I occasionally glanced over at it and the effect was surreal as I watched the images of a smiling woman holding a bottle of Ivory dishwashing soap, showing off her young-looking hands, and then turned to see the chaos in the street below. Cars blazed, people ran through the streets carrying clothes, toasters, food and whatever they could get out of the stores, and shards of glass gleamed on the sidewalks.

"We could go get some records, Eli," Gretchen said. "I want the Led Zeppelin album."

"Shut up," Wolfgang said.

"I was just kidding," she answered, chagrined.

In all the excitement I had forgotten about Mattie, but suddenly I felt a tightening in my chest as if my heart were a clenched fist. What if they got to our house? Would she be okay?

"Can we go back home soon?" I asked.

Wolfgang shook his head. "Not for a while."

And so we waited. By late afternoon the rioters had moved to other parts of town, but we were still afraid to leave. We sat at Pete's spool table and watched the news when it came on. Augusta got a brief mention. The governor, they said, would be calling in the National Guardsmen—the same guys who killed those college kids. I didn't know how you were supposed to handle riots and demonstrations, but shooting people didn't seem to be the way to do it. Surely they would not do that again.

I looked over at Gretchen. Her hands were trembling. Wolfgang reached over and placed his own hands on top of hers. He had small hands for a guy but they were beautiful. Mixed into this crazy day was my dumbfounded admiration for everything about him.

"Well, frauleins, now you've seen a real riot," he said.

"I need to get home," I said. "Mattie's going to be worried. And I'm worried about her."

Wolfgang agreed. We stood up. Wolfgang thanked Pete for letting us hang out.

"No problem, man. Anytime the niggers go crazy you can come up here and watch," he said. That was a dangerous word, I thought, and Pete was too stupid to know it even after all we'd seen.

We came out of the doorway onto the sidewalk. The smell of gasoline and smoke hung in the air. The windows of the department store were shattered. A mannequin tilted to her side like a petrified woman, still smiling though the clothes had been ripped off her. I could see a few shadowy figures slowly wandering through the debris inside. I suddenly had a terrified thought. The Opera House! It was only a block away.

I started running down the street. The trees in the park looked steadfastly on.

"Wait, Eli!" Gretchen shouted.

"The Opera House," I said over my shoulder. She and Wolfgang trotted after me.

Panting I stopped short across the street from the old building. Beside it, the ladies' clothing store was nothing but naked mannequins amid piles of clothes and shattered glass. But the Southern Opera Guild stood untouched. In a chair in front sat Curtis, the janitor, wearing his old hat and holding a shotgun across his lap. He lifted a pint bottle to his lips and drank. When he saw me, he raised the bottle as if to say, "Cheers."

"Come on, Eli," Wolfgang said. "We must go."

We walked quickly over the glass, which crunched beneath our feet, to find the car. We all breathed with relief when we saw the old dented Falcon had not been torched.

Wolfgang took a side street to Greene Street. We turned north, and headed back up to the Hill. As the light bled from the sky, we passed random groups of people roaming the street. Wolfgang didn't stop for stop signs, but at one intersection there was a barricade of debris—old couches, pieces of wood and boxes piled up with some teenaged kids tossing gasoline on it and getting ready to light a bonfire.

"I don't like the look of this," I said.

"Me either," Wolfgang agreed.

"Turn around, Wolfie," Gretchen said in a pleading voice. Just then the kids noticed us. They turned as one and grabbed sticks, bats, anything they could find and started running toward us. Wolfgang threw the car in reverse and then turned his head around to look out the back window. He drove backwards fast. A brick flew toward the car and busted out one of the headlights. Wolfgang didn't stop. He backed onto the sidewalk and turned the car in the other direction and hauled ass. We heard something hit the trunk but we kept going.

"Oh, God, Mom is going to kill us," Gretchen said.

"If the rioters don't kill us first," Wolfgang said.

A car in front of us was on fire. Bright yellow like the sun as if Apollo's chariot were an old Chevrolet, the flames swarmed underneath the car and wrapped orange arms around its sides, filling the interior. The smoke that billowed from the flames was thick and black like rubber and seemed too heavy to float into the sky.

The once quiet streets of my town were filled with sounds. Screams, laughter, shouts, glass breaking and then suddenly an explosion about a block away. A building, a gas station, lit up the black sky. I was terrified. All of us were. Even Wolfgang's unflappable exterior was showing cracks.

"What do we do?" Gretchen whimpered. We were stranded down in that part of town that belonged to Augusta's black folks. It was filled with restaurants offering hamburgers for a quarter, fried chicken, sweet potato pie and other things to eat. There was a bank, a theater, a billiards parlor, some nightclubs and a shoe repair shop where Miz Johnny always took our shoes when they needed mending, and outside there was a little stand for shoe shines, where a teenage boy shamed men into getting their shoes shined. I had walked these streets carelessly my whole life, feeling a kinship with the people who worked in the businesses, the lady at the bakery who always gave me a sugar cookie for a cent, the man at the Penny Savings bank who smiled at me and asked if I wanted to open an account when I came in with Miz Johnny to do her errands. This part of town was originally settled by free blacks back in slave days, and Miz Johnny said it was the heart of the city. Now it looked and sounded like a war zone, as if the havoc we were creating in a small country on the other side of the planet had traveled the molten layers of the earth's core and erupted here in the midst of our tranquility.

We'd lost the marauding kids who had chased us with bats and pipes, but we had no idea how to get out of the area. Ahead of us was the burning car, and behind us the crowds ready to set their torches to us. The smell of smoke, of burning tires, lacquered my throat.

Wolfgang looked down the side streets, confused, not knowing which way to go. Gretchen and I were squeezed next to him in the front seat. I chewed my lip, looking for help when suddenly I saw the twin towers of the Tabernacle Baptist Church and I knew that we might be saved though not in the sense that the Baptists usually meant that word.

"Turn down here," I said just as Wolfgang had edged the car forward. He didn't stop to ask me why, just cut the wheel sharply to the right.

"That church," I said. "Go park in the parking lot. Miz Johnny lives about two streets down. We can cut through the yards and get there. The car'll be safe in the church lot."

Wolfgang obviously didn't have a plan of his own, so he crept along the street to the big church. He pulled to the very back of the lot and shut off the car.

"Maybe we should just stay here," Gretchen said.

"We can't," I said. "Someone's gonna see us if we stay here."

From the car we could see flames tearing down the walls of a building down the street. I couldn't even remember what used to be there.

"Okay, then we go," Wolfgang said. "I hope you know where you're going, Eli."

I hoped so, too. I couldn't stop shaking from fear and, yes, from excitement, too. It was like an electric current running through the city and if you got close to it, it leapt inside your skin and jittered your bones. We dashed around the back of the church through the bushes and into a backyard. The house in front of us was dark. A dog in the yard next door started barking at us, but dogs everywhere were barking so we paid it no mind.

"Which way?" Wolfgang whispered.

I wasn't really sure. I knew Miz Johnny's house was either on this street or the next one. We slid along the side of the house and came to the front. We could see the main road from where we were.

"Her house is across the street," I whispered. A car filled with men hanging out of the windows, yelling and throwing bottles, passed along the main street. A siren shrieked. Gretchen and I jumped. Crossing the street seemed perilous. Then we heard them, the crowd running along Gwinnet Street. There were curses and yelling and things banging. We shrank back into the shadows of the house.

"What do we do?" I asked.

"Just wait," Wolfgang muttered.

In a few moments we could see a throng of maybe thirty or forty people running along the street. Some of them carried things they had taken from stores. A few people were just watching with wide eyes. Then there was a scream: "Police coming!" A moment later, we heard the police car squealing down the side street where we were hiding. It pulled to the stop sign and a man got out of the passenger side of the car. The crowd yelled at him from a distance. He lifted a shotgun to his shoulder. Most of the people turned and ran when they saw the gun. Then a flash erupted from the gun. The explosion echoed against the houses and the people ran helter skelter screaming. The sound was terrible. I closed my eyes and felt Gretchen's fingernails digging into my arms and hot tears of fright swelling against my eyelids. When I opened my eyes again, the police car was speeding down the street.

"*Ach du sheisse,*" Wolfgang whispered.

"No, God, no," a man wailed as he stood over a lump in the street. "They killed my brother! God, please, no."

My lungs felt as if they'd been singed and my legs were like noodles. We stood unable to move, unable to breathe, the shock of what had just happened like nails in our hearts.

Then I realized we had to move. We had to forget the lump lying in the street, and we had to get to safety.

"Come on," I said. I ran across the street with Wolfgang and Gretchen following. Instinct took me to Miz Johnny's dark porch. I flew up the porch steps and banged on the door.

"Who's that?" Miz Johnny asked from the other side of the door.

"It's me, Miz Johnny. It's Eli. Let us in. Please let us in."

The door swung open, and Miz Johnny wrapped her fingers around my arm, pulling me inside. Wolfgang and Gretchen stumbled in after me. She slammed the door shut behind us and locked it with a deadbolt.

"What in the name of Jesus are you all doing out in this mess?" she asked. She was close to screaming. I had never before heard her say Jesus' name except after the word "praise." "Eli Burnes, you have pulled some stunts in your time, but this is . . ." She was at a loss for words. She had her hands on her hips and her eyes looked like they were full of jet fuel. "I oughta slap you upside your head."

"I'm sorry, Miz Johnny," I said. "I didn't think we'd get caught in it."

"It's my fault," Wolfgang said. "We wanted to know what was going on."

"Who are you?"

"This is Gretchen's brother, Miz Johnny. We didn't mean to do anything bad," I said.

"You're lucky you ain't dead," she said. "Who's looking after Miz Mattie?"

I looked down at the rag rug on her pristine floor.

"And she sick?" Miz Johnny waited for me to say something. When I didn't, she turned around and went to the kitchen where she had a phone on the wall. She picked it up and started dialing.

"Miz Mattie? You okay?" she asked. "Good. I'm glad you got someone there with you. Eli is over here. Yep. Don't worry. She's okay. I'll take care of her tonight. Yes'm, I heard the governor has called in the National Guard."

After Miz Johnny hung up, she pointed at Wolfgang and said, "You'll sleep on the couch. These two girls can sleep in my boys' old room."

"Is Mattie okay?" I asked guiltily.

"Carl's over there with her. She's all right."

Next Wolfgang called his father and offered some sort of explanation in German. Gretchen shrugged her shoulders. She might get grounded for a week but then it would blow over. I could tell she thought it was worth it. I didn't regret coming out either. This was my city, and in some confused way, these were my people. At least they were now. I knew I could never be on the side of the ones who shot them down.

Wolfgang took off his shoes and stretched out on the couch under an afghan. Gretchen and I got the twin beds where Miz Johnny's sons used to sleep. It took a long time for us to fall asleep but eventually we did, our dreams punctuated by the sound of sirens.

***

When morning arrived, there were state troopers and National Guardsmen stationed at just about every corner. They stood posted by their cars, holding shotguns. The street where the man had been shot the night before was empty. But we stopped and looked at the road. A dark spot like a giant amoeba was all that was left. The air smelled sour with smoke and wet ruins. A firetruck was parked down the street, and we came upon some firemen standing on the broken walls of a still burning building. Their hoses sprayed over the black bricks in a rainbow arch. We drove home silently. A police car passed us, its single red light on top pulsing for no reason. A shotgun hung out the window. It made me feel sick.

Our world was scarred, and we felt a stupefied grief.

Wolfgang pulled in front of my house. My neighborhood didn't look much different. Some trash scattered around the yards, but nothing like what Miz Johnny's neighborhood looked like.

I walked in the house. On the living room couch, Carl slept underneath a quilt. Mattie was in the kitchen, fixing tea.

"How are you feeling?" I asked.

"Better. Are you all right? You know you shouldn't have done that," she said. "If I'd realized where you were I would have been worried to death. I thought you were at Gretchen's."

"I'm sorry," I said. I wanted to talk to her about the man who was killed, but it was so good to see her up and dressed that I didn't want to say anything that might upset her. She seemed unaware of what I had seen and heard.

The news came later that day. Six black men had been killed by police in the riot. Six of them. And lots of people were injured. Two of the dead had been looting. Three were by-standers. No one knew why the sixth one was killed.

4

Gretchen's sister, Lana, struck a match against the brick wall, lit the papery end of the joint and took a long deep hit before passing it on to me. Lana had a sharp face and scornful dark eyes. Her hair was brown and short and greasy but she was pretty in a frightening kind of way. The boys got quiet and furtive when they saw her. She had an effect on them that a girl like me could only dream of. Generally, she ignored them, but if she deigned to laugh at one of their jokes they would become like monkeys vying for her attention. Her laughter was like a drug. And it made sense that she would be the one to introduce Gretchen and me to the "terrible maryjane" that our teachers warned us about.

When that paper burning smell hit my nostrils, I forgot about the woolly feeling of sadness that had been wrapped around my neck for weeks. I inhaled the smoke and tried not to cough before passing the joint to Gretchen's waiting fingers. We were sitting out on the balcony of their apartment with our legs dangling through the iron bars. The summer evening felt dreamy and endless. School was out; the riots were not forgotten but at least they were not part of our every conversation anymore. James Brown had come to town to help restore peace, and it had worked.

Wolfgang came out on the balcony with us.

"You shouldn't be smoking that shit with them," he said to Lana.

"I'm not forcing them," she said in a flat voice. "It's a free fucking country."

Wolfgang was lanky like a scarecrow with dark brown hair. He was only seventeen but seemed smart like a professor. His quietness was like a fire that drew everyone to it. He went back in the house to look after Prissy, the youngest sister, who had just been a toddler when I first met Gretchen. Prissy had some kind of brain damage and she cried a lot.

After we smoked the joint, Gretchen and I got giggly. We had never smoked pot before, and we weren't sure what to expect, so probably we were acting crazier than we felt. Lana stood up and warned us not to fall off the balcony before she slid open the glass door to the apartment and disappeared. Gretchen's apartment was on the third floor. Looking down you could see the big gravel parking lot and trees and old beat up cars.

Gretchen and I suddenly realized our throats were parched and our tongues thick and dusty, so we went inside. Lana looked up from the couch where she was watching TV with Prissy and glared at us. Even high Lana had the temperament of a scorpion. Gretchen said, "She's always on that rag." Of course, Gretchen said "dat" instead of "that."

We went to the room that Gretchen shared with Prissy. In Gretchen's room we sat on the floor, examining Prissy's toys as if it were all stuff we hadn't seen before. In a few minutes we began to play with the teddy bears and stuffed dogs. We put on a fashion show, dressing up the toys in outlandish outfits. Gretchen and I laughed so hard we almost peed on ourselves.

"We got to get more of dat reefer," Gretchen said.

"Where would we get dat?" I asked, having caught her German accent like it was a virus. It wasn't hard for me to acquire and drop accents from sentence to sentence. I had learned from Mattie how to sound like British royalty or Eliza Doolittle. Then there was the deep poetry of Miz Johnny's southern Negro language. I constantly sampled the sounds of words like someone at a buffet who has to try everything.

Gretchen's big jello-y breasts jiggled as she laughed, and normally I would have been envious but everything seemed so silly that I just snickered. Suddenly her little blond-headed sister came in and demanded to know what we were doing. I placed a big purple poodle on my head and twisted my head from side to side, saying in a sing-song voice, "I'm poodler-moodler." This sent Gretchen rolling onto the floor once again. The little girl snatched the purple poodle from me and said we had to leave her stuff alone.

I had no idea what time it was but maybe a half hour maybe an hour later, Gretchen's father stood in the doorway of Gretchen's room and said it was time for me to go home.

"Mrs. Burnes will be worried," he said. "Wolfgang will walk you home." Gretchen's dad had deep downward slanting eyes that always seemed on the verge of tears even though he was in general a cheerful man. He was a mechanic. Mattie took her Bonneville to him whenever it needed an oil change or a tune up.

I got up and left the apartment with Wolfgang. Gretchen waved to me from the balcony as I walked a few paces behind his lanky frame.

"Don't let the boogie man get you!" she yelled down at us. Wolfgang ignored her—and me. I waved my middle finger at her and she waved hers at me. We wanted to be bad kids, Gretchen and I. But it was hard for both of us. Her parents didn't know enough to care what she did, and Mattie—well, she always said you can't rebel against a rebel. I didn't want to think about Mattie, and in fact, I was in no hurry to get home. Since the riots, she slept most of the time. The doctor gave her drugs for pain, and when she tried not to take them she whimpered like a strangled kitten. It was so dreadful to watch, and tonight I had fled to Gretchen's rather than be there for another quiet night as Mattie slept fitfully and Miz Johnny padded around the house, cleaning up for no one.

Wolfgang and I walked away from the apartment building and

down past the elementary school. I thought we would take the streets because it was night but then Wolfgang cut across the street toward the playground. I would never have ventured into the playground at night by myself. I raced to catch up with him. I didn't know what to say to him but he didn't seem to need me to say anything. We cut across the big field of grass. There were plenty of streetlights but when we passed under the trees it was dark. I took a deep breath.

"Isn't this exhilarating?" I asked, trying out this word that felt like marshmallow cream in my mouth.

Wolfgang grunted a short quick laugh.

When we got to the swing set, Wolfgang sat on one of the swings and lit a cigarette. He was way too tall for the swing and his skinny legs stuck out, his big shoes scraping across the dirt. He didn't offer me a cigarette, and I didn't question why we had stopped. It didn't matter. I was still somewhat stoned and lost in this otherworldly feeling. Maybe he had forgotten what we were supposed to be doing. I lay down on one of the rubbery swings on my belly and held my arms out like I was flying. My shadow sailed back and forth underneath me.

I looked over at Wolfgang, and for a moment his glance fell into mine. Then he looked away. Wolfgang was not like any other boy I knew, not that I knew very many very well. He tolerated Gretchen and me. It wasn't that he liked us much, but he didn't hate us either. I sat up in the swing and placed my legs on either side swinging sideways instead of back and forth.

"Wolfgang," I said, "Gretchen has been kissed lots of times."

He looked over at me with his bushy eyebrows slightly arched. "So?"

"I've only been kissed once, and that was by that creep Freddy in the seventh grade and he went and told everyone I was a lousy kisser. Do you think I'm ugly?"

Wolfgang looked down, which only confused me until I realized he was trying to hold in his laughter. Then he cocked his head sideways and said, "Do you want me to kiss you, Eli Burnes? Is that what you want?"

I nodded my head. I did want him to kiss me. I didn't want any of those boys who kissed Gretchen to kiss me. She said Marvin touched her tits, too, but I didn't tell that to Wolfgang.

"You're too short," Wolfgang answered.

I shrugged my shoulders and made circles in the dirt with my sneakers. Wolfgang smoked his cigarette.

"Come on," he said, standing up from the swing. "You need to get home."

I looked up at him.

"I could stand on something," I said.

Wolfgang placed his hands on his hips and rolled his eyes. I got out of the swing and walked over to a railroad tie that bordered the little kids' jungle gym. It raised me about four inches off the ground. Wolfgang came over and stood before me, looking down at my face.

"Boys don't kiss you because they don't understand what the hell you are saying," Wolfgang said. "You scare them."

"They think I'm weird."

"You are weird," he said. "That's okay."

I didn't mention that he was a little weird, too.

Then he put his hands gently around my waist and closed his eyes as his face lowered toward mine. I placed my hands on his arms. I could feel the smooth cotton of his t-shirt under my fingers and decided I'd better close my own eyes. His lips landed on mine like a cloud descending on a mountain. It was that soft. I could taste his mouth and smell the fresh smoke on his skin. Then his tongue glided over my lips and I thought I would fall off the railroad tie. I swear it felt like my bones were vibrating into tiny molecules in my body. If this was what a kiss was supposed to feel like, then what happened when they touched you somewhere else, somewhere underneath your clothes. I wanted to start screaming. I wanted him to keep kissing me. I wanted my lips to catch fire. Then the kiss ended, evaporated, my lips steaming. Wolfgang strolled away towards my house on The

Hill.

I ran to catch up to him. In a few blocks we were there. I had managed not to think about Mattie all night long but I would have to think about her as soon as I got inside and saw her lying sick and spidery in her bed.

"See you later, Eli," Wolfgang said.

"Wait a minute. Am I good? A good kisser, I mean?"

Wolfgang chuckled and said, "Go inside, Eli Burnes, before someone puts me in jail for statutory rape. You're jail bait."

I was pretty sure that a seventeen-year-old boy would not go to jail for kissing a fourteen year old girl. I figured that jail bait was an insult and some sort of compliment at the same time. I also suspected that I would never get kissed by Wolfgang again and that no one would ever believe he'd kissed me. But the fact was that he had kissed me, and no other girl that I knew could say that. And I thought I knew something else—that I was a damn good kisser. Because it didn't really take much except that you like it. And I did. I loved it.

"Good night," I said. "Danke for taking me home."

"Güten nacht."

He walked away. And I looked up at the doorway to the big house where Mattie was lying upstairs in her four-poster bed.

5

When I came inside, the air felt like it was seeping in from another dimension. I slowly climbed the stairs and entered her room. Miz Johnny was lying on the divan, sleeping. I shook her awake; she struggled to a sitting position, placing her hands on her knees.

"Was the doctor here?" I asked.

Miz Johnny nodded. "He give her something for the pain."

"What else did he say?"

"He said, not much longer. That's all. Not much longer. I think she's ready."

I looked over at the bed. How had she managed to fool so many people? She told them she had a virus, she told them any number of tales. But Carl knew, and Fallene had figured it out, too. Still they would not be prepared for this. Mattie's hair was still lustrous and thick, splayed against the white pillowcase. The thick purple quilt covered her body, and the room air conditioner hummed.

I took her hand, afraid of hurting her.

Mattie's eyes fluttered open when I touched her hand. When she saw me, she smiled. I crawled into the bed with her and wrapped my arms around her. She struggled for each breath. I felt a few tears melting along my face, and if her life wasn't flashing before her eyes, it was certainly appearing before mine.

I remembered once when I was about ten after her performance of Aida. Even the big newspaper in Atlanta had written about it— the stunning performance by Mrs. Mathilda Burnes, the former

Metropolitan Opera star who founded the Southern Opera Guild in Augusta, Georgia. "Who would have thought that a world-class soprano could be heard in an outpost such as Augusta" the reviewer had written. "Brava, Mrs. Burnes, Brava."

That morning after we read the review and we were lounging in the dining room, drinking our cups of coffee, I asked her if she ever missed New York.

"Darling, I had my moment. To hang around New York or London or Rome would have simply meant fading away into obscurity. Here I get to do it on my own terms. Here I am a queen, not a courtier."

She shook her auburn hair from her face and gazed at me with her gray eyes and smiled.

"Besides," she said, "if I'd stayed there I wouldn't get to be here with you, would I?"

I got up from my chair and slipped onto her lap where she fussed over me as if I were an oversized cat. I fell into the moment's spell, staring at the roses in a large green vase on the table, the delicate cup with flowers painted on the white china and a gilt handle, feeling the breeze traipsing through the sheer curtains.

Now I was losing her, and it wasn't fair. I wanted to scream at someone, but I didn't. I held it in the way people will hold back a snarling dog when a stranger comes to the front door. I muzzled the anguish in my heart.

"I love you," I whispered. I don't think she could hear me. Something seemed to be pulling up from her chest. Her hand on my back tensed and relaxed. I thought the moment had come but then she settled back into herself. Eventually I fell asleep, and I never knew when the end came. I only knew that when Miz Johnny shook me, Mattie was cold and her face was not one I recognized.

"Eli, Eli, girl, wake up. Miz Mattie has passed. You need to get up. The doctor's coming to write up the death certificate."

I looked at Mattie's motionless form. There was no trace of her there. It was as if a costume, a wig, and a mask were lying in her place. Where did *she* go? That was the first time I realized how you not only see and hear a life but you can feel it against your skin even if they're nowhere near you. Their absence is an even more palpable thing. Standing in Mattie's room with her mirrors, her make up, her perfumes and her closets and bureaus overflowing with clothes I suddenly felt that Mattie's absence was like a hole in reality. And it followed me as I went into the hall and down the stairs.

I wandered blindly into the living room, that absence lagging behind me like a recalcitrant shadow. Standing in the middle of the room on the Persian rug, I gazed up at the enormous portrait of her. She wore her crimson gown, her hair was swept away from her face into some sort of French twist, and her pearls rested on her collarbones and hung just below her long slender neck. Was it possible that someone that gorgeous had come into this sleepy southern town and lit it up like a bright jewel? And that she had loved me?

I glanced at the coffee table littered with programs from years of her operas. Everyone said they were extraordinary, but I hadn't seen any others so I didn't know. All I knew was that Mattie spared no expense. "Break the blooming bank," she used to say. "Do it right or don't do it at all."

I stopped at the Steinway where Mattie sang while Carl accompanied her. I plunked a few notes. I had gotten pretty good at the piano these past few months, but I didn't care much for practicing unless I had a song I especially liked. Now it was over. All over. I fell down on the floor and sobbed, my body shaking hard and uncontrollably. It seemed that I would never stop crying, but eventually the sobs subsided. My nose was full of snot. I found a box of Kleenex on a shelf and blew into a tissue. Then I sat, empty as an old bucket with a hole in the bottom.

Miz Johnny slowly shuffled in the room.

"I called your daddy last night. He should be getting in sometime today. He wants to have the funeral right away."

She picked up a figurine and wiped off the dust.

"He's gonna take you back to St. Louis to live with him," she said.

"Why can't you and I stay here in the house?" I asked.

"They're gonna sell the house, Eli. And I am retiring. I'll miss Miz Mattie, but I'm old, child. I want to stay home and take care of my great-grandbabies and fiddle with my garden."

Miz Johnny had her own life. I should have realized that before now, but I hadn't. I mean, I knew she had two sons that she loved and she had grandchildren who were growing up, but she didn't seem to care that she was leaving me. Miz Johnny had never been one to coddle me. Mattie spoiled me and Miz Johnny administered the discipline. But to me the two of them together had been my world, and now my world was being dismantled like the set after a show was over, flats taken down, furniture returned to wherever it had come from, props stored back in the prop room, the musical instruments packed in their black cases and taken home.

Miz Johnny absently pulled a rag from her pocket and began to wipe down the shelves of the bookcase.

"I don't know what's going to happen to all this stuff," she said.

I looked around. What would happen to it all? Someone comes along and creates such beauty in the world and then they go away and the beautiful things are suddenly just stuff. I wished I could create a museum like they do when really famous people die and you go to visit their houses. I could put velvet ropes at the doorways so people could look in and I would be the guide who explained, "Yes, this is where she had her parties. She stood here by the piano and sang. It wasn't always opera that she sang. Sometimes it was songs from shows. Like 'My Funny Valentine.' 'Stay, funny valentine, stay.' Those are the words. And she'd look right at me when she sang, her voice like a lace ribbon leading you to wherever she wanted to take you." I realized I was getting sentimental. I was afraid that was my great failing in life.

But I was only fourteen and I had just lost the one person I was sure who loved me totally and completely.

"Look here," Miz Johnny said. "Here's that book she loved."

She handed me the broken-backed copy of *Jane Eyre* that I'd read to Mattie at night. She loved to have me read to her. I thumbed through the pages and remembered Mattie saying, "Every family has its secrets, darling. Maybe not a crazy lady in the attic, but secrets all the same." We'd finished the book about a month ago. I sniffed the book as if I could sniff out its secrets. It smelled like rain.

The doorbell rang. It was probably the doctor come to do whatever it is they do with dead bodies. Miz Johnny went to answer it, and I gazed out the window. Dawn was already creeping in among the houses and the garages, stealing over the dogwoods, jostling the birds awake as if were just another day.

6

Mattie's body was taken to the funeral home. The funeral would be the next day. Fallene and Louise and Max had shown up and were sitting desultorily on the claw-footed sofa. Carl moped around, nursing a whiskey and soda on ice that I had fixed for him. Miz Johnny, who had been up most of the night with Mattie, was running around trying to make sure that everyone had plenty to eat and drink. Other people began arriving, bringing ham and potato casseroles. Who was going to eat all that food? As long as I was in this house, I would eat Miz Johnny's food. She answered the door. Edward and Lawrence entered soberly. They were both ashen-faced. Lawrence kissed me on the top of my head, and Edward went immediately to stand before Mattie's portrait.

"Lemme get you something to eat," Miz Johnny said and hustled off to the kitchen. All my life I had seen Miz Johnny work. That's what she did. But today she should be allowed to grieve.

I went up to my room and called downstairs.

"Miz Johnny, I need you. Please come here."

After a few minutes, she came trudging up the stairs, grumbling.

"What is it that a grown girl like you can't do for yourself?" she asked, standing in my doorway.

"Miz Johnny," I said. "Mattie wouldn't want you to wear yourself out. You should rest. Let them take care of themselves for once."

"I can't do that."

"Why not? Slavery has been over and done for about a hundred years. Lie down on my bed and take a nap."

I had never spoken to Miz Johnny like that before, but she didn't get mad. She just shook her head.

"I'm scared to lie down, baby. I'd rather be busy," she said.

In an instant I knew the same thing was true for me. The last thing I wanted was to be alone, trying to go to sleep. So we both went back downstairs and began serving the streams of people who trailed into the house with their sad, curious looks.

***

By early afternoon, the only ones left were Mattie's closest friends—Carl, Fallene, Max, Louise, Edward and Lawrence. Tears fell down Carl's face. I felt sad for him because he had loved her so much and though she cared for him, I don't think she loved him like that. The rest of them didn't have anything to say but they couldn't seem to tear themselves away from the room where they had spent so many hours drinking and singing with Mattie. I was glad for their company. Even Miz Johnny sat down with us, pretending to dust something once in a while as if that way it would be okay. Carl put a hand on her shoulder and asked if he could get her anything. I knew that there was no other living room in Augusta where a black maid could sit among the guests. But then again this was as much Miz Johnny's house as it was anyone else's. She had been here for fifty years at least, working since she was just a little older than me.

A loud bang in the driveway startled us all, and I went to the front porch to see what the noise was. A rusted, falling apart blue pick-up truck that looked like it was older than me sat in the driveway, chugging. It backfired once more before finally shutting off. Willie got out of the truck and came toward the front porch. His hair was so long now he wore it in a ponytail.

"Hey, kid," he said.

"Hey, Willie." I wasn't exactly overjoyed to see him. I hadn't ever thought it bothered me that he wasn't a real dad to me, but that day I couldn't help but feel he was an imposter, someone who had pretended to care about me when it wasn't inconvenient.

He stood next to me and looked down at me as if he didn't know what to do next.

"Rough night?"

"Yep."

"Sorry. Very sorry."

He gave me a stiff hug.

"You know my mom died when I was ten," he said. "It's not easy."

So here we were—a couple of orphans. Now we would have to live together like a real father and daughter. What a joke.

I led him inside.

"Oh William," Fallene said, rushing over and falling on him, weeping. Max strode over to my dad with his hand outstretched. Carl slunk over by the piano as if that gave him a reason for being there, while Edward and Lawrence stood at the far end of the room holding each other and wiping their eyes. I'm sure they all mourned Mattie deeply, but the fact that they were all performers in one way or another did mean they couldn't help but create a poignant scene.

***

Gretchen's father came to the house and got the keys to the Bonneville. He was going to sell the car for us. He stood in the foyer of the house on the shiny hardwood floor and gave me a sad smile.

"You vant to come to the house? You eat mit us, I think," he said, nodding his head.

"Okay," I said. It would be good to get out of the gloom-ridden house for a while.

I got in the passenger seat of the Bonneville.

"Do you think we'll get much money for it?" I asked.

"It's pretty old," he said. "But someone vill take it."

He started humming. The car smelled like Mattie to me, or

rather it smelled like me riding with Mattie. He cranked up the air conditioner, and luke-cold air came rushing out of the metal slots. I rolled up the window and felt as if I were in a glass casket.

We pulled up to the old hotel that had been turned into apartments; Gretchen's dad parked the car. We climbed the three flights of stairs to the apartment. The smell of cooked cabbage and meat seeped into the hallway. Inside the apartment, Gretchen's little sister sat staring at the color TV, enraptured by *Wild Kingdom*.

"Gretchen!" her dad called. "I brought someone home for supper!"

Gretchen's mother called back from the kitchen, "I just sent her to the store. Who is it?"

She came to the kitchen doorway and saw me. She was a tall woman with a red face which managed to get even redder when she saw me.

"Oh, it's you, Eli. I'm so sorry about Mrs. Burnes. What a horrible thing for you to have go through."

I shrugged and couldn't answer.

"Gretchen's not here right now. You can go wait in her room if you want."

I peeked into Gretchen's room. Lana was in there painting her fingernails a dark purple. I didn't want to see Lana. Lana would not be able to spare an ounce of sympathy. Not that I wanted any, but I didn't want her to torture me either. If Lana had been born thirty years earlier, I was sure she would have been held in high esteem by the Gestapo. Gretchen's father was already making for the bathroom and her mother had disappeared back into the kitchen.

I walked down the hallway past Gretchen's room and stood at Wolfgang's door. It was a plain white door. I knocked.

"*Ja?*"

"It's me. Eli," I said and held my breath. I could hear the TV voices murmuring from the living room, and Steppenwolf playing behind Wolfgang's door which finally opened just as I was about to walk away. He stood there, his wire-framed glasses slightly askew, his dark hair sticking out of his head like deranged blades of grass.

"Mattie died," I said.

His face softened and he stepped aside. I walked into his room. I'd only glanced in a few times. On the wall there was a poster of a man in a beret and underneath him the word *Che*. I had no idea who it was. A bookshelf made of boards and glass bricks covered one wall. The top shelves were all books and the bottom was records. A single window was covered by an American flag.

"So this is your room," I said.

He refrained from telling me what a stupid and obvious comment that was. He merely sat down on his bed and propped some pillows behind his back.

"That's bad about your grandmother," he said. I didn't correct him. Everyone thought of Mattie as my grandmother.

"I know." I sat down at the opposite end of the bed. I felt somehow comfortable around him as if we'd known each other a long time though in fact we hardly ever spoke to each other. Still, we had been through a riot together and we had kissed. He knew what my lips tasted like. But death numbs you in a way and so that shaky terrified feeling that usually filled me when I was too close to him did not happen. I would never have been able to believe I would be alone with him in a bedroom. But here I was.

His closet door was open and inside was a green duffel bag with clothes and books jammed inside of it. I wondered why.

"Are you going somewhere?" I asked.

Wolfgang didn't answer me. Instead he scratched his ear and ran a hand through his hair.

Just then Gretchen burst into the room.

"Here you are," she said. "Mom told me you were here. Poor, sad girl."

Then she hugged me and I wished she hadn't because the tears that had been down hiding deep in my chest spilled upwards and caught in my eyelashes. I wiped them away quickly.

We ate dinner. Gretchen's family dinner was a feast of noise. Lana cursing under her breath. Gretchen laughing. Her father talking about the old country. Her lean mother trying to persuade everyone to eat more. Prissy babbling about boogers. Only Wolfgang was silent. But no one seemed to notice. After dinner, Gretchen helped her mom with the dishes while Lana had to bathe poor Prissy.

I stood for a minute without anything to do. They wouldn't let me help with the dishes. Then I saw Wolfgang go out onto the balcony for a cigarette, and I followed him.

"Where are you going, Wolfgang?" I asked, leaning into the night air.

He paused and then said softly, "Canada."

"Canada?" I was utterly confused.

"My draft number is 37," he said, his hands in his pockets as he gazed over the railing into the parking lot below.

"I don't understand," I said.

"My number. It's low. Real low. I'll be one of the first ones called up in the draft."

"Shit," I said. The balcony suddenly felt shaky or else it was my legs.

"Vietnam," he said as if it were the name of a flower. Then he turned to face me, his lips screwed up, his eyes wide.

I stared at him, at the disbelieving look on his face, and in that moment my destiny was clear. I would go to Canada, too.

7

Being an Englishwoman, Mattie was an Episcopalian who went to church for Christmas Eve, Easter and a few select Sundays of the year. The priest professed to adore her and had season tickets to the Southern Opera Guild. The church was filled with all sorts of people that day—Augusta's high society patrons of the arts, opera singers who had flown in from New York, and then people who were just curious. They'd seen her die many times before. Maybe now they were just coming to make sure it was really true.

Churches in Augusta were usually black or white, but for this service the rules were forgotten. Curtis, the Opera Guild janitor, was there dressed up in a suit and his battered fedora along with Mort and Randolph, two jazz musicians from Atlanta who had played at our house with Carl in the wee hours of the morning on their visits to Augusta. Gospel singers from the black churches were there. They had loved to hear Mattie sing. And there was a wreath of flowers from a young black opera singer from Augusta who had already gained fame around the world.

Gretchen was there with her parents and Wolfgang had come as well, which made me feel nervous. I sat with my dad in the front row. Miz Johnny was in the second row with a tall handsome man I didn't recognize. She wore a pretty navy blue dress and a little hat with a veil hanging over the top half of her face.

As sad as I was, I couldn't help feeling that this was one of Mattie's parties done really big. I hadn't really thought much about death before. There was, of course, the distinct possibility that my mother was dead, but as I couldn't remember her, that was more or less an abstract notion to me. This, on the other hand, was real. Sitting in the hard pew I sensed something. Earlier I had thought that Mattie had left a gaping hole in the fabric of the universe, but now it seemed different. Now I had the feeling that Mattie knew everything that was going on. I had never considered the whole life-after-death phenomena before, but it seemed as if a part of Mattie was now attached to me, an extra appendage that only I knew about.

As we stood outside the church, people filed past us. Mattie had been adamant that there would be no additional graveside service. So Willie and I had to stand there and shake hands with people. At the end of the line, Miz Johnny came by with the tall man. When they stood before us, I realized he was her son, the one who had moved away a long time ago and was now some kind of businessman. His eyes fell on me but his gaze was unreadable.

"Hello, Randolph," Willie said. They shook hands. I wasn't really paying attention. Instead I was trying to see where Wolfgang and Gretchen were, but something about Willie's voice and a feeling of electricity crackling in the air made me turn and watch the two men.

"This is Marguerite's girl?" Miz Johnny's son asked. Miz Johnny herself had moved on, looking distracted and at a loss.

"Yes," Willie said stiffly. A strange strangled silence formed around us.

Then Miz Johnny's son said, "She's got her eyes."

"Come on, Randolph," Miz Johnny said, coming back to us. "I need to get over to the house. People will be coming by."

They left, and I looked at Willie's face. It might as well have been made of plaster for all the emotion I could find there. Didn't he care about anything?

I noticed Wolfgang standing off beside a no parking sign in front of the church. Willie was deep in conversation with someone and I was able to wander away.

"I'm sorry about your grandmother, Eli," Wolfgang said.

"Yeah, you told me that. Have you thought about it?" I asked.

"Why do you want to leave your dad? He seems like a good guy," Wolfgang answered, looking over his shoulder at Willie. An opera patron stopped and squeezed my arm.

"So sorry for your loss. She was a wonderful, wonderful woman," the woman said.

"Thank you," I said. I turned away before she could continue.

Wolfgang shucked the jacket he was wearing. He looked odd dressed in anything other than jeans and a t-shirt.

"He's got a family," I said. "A wife and two little boys. I just . . . I just don't want to live with them. That's all. I want to be free."

"Free from what?"

"Everything," I admitted.

Wolfgang looked down at the ground.

"You'll have to bring your own money," he said. "I can't feed both of us. And you'll have to get a job. And we're not going as boyfriend and girlfriend, okay?"

Rules, of course. There were even rules to freedom.

"That's okay. I have a little money." I had almost fifty dollars saved up in my treasure box.

Wolfgang looked at me. His eyes seemed full of pain. They matched my own pain, the pain I didn't want to feel. I shivered in the heat.

***

After the service our house filled with people. I savored a ball of melon in my mouth. It melted, breaking, dissolving into sugary juice and soft pulp. The pain of Mattie's death came to me in waves: a clutching sensation right above my breast bone like a fist trying to pull my body in upon itself and then it would release and I would feel almost normal.

Carl took his seat at the piano while Mattie's other friends sang and drank and told stories.

"Remember when Maxwell's cummerbund burst open on the

stage? I'll never forget the tears streaming down Mattie's face as she tried not to laugh," Fallene said. Max blushed.

"But she kept on singing. A true professional."

"What about the time the orchestra conductor was drunk, and she fired him on the spot. She went down in the pit and conducted the show herself. Thank God she wasn't in that one. She would have had to sing from the orchestra pit." Followed by peals of laughter.

"And the union blackballed her. Remember? That was a doozy. She didn't even care."

I listened to the stories and eventually realized my father was not in the room. I slipped out to try to find him. As I wandered through the house, I heard some low voices coming from the breakfast nook. I quietly sidled up to the wall next to the doorway.

"You've gotta be kidding me. There's nothing left?"

"It costs a lot of money to put on the productions your step-mother put on. And the investments your father made before his death were not good ones. Not to mention that his bookkeeper made off with about fifty thousand dollars several years ago."

"The old capitalist. He was always threatening to disinherit me. It never would have mattered."

"There is a small trust fund for the girl."

"For Eli?"

"Yes. Basically it's enough to get her through college. A good college. She'll get a portion when she's 18 and then a sum each year till she turns 21."

"What about the house? The furnishings."

"Better take what you can get now because the creditors will be here tomorrow."

Silence.

"I guess that settles that." My father's voice.

"I'll handle the sale for you, William."

"Good, because to tell you the truth, I never wanted any of it anyway. It's tainted."

"Tainted?"

"You know. After what they did to her?"

"Oh, you mean Marguerite? Willie, you know she did most of that herself. Anyway, that's water under the bridge."

"Lousy analogy."

"Sorry. I'm truly sorry."

"Nothing to be sorry about. I'm glad Mattie did something good with the old man's money."

Silence.

"When will you leave?"

"Tomorrow."

"So soon?"

"Yeah. You'll send Eli's stuff to my place?"

"Certainly."

I stole away from my listening post. Everything would be gone? I stood in the dining room, looking at the silver service set, the china, the linens that had been in our family since the Revolutionary War. I felt Willie come behind me.

"It all came from the blood and sweat of slaves, Eli," he said. "We're better off without it." I didn't know if he knew I had been listening, but I nodded.

The guests left. Carl was the last one. He looked up at Mattie's portrait. He had a beakish nose and thin hunched shoulders. I knew he was wishing the painting would come to life and step down off the wall into his arms. He turned to me.

"I want to give you something," he said. Then he handed me a small square box just a half-inch thick. I opened it and saw the plastic reel of recording tape inside.

"What's on it?" I asked.

"Some of her best arias. I thought you would want to have them," he said. Then without waiting for me to say anything, he dashed out the door. Poor Carl! I put the reel into my treasure box along with the picture of Willie and my mother and all my other treasures.

8

I woke up at 4:30 the morning after the funeral. Wolfgang had said to be ready to leave at 5:30 or he would go without me. That gave me forty-five minutes to decide if I was really going to do this. Could I? Could I leave my dad sleeping in the next room, thinking I was going to go live with him and his kids and Cleo in goddamned Webster Groves? But I knew that wasn't what I was running away from. Cleo had seemed okay the few times I'd met her and Willie was easy enough. Would he even care if I didn't go back with him? He would probably be relieved. I knew he had money problems. Look at that piece of shit truck he was driving. No, it wasn't so much Willie that I had to get away from.

I had to get away from anything that reminded me of Mattie. It was such an awful feeling like a vat of boiling acid, like I'd eaten my weight in tar, like I wanted to rip my hair out and strangle myself with it. I didn't want to be around Willie and Cleo and their kids and pretend like we were one happy family. No! I needed to erase my life.

And there was something else. There was the idea of adventure. I wanted an adventure. Somehow it felt that Mattie had been instilling this desire in me my whole life with her stories and operas. Now I felt it coming to life, pricking out of the shell of Augusta. And that adventure looked to me like Wolfgang, a suitcase and a bus ticket north.

Yet still I lay there, listening to the ticking of the clock by my bed and the hum of the air conditioner in my window. When I glanced at the clock again, it was 4:55. I slowly extracted myself from the warm nest of my bedcovers. Night had blindfolded the windows. I got up and turned off the air conditioner, shivering in my cotton nightshirt. Pajamas, I thought. I'll never wear pajamas again, and I pulled off the nightshirt and dropped it to the ground. From now on I would sleep in my clothes. I slipped on a clean pair of underwear, some blue jean cutoffs and a Santana Abraxis t-shirt that Gretchen had given me. Then I stepped into my sandals.

I saw my big trunk full of everything I owned ready to go into the back Willie's pickup truck. I could never drag that around the country with me. And what did I need with all that stuff anyway? Maybe he would take it back with him and keep it until I came to claim it. I had put my treasure box inside. I would have to leave that behind.

Instead I picked up the smaller navy blue duffel bag. My hands moved automatically, putting a few necessities into the bag—my toothbrush and toothpaste, deodorant, some extra underwear, t-shirts, a pair of shorts and a pair of jeans. I grabbed an old book off the book shelf so I'd have something to read on the bus. I stared down into the bag. I still hadn't started my period yet so I didn't bother to pack the bag of Kotex in a drawer that had been stored there for that eventuality. I figured I was never going to bleed. I was the only girl my age who hadn't started.

Then I realized I did need something else. Mattie's pearls. Carrying my little duffel bag, I stole out of my room out into the hallway. The door to the guest room was cracked open just a sliver and I could hear Willie snoring. My feet padded on the warm wood. Only the bedrooms had air conditioners. I stepped along the hallway and froze for a moment as Willie shifted in his bed. Then I hurried forward and went into Mattie's room. The emptiness was appalling, and for a moment I forgot why I was in here. There was the high four-poster where Mattie and I had curled up together at night while she told me stories. There the vanity where she sat to put on her face and gaze critically at her work, pretending she didn't notice how beautiful she was. But now the bed where she had died was empty, bed clothes stripped off. What would happen to her stuff? Her closet full of dresses? Her creams, her scarves, her little knick-knacks from all over the world? I couldn't take them, and Willie didn't want them. The only thing I knew I must have were Mattie's pearls, the strand that she had always promised me. Pearls some rich Greek fart—a shipping magnate, she'd called him—had given her a million years ago before she met my grandfather, back when she was a young diva who thought her life would never end.

I shook the sadness off me. The boy I worshipped was taking me away to Canada with him and who knew what grand things awaited me. My invisible and unknowable life stretched a hand before me. I rummaged through Mattie's jewelry box quickly. Damn, where are they, I wondered. I looked in each drawer, nothing but paste and rhinestones except for one drawer that was completely empty. And now it was already 5:15. I would have to leave them behind. My mood darkened. I glanced around at Mattie's empty room once more. For the first time in my life I understood that things change and they change irrevocably. Mattie was gone as if she'd never been here and my perfect childhood was over.

"Goodbye," I said and stepped out of the room without my pearls, shutting the door behind me. I picked up the duffel bag that I'd left in the hallway and tip-toed down the steps. It would be nice to have a cup of coffee and one of Miz Johnny's zucchini muffins before I left. But there was no time for coffee, so I grabbed a napkin full of muffins from the top of the bread box and crammed them into my purse. Then I waded through the early morning stillness toward the front door. I could hardly believe what my hands and feet were doing. My new life was out there, and it was bigger than I'd imagined.

9

I had left a note on my bed that said: "Dear Willie, I don't want to be a burden to you and Cleo. You've already got two kids you have to take care of. Don't worry about me. I'll be fine. I will call you in a week or so. Love, Eli."

As I walked behind the silent loping Wolfgang to the bus station, I realized that I could finally identify a feeling back behind my eyeballs. I was pissed. What right did Mattie have to go and die? She probably did it on purpose just to keep from growing old. Yesterday this going to Canada had seemed a great adventure, but now with Wolfgang acting as if I weren't there and me realizing I needed to pee something fierce and not sure where we would sleep that night, it didn't seem like such a great idea. And I wouldn't be in this spot if Mattie hadn't let herself go and die. Well, goddamnit, I would show them. I didn't need to be mothered or fathered. I was a 20th Century Athena, sprung out of some old god's head, ready to fight.

At the bus station after I made a stop in the smelly bathroom, Wolfgang handed me my ticket. The bus grunted and belched. The smell of diesel fuel in the morning soothed me and the anger I had felt just a moment earlier dissipated. Now I was only hoping that Willie hadn't somehow woken up early and found my note and was even now on his way here to stop me. Yet another part of me sort of hoped he was. Then Wolfgang turned to me.

"You shouldn't come," he said. That was the deciding factor.

"Of course I'm coming. You can't stop me. I paid for this ticket with my money."

"I'll probably get busted for kidnapping," he said.

"Well, you're a damned draft dodger now, so what difference does it make?"

He shrugged. As smart and worldly as Wolfgang was, I think he wanted to have some company. We climbed onto the bus. The sun was blooming like a rose on the horizon as the bus doors closed; with a grudging squeal the bus pulled away from the curb, and we rode through the outskirts of Augusta on our way north.

I felt like I had never been anywhere before. Suddenly it was easy to forget about Willie and Miz Johnny and the house on The Hill. The only trip I could remember taking was one time with Mattie when we went to Daytona in Florida to see the London symphony. As we rode through the day, watching America build and unbuild itself, Wolfgang played with the dial of a transistor radio trying to catch radio stations along the way. I rested my knees on the seat in front of me and stared out the window. For the first time in a long while, it occurred to me that perhaps my mother wasn't dead. Hadn't she done this same thing? Gotten on a Greyhound bus and just disappeared? Maybe she was in New York, and I'd be walking beside the Statue of Liberty, which was the only thing I could picture, and she'd see me and somehow we'd know each other. I couldn't get very far with this scenario, however. I couldn't picture her. And besides, did I really want a mother who was a drunk?

"Why are we going to New York?" I asked.

"There's a lot of people underground there. We can get some ID. Somebody will put us up. I got the number of a guy from my friend in Washington."

"Wolfgang, how do you know people like that? I mean, no one in Augusta is against the war," I said. "No one goes to marches or anything."

"It's not hard to find out if you really want to. I thumbed over to Washington a couple of times. The SDS had offices there. You just go in and start talking to people. They give you names, people to talk to. And there's magazines."

"SDS?"

"Students for a Democratic Society. You know all those protests and riots at the colleges? SDS organized those. They have chapters all over the country. Or they used to."

"Used to? What happened?"

"I don't know. Some had to go underground."

"Oh," I said. I stopped asking so many questions because it made me feel stupid that I knew so little. I had no idea what he meant by underground. Did they live in tunnels?

There were only two ways I knew the world: opera and books. My favorite opera was *Carmen* because Carmen was a gypsy and men adored her and she didn't care about much of anyone. I admired that. My favorite book was *The Adventures of Huckleberry Finn*. I could remember the very day Huck and I discovered each other.

A narrow park cut through the center of town. It had a fountain and trees with their limbs so full of summer leaves they could barely hold them up. I was about twelve and just as I passed alongside the park, I saw three girls from my school walking through it. They glanced at me and then turned away as if I were nothing more than a buzzing fly. Girls from my school had no use for me. They were already starting to wear make up and trying to find boys to go steady with. I don't know what got into me, the devil Miz Johnny would say, but I hollered at them, "Ugly bitches!"

Now, why would I do that? In a small town like Augusta? In fact, Miz Johnny wouldn't even have to hear it from somebody else. Her radar was probably going off before the exclamation point was even out of my mouth.

I pedaled to the library and decided to hide out in there as long as I could. Maybe a good book would save me.

"I like that Tom Sawyer book," I told the librarian. "Do you have something like that?"

"You could try reading The Adventures of Huckleberry Finn," *she*

said, gazing down her pointy nose at me. "It's got some bad language in it, but you probably won't mind."

Word travels fast in a small town. Especially if it's a bad word and a girl said it. The boys could cuss and no one cared, but the granddaughter of Will Burnes Senior was held to higher standards and almost always failed to meet them.

I checked out the Huckleberry Finn book and stuck it in my tote sack. Then I was back on my bike and riding across the Fifth Street Bridge. The Fifth Street Bridge had walkways along both sides of the bridge with thick stone railings. On the other side of the bridge, I was sure to find a grassy reading spot not too far from the water so I could hear a fish splash if it decided to jump up and take a look at the land world.

It was one of those books that wouldn't let go of me. I found myself yelling at Jim and Huck, trying to keep them out of trouble, but there was nothing I could do as they got themselves in and out of one scrape after another. Finally I noticed the mosquitoes that were drawn to all the sugar and salt in my bloodstream. And I looked up. Damn. The sun was washing its hands of another day, and I was supposed to be home before dark, which meant before even the suggestion of dark. Miz Johnny was going to swat my butt with her bare hand even though we both knew I was too old for that.

But today the only book I had brought with me was that old copy of *Jane Eyre* which I had read aloud to Mattie curled up in a chair on a rainy Thursday because it always seemed to rain on Thursdays: big, drenching thunderstorms and that seemed only fitting on the day belonging to Thor, god of thunder. Of course, I read it to her other times as well, but I only remember that Thursday.

Wolfgang was reading a book called *Twilight of the Idols* by someone named Nietzsche, a name I didn't dare try to pronounce. So I pulled out my copy of *Jane Eyre*. The thing about *Jane Eyre* is that no matter how shitty your life is, you know Jane's was worse. I compared Mattie with her laughter and her voice that exploded like the sun from her throat to that awful aunt who hated Jane and locked her in that terrifying room with the ghost. I realized I had it good. And on top of everything I'd had Miz Johnny with her blackberry preserves that we would make every June from blackberries we went out to the country to pick. But in a way, not having had a deprived childhood made things worse. Jane had nothing to grieve for, nothing to miss. Things could only get better for her. For me, the best part of my life might already be over. And here was my own brooding Rochester. I glanced at Wolfgang, his pale skin, the wire-rimmed glasses, the sturdy cheekbones and the jawline with its little bit of hair. Well, at least I was sure he didn't have a crazy wife hidden in the attic because he damn sure didn't have an attic.

Wolfgang caught me looking at him, and I felt my face turn hot.

"What are you reading?" he asked.

"*Jane Eyre*."

He took the book from my hands and opened the front cover. There he saw Mattie's handwriting, "To my most precious Elisa."

"Elisa?" he asked.

"Don't call me that, okay?" I said.

I dozed off eventually and when I woke up, we were in the Port Authority in New York City, Wolfgang shaking me awake.

I'd never imagined such a place as this. It's one thing to see New York in movies, but there's nothing like the actual feel of the bodies. Bodies everywhere. Throngs of people. Men in their suits, young straight guys with their short hair and goofy smiles, old ladies clutching bags, black guys in their flare pants and their 'fros, freaks and hippies, smelling like patchouli oil, bums that smelled like something rotted, and these strange guys with long black beards, black suits and black eyes. I was agog and we hadn't even left the Port Authority.

Wolfgang took my wrist and pulled me through this mass. He found a payphone and pulled a dime from his pocket which he dropped into the slot. Then he looked closely at a scrap of paper he held between his thumb and his pointer finger and dialed. I was getting hungry. I hadn't had anything since we'd transferred buses in Richmond. All in all, the trip had taken a little over 24 hours. I noticed a hotdog stand just outside the door.

"Food," I said, nudging Wolfgang.

"Forget it. We need to save our money. Someone will feed us."

"Who?" I asked.

"There's a whole network of people up here helping draft resistors," he said and then he turned to the phone. "Hello?"

I continued to stare at the people, sitting on benches or begging or walking by with their eyes pinned in front of them. It was so different from the south. In the south, you had to say hi to everyone you passed, but that would be impossible here.

Wolfgang hung up the phone.

"Okay," he said. "We're near Times Square and there's some kind of coffee shop a few blocks to the south where Frank wants us to meet him."

"Frank?" I asked.

"Yeah. The people in Washington told me to contact him. He's gonna help us. Did you see a cigarette machine anywhere?"

I pointed out a cigarette machine not far from where we were standing and watched as he went over and spent 35 cents on a pack of unfiltered Raleighs. So as soon as we walked out the door, I went up to the hotdog stand and got a hotdog with mustard and onions, not caring if my breath was bad. I ate it standing on the street with people walking around me, and Wolfgang smoking his cigarette, shaking his head. I'd never eaten a hotdog while standing on a sidewalk. I had a feeling I was going to be doing a lot of things I'd never done before.

As we walked to the coffee shop, I gazed up at the buildings that seemed slapped up against the sky. The sky was a different entity altogether—white and distant. We had to walk through Times Square, and every few feet there seemed to be a guy yelling at us to come look at the exotic dancers. Or else some other guy wanted to sell us Jesus. Wolfgang held onto my arm tight and kept me near him, which I was glad of. Finally, we found the coffee shop where we were supposed to meet this guy Frank and we slipped inside.

"What do we do now?" I asked, playing with the salt and pepper shakers.

"Wait for Frank," he said.

A waitress came by and asked what we wanted.

"Two waters," Wolfgang said.

She stood by the table, looking down on us with her arms crossed.

"Sorry, Charlie. You have to buy something," she said.

Wolfgang looked away from her. I knew he was afraid of not getting to Canada, but he was going to have to loosen up a little.

"Two coffees," I said.

The waitress wrote that down on a pad as if she couldn't remember such an enormous order.

"Anything else?"

I shook my head and she walked away from us.

We were just finishing the coffees which we had sipped as slowly as possible when finally a guy in black bellbottoms and a t-shirt with a picture of a leaf on the front of it showed up. He sat down at the table with us.

"Wolfgang?" he asked.

Wolfgang nodded.

"Frank Zappa," the guy said.

"Zappa?" Wolfgang echoed.

Frank laughed. "Not really. But I sure as fuck don't use my real name anymore. Look, I got bad news for you. Our office has been disbanded for the moment. The FBI is crazy, man. Ever since the townhouse explosion last March, they've got their noses so far up our asses they can smell our Twinkies before we swallow them."

"What happened to the SDS?" Wolfgang asked.

"They're history, man. It's Weatherman now. Or Weather Underground. Depending on whether you're wanted or not. The movement is in total disarray."

Wolfgang looked discouraged.

"Hey, it's not so bad. There's plenty of us still helping people elude the long arm of Uncle Sam."

Then it seemed as if he saw me for the first time.

"Who's this?" he asked.

Wolfgang hesitated and then said, "My girlfriend."

I smirked at Wolfgang. How else to explain me?

"How old are you?" Frank asked me.

"Sixteen," I lied.

"Runaway?"

"Orphan."

For some reason that made him laugh. Then his face grew serious and he wiped his hand over his mustache.

"Okay, Wolfgang and Orphan, I know a place that will keep you for a few days. We've to get you some IDs and you," he looked at me with his eyebrows raised, "you need to start wearing make-up or something. You should look eighteen and not twelve."

I wanted to hit him. I didn't look twelve.

"Make-up?" Wolfgang asked.

"Steal some. You've got to learn how to live on the streets now, kids. Live by your wits. You can't go out and get a job for *the man*. Stealing is a form of social protest. It's a way to weaken the capitalist system. Never, ever pay for anything if you don't have to, man."

He gave Wolfgang an address and a code phrase to use. Then we aided and abetted the capitalist pigs by paying for our coffee. And we left.

As we stood outside on the sidewalk, Frank leaned his lanky body close to us and said, "The people you'll be staying with are black militants. They're armed. They have to be. If we're ever gonna have justice in this country, the pigs aren't simply going to hand it over to us. But that means you need to be really careful. If they think you're pigs, they'll kill you."

"Do we look like pigs?" Wolfgang asked and lit a cigarette.

"Well, pigs don't usually travel with underage girls. I'm just saying, be cool, man. These guys owe me a couple favors. I got the pigs off their asses a few nights ago, so I don't think you'll have any problems. You cool?"

We nodded. I wasn't sure whether I adored this guy or despised him. I figured it didn't matter because he wouldn't be in our lives for long.

"All right. The place is in Spanish Harlem, so you should be safe. Know any Spanish?"

"Not much," Wolfgang said.

"You?"

I shook my head.

"Well, just fake it. If anyone messes with you, tell 'em you're friends with Bobby Seale. All right. Sayonara, kids."

He turned his back on us and walked away, disappearing into a throng of people.

"Wow," I said.

Wolfgang looked down at the address.

"We got to figure out how to get to this place."

"Should we ask a policeman?" I said.

"Don't be a smartass." He tossed a cigarette to the sidewalk where it smoldered before a shoe obliterated the fire.

10

We were in Spanish Harlem. I'd never seen or smelled or heard anything like this. Voices calling from everywhere, cars honking and buses rumbling by, and under the ground a rumbling from subway trains. Steam swept out of grates in the sidewalks, food smells wafted from open doorways. People walked past us as if we were patches of thickened air. Wolfgang said he had been to New York when his family first came over from Germany. We had walked for miles it seemed along the sidewalks. No one bothered us. We were just a couple of hippies like all the other thousands of hippies.

We finally found the address, and Wolfgang opened the front door, which wasn't locked. Inside the hall it was dark; the floor was made of small tiles. Spanish words leaked under a doorway. We climbed six flights to the top floor and then walked along a narrow hallway to 6F. Wolfgang knocked on the door. After a few minutes, we heard a series of locks opening, and then the door swung wide. There stood an imposing girl about 20 years old with caramel colored skin, a short afro and a tiny gold ring hanging from her right nostril. I stared at it, fascinated. She stared back at us. Even Wolfgang seemed at a loss.

"What do you want?" she asked.

"Mother Jones told us to come here," Wolfgang managed to croak out. She stared at us for another minute, then turned her back and walked inside, throwing a "come in and lock the door behind you" over her shoulder as we followed her inside.

Since I was last, I turned and stood bewildered at the array of locks on the door. I fumbled with the deadbolt and then Wolfgang came back and took over, deftly turning the right knobs and sliding chains and bolts into place. Then the two of us meandered down the hallway to a living room with windows overlooking the street. The girl was sitting on a stool, intently watching the street below. I figured she must have seen us searching for the place. A dark-skinned guy in a suit sat in one chair reading a paper with his legs crossed. He barely glanced up at us, but another guy—a light-skinned guy with a halo of soft-looking hair—stood up and smiled.

"I'm David," he said, holding out his hand. Wolfgang took it in a hippie handshake. "That's James sitting down reading some commie newspaper, and our lookout is Val."

Val continued to stare out the window.

"Hi, I'm Wolfgang and this is Eli," Wolfgang said.

"Shit, what kind of accent is that?" David asked.

"German."

"And you're running from Uncle Sam? How can they draft you?"

"My family are American citizens, unfortunately," Wolfgang said, looking for a place to sit.

"Here ya go," David said, and began clearing off magazines and newspapers that were piled up on the couch.

James stood up and dropped his newspaper on the floor. He wasn't tall, but he was the most commanding person I'd ever seen. His eyes kind of burned, and I felt immediately intimidated.

"We don't bring any drugs in here," he said. "We don't keep weapons or build bombs in here. And we don't eat pork here. Is that clear?"

Wolfgang and I silently nodded our heads. I wondered about Frank telling us these guys were armed. Maybe he'd just been trying to scare us.

As I stared at James, I understood what was so wrong with the south, and I understood the fuel behind those fires that had raged during Augusta's riot. No black man spoke like that in Augusta. James obviously didn't "know his place." He was the most fearless man I'd ever met. I'd been so accustomed to a world where fear was the coin of the realm that I hadn't even been able to see it.

"Are you Muslim?" Wolfgang asked.

"Black Muslim," James answered. "We're doing you Yippie Weather people a favor. Don't abuse it."

"We won't," I spoke up. James cocked his head at me.

"Was that a cracker accent?"

Panic filled my throat. I never had an accent in Augusta, or so I thought. But I guess all Mattie's elocution lessons had fallen by the wayside if two words were enough to give me away.

"I'm from Georgia," I said.

Val turned from her window.

"You shuwa ah," she said, laughing. "Say something else."

I sank into myself mutely.

David chuckled and said, "Don't worry about it. Hey, there's a bathroom down that hall if you want to get cleaned up. I'm going out to do some business. Coming, James?"

The two of them left. David swaggered when he walked. James walked in a crisp manner—a man on a mission. Wolfgang took a shower while I sat on the couch and read an old copy of *New Left Notes*.

That night at dinnertime, we ate some red beans and rice and a salad that Val made.

"So tell me something, Georgia. Were you raised by your Mammy?" James asked, squinting one eye at me from across the table. I was still nibbling on my rice and beans. Wolfgang had gotten up and found a chair by the window and had his head deep into a book.

I didn't understand what he meant by *Mammy*. I thought maybe it was a strange pronunciation of "mommy," so I answered him, "My mother ran off when I was little. I was raised by Mattie, my step-grandmother, and Miz Johnny, our maid."

It only took a second or two of silence for me to realize I had said something wrong.

"Was Miz Johnny a black woman?" James asked.

I nodded, wishing I could extricate myself from this interrogation.

Val cleared her throat and said, "It's not her fault, James. She's just a kid."

"And I'm about to educate this kid," James said. "So why don't you stay out of it." Then he turned to me, "Now why was this black woman cleaning your house and wiping your backside for you when she probably had her own house to keep clean and her own children to take care of? Have you ever wondered about that?"

I shook my head. Then I ventured, "Her sons were grown. I think she loved me."

James threw back his head, and his perfect white teeth flashed in laughter.

"She didn't love you, white girl," he said.

I brought my hand to my face as if he had slapped me. I felt my own cheek under my fingertips, my skin that angered James. Was he right? Had Miz Johnny never really loved me? She had never said that she loved me. I simply assumed she did because she fed me and scolded me and taught me manners.

"Well, I guess she needed a job," I said.

"That's right," James said, "but I bet she couldn't get a good-paying job. She couldn't be a secretary or a teacher or a nurse because the only work fit for a black woman is cleaning up behind white folks, right?"

Val slapped her thighs and groaned.

"James, why is it that you only mention certain jobs like nurse or teacher? Is that because those things are women's work? You're just as bad."

James glared at her. "I'm just being realistic."

"Well, so is this kid. She's from Georgia, for God's sake. She didn't make the rules."

"But if no one points them out to her, how is she going to know they're wrong?"

"My point exactly," Val said, shoving herself away from the table and opening the refrigerator door. "You want a Coke, kid? What's your name again?"

"Eli," I said. "Eli Burnes. But I do know it's wrong. Mattie, the woman who raised me, she wasn't from the South. And she got a lot of people in Augusta mad at her because when she married my grandaddy, she raised Miz Johnny's weekly salary by about ten dollars. And she wouldn't just call her 'Johnny' like my grandaddy did. She always called her 'Miz Johnny.' So did I. But we couldn't just take her job away from her."

James leaned forward and said, "I'm trying to make you see that the system is rotten. Racism and bigotry are pervasive. You white hippies think you can call us brother and sister and just wipe out hundreds of years of beatings, lynchings, raping our women and starving our babies. Isn't that what you think?"

"No," I said, but my voice was weak because I did think that we were making a difference. "I hate racism."

Of course, I hadn't hated it. Not really. I didn't think about it much. Even during the riot I hadn't really thought about what made them so angry. I looked up and saw Wolfgang staring at me from the other room. Maybe he was thinking the same thing.

That night Wolfgang and I slept on the pullout couch. I'd never slept with a boy before. Wolfgang pretty much turned his back on me, but in the morning when I woke up, his arm was across my belly. The weight of his arm made me feel warm and calm. But I had to pee so I slipped out from under it and padded into the bathroom—a narrow room with a barred open window over the toilet. I had slept in my clothes so I changed in the bathroom. Then I stood up on the toilet and looked out the window. There was a brick wall about ten feet away and windows into a thousand lives. Everything was so different here. And I was different because I had been here. One night and I was not the same girl.

I wanted to get out into the city, but Wolfgang seemed to think we should stay in the apartment. James and David were busy writing some kind of "manifesto" and they spent most of their time at the kitchen table. Val had Smokey Robinson on the stereo as she looked down at the street below her perch by the window. Wolfgang might as well have been in heaven. He was immersed in the books that were stacked in piles around the living room. I tried to read as well, but none of the books had stories in them. They were about capitalism and socialism and colonialism and imperialism; my eyes got crossed in all those isms. I would have given anything for a few comic books.

Then Wolfgang and Val started talking about someone named Angela Davis, whoever the hell she was, and I could have screamed from the boringness of it all. Eventually I went in the bedroom where there was at least a fan blowing and lay there under the wooshing air and thought about how I wanted something, anything to happen. I fell asleep. When I woke up, I stumbled groggily into the living room.

"Where's Wolfgang?" I asked.

"He and James went out to mimeograph some leaflets. You might as well be useful while you're here," Val said.

"Oh."

David scratched his head and looked at me in his friendly way. He had small even teeth and curly eyelashes.

"Val was thinking of a way you might be useful," David said.

I wasn't sure I'd ever been useful before. Well, I had helped around the Opera Guild, but I had a feeling that Val's idea of being useful would be something quite different.

"I'm gonna teach you how to boost," she said.

"Oh." As if I knew what that meant.

"Have you ever boosted anything before?" David asked me.

I sat down on the floor and stared at the Olivetti typewriter on the coffee table. I had no idea if I'd ever boosted anything before.

Val laughed.

"She doesn't know what the hell you are talking about, boy."

"Your mama's a boy," David responded.

I laughed at this absurd statement, and then stopped laughing as Val rolled her eyes at me.

"Shoplifted, girl. Have you ever stolen anything before is what he's trying to find out," she said, exaggerating each word as if I were deaf in addition to being an idiot.

"Oh," I said for the third time. I sat for a moment, gazing at the letter "h" on the typewriter and thinking that was the first letter of the word "home." Then I said, "I stole a Three Musketeers bar once from The Hill Drugstore." I didn't add that I felt so guilty I couldn't eat it and in fact never ate a Three Musketeers bar again.

Val smiled. "Well, see there, you've even got experience."

***

"I don't know," I said, as we hustled down the street. "How is stealing useful to the cause?"

"First of all, it disrupts the capitalist system. The people should not be denied the right to live, hell, to eat like anybody else," Val answered. She was wearing a little beret and sunglasses. Her hips were wide and she walked fast with a forward tilt. "In our case, the people are being so harassed by the police that the people can't go get a job. So if we don't boost, we starve. There's a higher law: the law of survival."

I had to practically run to keep up with her, but then she stopped and pulled me down on a bench. Her mood earlier had seemed somewhat playful, but now she frowned bitterly.

"We set up free breakfasts for children in California. We empowered the neighborhoods all across this country. We're trying to give black folks a fighting chance to have lives of dignity and *they* want to kill us for that."

I took a deep breath. I hadn't understood those books and magazines back at the apartment, but I did understand this. I was from the south, after all. I had heard the boys talk about "niggers" and tell "nigger jokes"—jokes that were short on funny and long on meanness—and now I realized there was something insidious underneath those jokes. If it hurt me, if it bothered me, how much more must it bother the people who were the targets of the ridicule.

Val continued, "The white power structure would rather see black folks in the ghetto fighting each other for a scrap of bread, hooked on drugs, stealing welfare checks from their grandmas than to be contributing, you know, making a better world. They somehow think they'll lose something if we, if our children, have anything more than crumbs and shit."

Val's face looked like a portrait of history, a thousand years of pain etched into the tiny lines around her eyes. Then she smiled at me and broke the spell.

"You oughta be a speaker, Val," I said. "I think people would listen to you."

"Not me. I'm not gonna stand up in front of people. That's for James."

We were silent for a moment. An old man came by and said to Val, "Sister, can you spare a quarter?" She reached into her pocket and gave him all the change she had. "Bless you," he said. "Bless you, Sister."

We watched him limp down the sidewalk.

"Well, I'll do it," I said. "Show me how to do it."

"Boost?"

"Yeah, boost."

***

We took the train to Brooklyn, and lo and behold there was a McCrory's. Val told me not to walk with her, told me to look at stuff, pick things up and then put them back. So that's exactly what I did. I handled various items—wallets, pots, flips flops, sewing kits, hair brushes, hand mirrors, sunglasses, magazines, tubes of Bryl Cream, cans of VO5 hairspray, and packets of bobby pins. A lady with beehive hair and glasses asked if I needed any help.

"No, thank you," I said as politely as I could. She lingered near me as I continued to inspect various items. After about ten minutes of this inspection, I noticed Val at the end of the aisle. With a nearly imperceptible nod of her head, she exited the store. I gave her a minute and then put down the picture frame I was holding and followed her. Val stood across the street. I dodged through traffic. As soon as I caught up with her, we started walking. She found a diner and the two of us went into the bathroom. She washed her face in the sink and looked at my reflection in the mirror.

"I got you some make-up, but all the make-up in the world is not going to put titties on your chest," she said and laughed.

I glanced down. She was right about that.

"Maybe we'll get you a padded bra."

"No way," I said, imagining Wolfgang suddenly pressing against two hard boulders on my chest. It was better to be flat.

"Suit yourself," she said and we walked back out. Soon we found our way to a park by the river. I instantly felt at home with the water rushing by. On the other side, Manhattan was beautiful. Val began to show me her haul: a transistor radio, some mascara and eyeliner, a couple of bracelets,

"My mother tried to get a job at a McCrory's," Val said. "Of course, they wouldn't hire a Negro."

"When was that?"

"Not all that long ago. Five years maybe. Right after my daddy died. That man worked two jobs to put me and my three brothers through school. He worked all the time, it finally killed him. He had a heart attack, and he was only 47."

"Shit," I said.

"Yeah, it was fucked up. Okay, now we're going to the grocery store. This time it's your turn. We need some steaks for dinner."

***

It was easier than I thought, my heart thudding like a hammer on the bone, the feel of the cold package of meat against my belly, under the loose shirt that Val insisted I wear. It was quite a trick to walk naturally with three steaks wedged into my clothes. But I remained calm as we stood in the checkout line with a can of green beans. Maybe all those years of watching operas had taught me something about being someone else. And it wasn't such a hard part to play. An innocent girl. I'd been one all my life so it came naturally to me. No singing was required.

11

After eating a delicious dinner of steak and green beans and biscuits, Wolfgang and I decided to head out for a while. Wolfgang wanted to go to Washington Square Park. That's where everyone hung out, he had heard, and he wanted to see what he could find out about getting to Canada. So an hour later we found ourselves sitting on a low concrete wall across from an enormous stone arch. The wall formed a circle, rather than a square, and inside it were hippies and a few old street bums just hanging out, enjoying the evening. A guy on a unicycle rode around in circles and nearly ran into a girl with a dozen bangle bracelets on her arm and a thick head of glossy black hair that floated to her waist.

"Hey," the girl said, plopping down on the ground in front of us. "I'm Sassy. Where are you guys from?"

Wolfgang laughed in surprise at this audacious black-haired girl. I stared in wonder. If you took her features separately she would seem to be one ugly duck—buck teeth, deep sunken eyes, eyebrows almost as thick as Wolfgang's—but combined together in one face she was astonishingly lovely, especially with that humongous smile beaming from her lips.

"We're from Georgia," I said. Wolfgang gave me a scathing look. The girl intercepted his glance.

"Don't be so uptight, man. I'm with the movement. I just wanted to make sure you're okay. Where are you staying?"

"Spanish Harlem," Wolfgang answered. The girl nodded.

"With James and Val?" she asked.

"Do you know them?" I asked.

"They're good people, so is David. But you can't stay there long. You'll draw down the heat on them, and the pigs are slaughtering the people in this fairytale." Her eyes were wide now and she seemed, to me at any rate, to be vastly wise.

"You know the FBI infiltrated nearly every organization. That's why it's all had to go underground. They stir up violence, man, whenever they can. They even pretend to be construction workers and then incite the hardhats to come and beat the shit out of hippies."

"The hardhats?" Wolfgang asked.

"The what?" I said.

"Working class guys who don't get that we're not out to hurt them," Sassy said. "It's easy to whip up fear and hatred. And we're an easy target."

I shuddered. When had the world gotten so dangerous? I couldn't imagine why anyone would want to hurt me. I hadn't done anything. But then I remembered that Christmas when Marvin and Freddy hit a black kid with a rock, and when I went over to see if the kid was okay, his mama came out of her house in a flowered housecoat and slapped me in the face. I went back to the park, and Marvin and I got in a fight—one of several we had that year—which I was in the process of winning until Wolfgang showed up and broke it up, calling Marvin a "poosy" for fighting with a girl.

"Hey, are you hungry?" Sassy asked. Out of a big cloth bag hanging from her shoulder she pulled out a couple of apples and a plastic bag of pistachio nuts. We ate hungrily. "Eat up, children."

"What's your role?" Wolfgang asked, dropping pistachio shells onto the ground.

"I'm kind of a messenger. I mean, no one talks on the phone anymore. They're all tapped. So I look out for people, and deliver messages."

"How about telling someone we need some ID to get into Canada with," Wolfgang said.

"It's already taken care of," she smiled again. "Meet me here tomorrow at noon and I'll bring you both passports."

"Cool," Wolfgang said. It suddenly struck me what we were doing, leaving our country. Well, it wasn't really Wolfgang's country, but it was mine. Love it or leave it, the people back home liked to say. So we were leaving it, but I realized that didn't mean I somehow didn't love it. What it meant to love a country, I wasn't sure. The one thing I knew I did love was the Savannah River, that iridescent serpent that pilfered from our banks and took what it could out to sea. But Georgia was far away, and Canada would have rivers, I consoled myself.

The air was warm and twilight was transforming the hot day into something else. A couple of guys began beating on conga drums, the sound taking over the big round concrete plaza. Sassy jumped up in her long Indian-print skirt and started swaying her hips. All around us people started moving to the jungle beat.

"Get up!" Sassy laughed. "Dance."

My legs obeyed. I was off my butt and moving my legs and my arms. The drums were a hundred beating hearts; my pulse echoed the rhythm. I whirled. My bare feet pitter-pattered on the concrete. Beside me Sassy shimmied and shook. Wolfgang watched with an amused look on his face while Sassy and I danced with a small throbbing tribe. I felt like a creature of the wild, I was a leopard, I was wind. Laughter stirred through me like a tornado.

When I stopped twirling around, I noticed Wolfgang sitting on the wall, talking to Frank.

"Hey," I said, walking over to them. "When did you get here?"

"A few minutes ago, Isadora," Frank said, chewing a piece of gum which smelled like Juicy Fruit.

"Isadora? You mean like Isadora Duncan?" I asked.

"Yeah, you're smarter than you look, Orphan."

Sassy danced up to us and plopped down on Frank's lap.

"Frankie," she said in a deep voice. "What's happening,

Frankie?"

"Pigs are happening. Hard hats are happening. Death is happening."

Sassy stood up.

"Okay, I get it. You don't need a weatherman to know which way the wind blows," she sang and held up a finger as if testing the wind.

"Let's go. We've got business to take care of," Frank said. I saw a serious look cross Sassy's face and I wondered if her free-spirited hippie act was just a cover. Frank, I knew, would have no problems resorting to violence if he thought it was necessary. Sassy, on the other hand, was an enigma.

"Okay. Meet me tomorrow morning like I said." Sassy was already gathering her stuff from the ground where she had dropped it.

They walked off together. I didn't think they were boyfriend and girlfriend, more like business partners. What a new and intriguing world this was.

The warm city air engulfed us as we walked down the street: exhaust, subway steam, the human sweat smell of summer. Wolfgang pushed his thick hair from his forehead and glanced around with wide eyes behind his wire-rimmed glasses. I could not see him carrying a gun through the jungles of Vietnam. Suddenly I felt sad. I was missing Mattie, missing our living room and the singers gathered around the piano.

"Why did we leave Augusta?" I asked.

"I shouldn't have brought you. It was a mistake," he said.

"But it'll be good in Canada, won't it?" I asked.

"Yes," he said. "And not so goddamn hot." He wiped at the sweat that was trickling along his thin face.

"And better than Vietnam, too," I said softly, remembering what this was all about. It seemed quite simple at that moment. There were people who wanted ordinary guys like Wolfgang to give up everything and go kill people they didn't even know, people who had done nothing to them personally. And then there were guys like Wolfgang who wanted to do something else with their lives. At that moment it seemed pretty cut and dried. Wolfgang was running for his life. And because I cared about him and because I was young and lost, I was running, too.

We found a subway station. Wolfgang bought some tokens. We weren't going to take a chance and leap the turnstile tonight. The train arrived in a clatter of steam and noise. After the doors slid open, we pushed through the crowd to get a seat. It took a couple of stops for the subway train to empty enough for both of us to sit down. When we did, we were silent, rocking back and forth, each lost in our own thoughts. I wondered if Willie was worrying about me. Miz Johnny crossed my mind. God, she would lay into me if she knew what I was up to. I wondered how much she knew about what was happening outside Augusta. What would she think of it all? It hurt me to think of anyone ever disrespecting her, and yet I knew that she must have seen awful things. It wasn't the kind of thing she would have ever talked about to me, but I did remember one time when she snapped, "Those white-sheet-wearing cowards ever come in my yard again, I'll take a shotgun to them, I swear before God!" I couldn't imagine why or when the KKK had ever messed with Miz Johnny, and she wouldn't say. Mattie finally told me that Miz Johnny's youngest son had been seen with a white woman a long time ago and the KKK didn't like that.

We got out of the train down at 115th Street. It was nearly dark when we got to street level; we had a couple of blocks to walk to get to the apartment. Spanish music flowed through open windows, and people sat out on the stoops with their babies, trying to keep cool. The music moved me. It was somehow sad and happy at the same time. I couldn't understand the words, and yet it felt as if I couldn't understand anything anyway. Why was there so much hatred? And was it all because of skin color and the length of someone's hair? Or was there more to it?

We passed some young guys on one of the stoops. They were

laughing, and the distinctly sweet smell of a joint burning wafted past us.

"*Que pasa?*" one of the guys asked.

"*Nada*," Wolfgang answered. Val had taught him one Spanish word.

As we approached the apartment building, I noticed a dark car with its engine running in front of the building and that's when I heard that voice I had heard once before when Mattie got sick. Once again it did not come with cheerful tidings. All it said was, "Watch out." But watch out for what?

"Something's wrong," I said to Wolfgang.

At that moment, David was walking from the other direction. I saw him stop and look at the car. Suddenly his face became a mask. He lowered his head and walked toward us without looking at us. Wolfgang and I froze, confused.

"Keep going, keep going," David said as he passed us. His eyes never met ours, and we didn't look back at him. We walked past the house not quickly, but not slowly either. Wolfgang began to whistle, which seemed a little obvious to me, but I couldn't think of anything better to do.

We were two buildings down when I heard the shots and then a woman screaming. A crowd quickly gathered. Wolfgang and I shrank into a doorway and watched. People milled about, trying to see what was happening. There was a strange moment of silent anticipation. Minutes later sirens were wailing and the small street was a kaleidoscope of light.

"It's happening again, Wolfgang," I whimpered. "It's happening again."

I was reliving the riot all over again, smelling the smoke and hearing that man screaming in the street. Wolfgang glanced out from the doorway.

"They're putting somebody in the back of the ambulance," he said.

I stuck my head out in time to see the back doors of the ambulance close and to see Val shoved in the backseat of the police car. I could hear her sobbing. That meant it was James who had been shot. But was he dead? I clutched Wolfgang's arm. We stood petrified in the brick hollow as the police car zipped away.

We stepped onto the sidewalk. Wolfgang slung an arm around my shoulder and pulled me around the corner.

"Don't look back," he said angrily.

I jerked away from him.

"Leave me alone," I said.

"Eli, don't make trouble. We have to get out of here," Wolfgang pleaded.

My breath was caught hard in my chest, but I knew he was right. And what did I have to be angry at him about? He was just as lost and scared as I was. I thought about my dad and wondered if he was worried about me. For the first time, I realized what a stupid thing I had done.

12

The road unraveled behind us like a spinning skein of black yarn. Wolfgang and I were squashed in the back seat of a red Corvair with patches of rust dotting it like leprosy. Sassy sat in the front seat with her thick hair whipping in the wind while Frank drove. An enormous St. Bernard was wedged on the other side of the backseat. He gazed down at me placidly, his big pink towel of a tongue hanging from between his drooping furry cheeks.

A thick coat of silence lay over us except for the dog who whined occasionally and grunted as he tried to turn around and stick his head out the window into the onslaught of hot air. Wolfgang and I clung to each other, not as lovers but more like terrified children on a life raft. James, it turned out, was still alive, but the cops would say he had resisted arrest. They would have planted weapons on him. Val's word would be meaningless. James was going down for a long time.

Finally Sassy turned to us and said, "Look, when they became activists they knew it was dangerous."

Frank banged the steering wheel.

"I shouldn't have sent you two over there."

We understood that the color of our skin had drawn attention to the three black activists hiding in Spanish Harlem. In New York even in this short time I had seen blacks and whites mixing together like you never saw in the South, but I guess we were somehow conspicuous.

Then Sassy countered, "The Feds probably had them pegged for weeks."

"Maybe," Frank said.

Sassy reached back and ran a finger over my knee. She wore turquoise and silver rings on all her fingers.

"You'll be okay," she said over the wind.

We were on our way not to Canada but to a town called Canandaigua to stay with Sassy's sister, who was also taking the dog, which had apparently been left behind by a couple of Weatherman bombers who had to go underground. In the confusion of getting out of town, Sassy had not gotten us the passports. And now we were pretty close to broke.

"Do we need passports?" Wolfgang asked. "It's only Canada."

"You need some kind of ID if you want to work there," Frank said.

Sassy rubbed her hand into the dog's fur and he began to thump his leg in pleasure. His big feet danced on the seat next to me.

Sassy's sister was nearly six feet tall with long wavy blond hair. From a distance it would be hard to tell they were sisters, but up close they both had the same deepset dark eyes and the same overbite concealed behind large soft lips. Her apartment just off Main Street was wonderful. It had a bay window with pretty white lace curtains, posters on the walls and, for some reason, a giant picture of Frank Sinatra above her bed.

Wolfgang and I had spent the previous night dozing on subway trains or in The Port Authority. Our other clothes were left behind. I did still have my copy of *Jane Eyre*, which always stayed in my purse. And Wolfgang still had his Nietzsche, whose name I had learned how to pronounce: Neechee. The only thing I knew about him was that he had once said God is dead. Judging from the looks of things I thought he might be right.

Sassy's sister set up a cot for me in her room, and I lay down, thinking about death—the rioters back in Augusta, Mattie, maybe my mother. If I hadn't grown up on opera I might not have been able to stand it, but tragedy was woven into the fabric of my world. I soon fell asleep and didn't wake up till the next morning.

***

I wandered into the long living room with the cool light slanting in through the white curtains and found Wolfgang lying on the floor. Before I saw him, I'd had the sudden fear that he might have left and gone on to Canada without me. We weren't boyfriend and girlfriend, according to him, and I wasn't much use to him. But there he was with his ear next to a stereo speaker listening to someone sing in a loud beautiful wail: "Sometimes I feel like a motherless child." The words pierced me and I sank down to the floor beside Wolfgang.

"Who is this singing?" I asked.

"Richie Havens," he answered.

"What are we going to do?" I asked.

Wolfgang shrugged.

"*Güten Morgen.*" Sassy's sister stood in the kitchen doorway, holding a steaming mug.

Wolfgang sat up in surprise.

"*Sprechensie Deutsch*, Sonya?" he asked.

"*Ja,*" she answered, coming in and sinking down onto the sofa. She set the cup down on a table beside the couch, turning her head so that her long neck stretched on top of a delicate set of collarbones, peeking out of a white peasant blouse.

Goddamn it, I thought. I knew just enough of Wolfgang's native tongue to understand that she had told him she could speak "*Deutsch*" which was not Dutch, which anyone with any common sense would have thought, but German.

They began to converse like two people on top of a mountain and I was just some rock far below their feet. Sonya said something that sounded like "Glock In Shpeel Mafia" and Wolfgang—that traitor—smiled broadly. Wolfgang smiled! His two front teeth overlapped and they were more yellow than white but it was undeniably a great smile sending beams radiating from his eyes. Right then I knew I was doomed.

I got up and went into the bedroom to sulk.

I lay down on my cot, careful not to touch the horrible bedsheets where that beast of a girl would probably lure Wolfgang. I rolled over on my side and faced a wooden bookcase full of college-girl books. My eyes landed on a paperback book called *Valley of the Dolls*. I imagined Ken, Barbie, Midge and Skipper living in a valley in a little trailer. But the cover had pills on it, not dolls. I put that book back and slowly slid out the others till one intrigued me. The title was *The Happy Hooker*. I vaguely knew that a hooker was something bad. The woman on the cover of this book seemed both happy and bad. I opened the book and started to read. It didn't take long to figure out what a hooker was. A hooker actually got paid to have sex. Just the word sex made me rub my thighs together. Sex to me was kissing and touching and best of all, being naked with a boy. I knew there was more to it than that. Mattie had given me the basic facts and even in Augusta there were girls who were loathed and admired for things they were said to do with boys. Of course, Lana had been only too ready to answer any questions that Gretchen and I'd had.

"The man sticks his thing inside you and gets cum all over you," she said.

Yet somehow even with all this knowledge, sex was a dark room that I could only peer inside. It was terrifying to me, and yet I had an ache inside that wanted me to plunge into that mystery.

Holding the book in my hands, I felt like a pirate who had discovered a treasure map. I couldn't put it down. The happy hooker informed me of many things, but the most useful piece of information, given my present circumstances, was that I should practice oral sex on an ice-cream cone, preferably in front of the man I wanted to seduce. Oral sex must be some serious tongue kissing, I decided. The next thing I decided was that I would seduce Wolfgang. I needed an ice cream cone if I wanted to out-seduce the blond Glockenshpeel Mafia, who was now standing in the doorway watching me read her book.

"Learn anything?" she asked.

What could I say to that? I sheepishly put the book back on the shelf, wishing I was a worm so I could slide out of the room. Then she said, with her hands on her hips, "You lost all your clothes back in the city, didn't you?"

I nodded.

She walked over to her closet and I thought she was going to give me some of her old clothes which would have been welcome but humiliating at the same time. Besides I couldn't imagine what apparel belonging to that Amazon would fit me. Instead, though, she pulled out a baby blue Singer sewing machine. Then she rummaged through a basket beside her dresser and pulled out various pieces of fabric that she threw on the floor.

"I'm gonna show you how to make a halter top," she said, plopping down on the floor in front of the sewing machine. Hating her at this point seemed useless so I sat down on the floor beside her.

"You make a kind of triangle of the fabric, see. Fold the top over . . ." She glanced around and found a leather string on the floor. "Like this."

She folded the fabric over the leather strip and then zipped it under the whirring needle of the machine. "Now, you just tie the ends around your back and the top around your neck and voilá, a fashionable halter top. Great for summer and very sexy looking."

Then she gave me a little smirk.

"Put it on," she said. "You can wash out your t-shirt in the sink and let it dry on the towel rack. If you want you can use any of that fabric to make yourself a couple more."

She stood and walked out of the room. I realized maybe for the first time how spoiled I'd been all my life and how ill-equipped I was for survival. It hadn't even occurred to me to wash out my clothes in the sink. I would have just gone on stinking until they rotted off me, I guess. So I went in the bathroom and changed into the halter top, found some soap and washed out my t-shirt. It was with an amazing sense of maturity and accomplishment that I went back into the living room, expecting Wolfgang to notice me. He didn't. He barely looked up from where he was still sitting on the floor, studying the jacket of a record album.

Sassy was sitting on the couch, running her fingers through the dog's fur. She must have just arrived because she'd been gone earlier. Then I suddenly felt a finger run across my back.

"Nice top," Frank said and walked past me, carrying a bottle of apple juice. I shivered from his touch.

"Thanks," I muttered.

Frank sank into a beanbag chair, and I sat down on the floor by Wolfgang.

"Look at this beautiful dog," Sassy said. "He's such an old soul sent here by the gods to watch over us."

Frank pulled out a baggie of grass and proceeded to roll up a joint. He licked the edge of the paper and then put the whole thing in his mouth and pulled it out through puckered lips. He caught me staring and winked. I felt heat rise to my face. Then with a flourish he pulled out a Bic lighter and hit the striker with his thumb. A flame danced from the top of the lighter; the joint took the flame and extinguished it to a red ember. Frank took a deep toke, held his breath and then seemed to melt as he exhaled. I was in awe of this ritual though I had only smoked that one time, and the memories associated with it were not good ones, considering that was the night Mattie had died.

"Yummy," Sonya said, taking the joint from his fingers and inhaling. Her eyes watered and she held a finger under her nose before she blew the smoke out into the room. She stretched her hand with the burning joint toward Wolfgang. He shook his head.

"That's unfriendly," she said.

I knew it was weird that Wolfgang didn't smoke pot, but that didn't make him any less radical than anyone else. Wolfgang was never one to do something because every one else did it. Sassy reached over and took the joint from her sister. The dog lifted his snout to sniff curiously at the smoke and then placed his big head back down on his front paws, grunted and closed his eyes.

Frank watched silently, his eyelids low, his full lips in a slight pout. He turned to Wolfgang and asked in a quiet voice, "Are you sure you're not a cop?"

"What?" Wolfgang asked, his face turning red. It was rare to see emotion on Wolfgang's face.

"Maybe Orphan here is some FBI pig's kid. Maybe you're the one who snitched out James, David and Val."

Wolfgang rose in rage.

"I don't smoke because I do not give control of my mind to anybody or anything else. Not to the U.S. Government. Not to some pseudo-Marxist revolutionary organization, and never to a drug." His nostrils flared as he glared at Frank. Everyone else was silent for a moment.

"Wow. Heavy," Sassy said.

Frank lowered his eyes and said, "Look, man, cool it. I believe you. It's just we have to be careful. The pigs would love to stop us from saving the likes of you and keep us from getting your asses into Canada."

Wolfgang sat down again. He'd used up more emotion than he generally used in a year.

"I need to get some money," he said forlornly. "Most of my cash was in my bag at the apartment in Spanish Harlem."

"You could get some quick cash panhandling," Sassy suggested.

"He can't panhandle," Frank said. "He looks like a draft dodger. They'll bust him so fast his little peach fuzz mustache will burn off." Then he looked at me and deliberately smiled. Traitor that I was, I smiled back and took the joint from Sassy's fingers. I touched the paper end to my lips and sucked.

"Eli can do it," Sonya said.

I immediately gagged on the smoke and started coughing.

"Me?" I asked between gasps.

Frank appraised me.

"Perfect. She's got that waif-like look. Poor little orphan child. She could probably scare up thirty or forty bucks in an afternoon."

First boosting and now this. If Miz Johnny could see me now, my spiny ass would be black and blue.

"Not in Canandaigua," Sonya said.

"Rochester," Sassy interjected.

"So we've got a plan," Frank said, standing up. He took a hit of the joint, squinting his blue eyes through the smoke. Frank was somehow strange looking and cute at the same time. Suddenly I was all for panhandling. I would impress him with how much money I could make. This was a dangerous life and I could someday wind up like Val and James and David, but in the meantime I would have a blast.

13

From Canandaigua to Rochester was not a very long trip. It was hilly and pretty. Frank and Sassy stopped at an A&P to get a bag of Oreos because Frank had the munchies. Then they dropped us off in downtown Rochester. Rochester was bigger than Canandaigua, but much smaller than New York City. We passed a huge hotel that looked like a castle. Frank had told us that the city was the home of Eastman Kodak, and that if we went a few miles farther north we would hit one of the finger lakes. Rochester did have a river, a muddy cut down its middle. And it had plenty of big stone buildings.

I had never even thought of these places before. Never really wondered what lay past the confines of my little world. Now it was as if I were pulling open curtains upon curtains on new and curious scenes. Yet even though it was strange, nothing could diminish my sense of boldness. Maybe that was because I had so few rules as a child under Mattie's benign neglect. So while Wolfgang parked himself on a bench in Manhattan Square Park, I found Main Street and without a qualm, held out my empty palm to strangers and said in my most polite voice, "Excuse me, do you have any spare change?"

Many were startled. some simply ignored me; others stopped and stared, men especially. Then they would dig into their pockets for quarters, dimes and nickels. Occasionally someone would give me a dollar. It was a game to me like trick or treat. I soon collected six dollars and stopped in a soda shop to buy an ice cream cone. I found Wolfgang still sitting on his bench with a book by some guy named

Eldridge Cleaver that he had borrowed from Sonya's bookcase.

I scooted down beside him and jingled the coins at him. I licked my ice cream cone suggestively and offered him a lick.

He shook his head, ignoring my skillful tongue work.

"I don't like this," he said. "When we get to Canada, we'll get jobs. It's disgusting to beg."

"It's not disgusting," I said. "It's fun. They can spare it."

Wolfgang shook his head. I wanted him to be glad he had brought me. I wanted him to see that I was helpful and good. The jealousy I'd felt that morning had been like a sour ball of wax in my belly. It had a bad aftertaste I wanted to wipe out. I also felt ashamed for taking a hit off the joint when I knew he thought it was bad idea. At least I had only taken the one hit, so I hadn't felt much more than a temporary light-headedness.

I finished the ice cream cone, forgetting about being sexy until I was almost finished. I looked up at the sky, which was blue and pretty here but a shade paler than back home. The trees looked naked without Spanish moss draping like old beards from their limbs.

"I'm gonna go get some more cash-ola," I said.

"Be back at six o'clock," Wolfgang said, looking at the pocket watch he kept in his jeans—a gift from his father.

"Yes, Miz Johnny," I said.

I strolled back to the busy streets. I wandered past a bank with pillars in front, offices, stores, and restaurants. An Italian restaurant caught my eye and I wished I could go in and get something to eat. I'd never been in an Italian restaurant before. I caught the eye of a couple just coming out.

"Hi, may I trouble you for some spare change?" I asked. They were taken aback, but the man gave me fifty cents before they hurried away. I didn't feel like I was begging. I felt I was exhanging the gift of my smile, my very self for a few pieces of silver.

After being rebuffed by my next couple of targets, I approached a stout little woman with gray hair. She walked purposefully down the street. When I spoke to her, she stopped short and looked at me with wide eyes.

"What did you say?" she asked.

"I wondered if you had any spare change?"

"What on earth for?"

"So I can eat," I answered, somewhat truthfully. She stood on the sidewalk before me with her leather purse dangling from her forearm, looking at me through a pair of brown-framed glasses.

"Well, then come on," she said. "I'll feed you."

I would have preferred cash, but the idea of food appealed to me, and she took me by the elbow and led me into the Italian restaurant.

"You are a bit thin," she said as she ushered me to a table. I sat down and put the linen napkin in my lap as I had been taught. She noticed and approved. A waiter came by and I ordered spaghetti with meatballs. The lady ordered a salad.

"Now why are you out here on the street without any food? Where are your parents?" she asked.

I told her a story of half-truths: how my grandmother was dead and my father didn't want me. My meal came and I told her that the only Italian words I knew came from operas. She wanted to know all about that so I told her about the Southern Opera Guild, about having the theater to myself during rehearsals and then I told her how Mattie came to be my grandmother.

"The night my grandfather met Mattie she was singing an aria from *Manon Lescaut*. Mattie played Manon Lescaut in Buenes Aires and she said it was one of her favorite roles," I explained in between bites of spaghetti. "When she sang that aria, it would sort of fly over your head and lift you in the air. I've heard it all my life and it always made me feel as if my heart were being taken away. In the song, Manon has left the man she loves for a wealthy man. She sings 'In quelle trine morbide.' Which is French not Italian. It means that in those silk curtains she feels a chill. I can only imagine what Grandaddy felt as he stood there in that chandeliered room listening to the most beautiful thing he had ever heard. Granddaddy was a southern gentleman but somehow he had managed to go his whole life without ever hearing an opera before."

The lady's head was tilted as she listened to me. I could tell she was impressed. You could always impress an older person by talking about opera and you could always make young people think you were a complete weirdo. After dinner she paid the bill. I asked if I could have a peppermint pattie and she bought me two.

"Where will you go?" she asked when we got outside. "Do you have somewhere to stay?"

I nodded and suddenly remembered Wolfgang in the park with his father's pocketwatch.

"What time is it?" I asked.

She looked at her wristwatch and answered, "Six fifteen."

"Oh, I have to go. Thank you for dinner," I said, turning and dashing down the street. I was like Cinderella and the clock had tolled midnight. I hurried along through the crowds of people until I got to the park. Then I went straight to Wolfgang's bench. It was empty.

I looked around in confusion. Where could he have gone? I walked every inch of the park and then ventured around some of the surrounding blocks, but Wolfgang was nowhere to be seen. Had he finally left me, after all? It felt as if the ground beneath my feet could envelop me. Panic rose in my throat. A large black bird flew out of a tree above in a flurry of wingbeats and cawed loudly. I walked back into the park and sat down on Wolfgang's empty bench. I had no idea what to do.

I kept waiting, kept looking, kept hoping. But Wolfgang did not come. Instead a drunk guy who smelled like piss sat down next to me and asked my name. I didn't answer. Then he reached out and put his hand around my arm. I jumped up and fled to the other end of the park. I didn't dare leave. What if Wolfgang came back for me?

So I skulked around, trying to avoid other people. I found a bathroom where I hid for a while. When I came outside it was dark.

I went back to my bench. The drunk guy was gone. Again I asked myself what should I do? I turned in a circle, wishing an answer would arrive, wishing that voice that occasionally spoke to me would tell me what to do. But there was no voice. There was no sign. I had no idea how to get back to Canandaigua. I realized I couldn't plan ahead, not even as far as tomorrow. The only thing I could take care of was that moment. So I decided I would find a hidden spot among the bushes and trees. I would lie down and I would wait till morning. Which is what I did.

When I woke up, I was freezing. My clothes were damp. I still had on the halter top I'd made at Sonya's. My hair was full of leaves. I had bug bites on my arms. I was hungry and lonely and desolate. But it was morning. I had survived. I'd heard people in the park during the night but no one had found me. I went back to the bench. It was still empty. I wondered what the nice lady who had bought me dinner what was doing. Thinking of the spaghetti dinner only made me feel worse because as I'd eaten, I'd been feeling happy, unaware of how awful my night would turn out to be. I couldn't stop shaking from the cold. I still had a little money from my panhandling the night before. Suddenly panhandling didn't seem much fun. It certainly wasn't how I wanted to spend the rest of my life. Was Wolfgang in Canada already? Or had he gone back to be with Sonya in Canandaigua? The latter thought made me want to vomit.

I got up and decided I should get some coffee to warm up.

After a cup of coffee and a couple pieces of toast with grape jelly, I wandered around the streets of Rochester for hours. I was not the same bold girl I had been the day before. People avoided looking at me. I smelled bad. I probably looked worse. I came to the river and sat down, looking at the water. The surface glittered in the sunlight like tiny scales as if it were a living thing.

"Hello," a voice said.

I looked up. A dark-skinned man in an orange turban was looking down at me.

"Hello," I said.

"The river is nice to look at, isn't it?"

"I guess so," I said. I looked down at my dirty feet. I didn't feel like exchanging pleasantries with some freak in a turban.

"Have you ever read the book *Siddhartha*?"

"No," I said.

The man sat down beside me.

"In the book, Siddhartha tries to find himself in all kinds of pleasures. But nothing brings him happiness. He tries strong drink, wild women, gambling. Finally, he turns his back on the world and he becomes a bridge tender. He finds peace beside the river. It is a nice story."

I shrugged, but I understood what he meant. This river was soothing. The sun had warmed me. I was alone and friendless, but somehow my spirits had risen.

"You will be all right," the man said. He got up. As I watched him walk away, I saw a red Corvair driving down the street. I jumped up and yelled.

"Hey! Hey!"

The car stopped. I ran toward it and reached the driver's window.

"Your boyfriend got arrested yesterday," Frank said.

I dropped to my knees. No, I thought. No. No. No.

***

I showered for a long time but when I got out I still felt cold inside. My t-shirt was clean now and I borrowed an Indian-print skirt that Sonya had made. The skirt reached to my toes and felt somehow comforting.

Sassy hugged me when I came into the living room.

"Poor orphan," she said.

"What's going to happen to Wolfgang?" I asked.

Frank was sitting on the couch.

"He'll be inducted into the U.S. Army," Frank said. "He's absolutely fucked."

"There's nothing you can do, Eli," Sassy said.

I wandered over to the bay window and stared out.

Frank came and stood behind me.

"Sorry, kid," he said, putting a hand on my shoulder.

I looked at him.

"What about me?" I asked.

Sassy spoke up.

"You can come with me down to Georgia. There's a rock festival in some place called Byron, Georgia. And since I never did get to Woodstock I am not missing this."

"Oh," I said. How ironic, I thought, that I would be heading back home. "Are you driving, Frank?"

Frank shook his head.

"I've got work to do. I'm going to Chicago to help out there."

I didn't ask what kind of help he was giving.

"Some guys I know are driving down," Sassy said. "If you want we can drop you off wherever it is you came from."

"I can't go back there," I said.

"Then come to the festival. You'll get to hear Jimi Hendrix."

"But what about Wolfgang?" I asked once again.

"Nothing you can do about it, kid." Frank shrugged.

"I guess I'll go to the festival then," I said. It wasn't like I had much choice. It seemed I would be open to suggestions for a while. Then I noticed Wolfgang's copy of Nietszche sitting on the table. I picked it up and put it in my purse. Now I had two books from people who were gone from my life.

14

We drove away from Canandaigua in the back of a Ford van. There were curtains on the back window which I pushed aside to stare forlornly back at the receding town. There was an amusement park by the lake that Sassy and Frank and I had gone to the night before. Maybe they were trying to cheer me up. I'd ridden on the wooden roller coaster and screamed and laughed, but inside my chest was hollow. It only felt worse as we left.

I didn't know the people in the van. They were friends of Sassy's. She had grown up in Canandaigua. They didn't seem to be part of the movement. They were just a bunch of people who liked to smoke dope and who liked rock music. I nestled down on the floor of the van and tried to sleep through the trip. I hadn't known it was possible to feel so lonely. They had a tape deck and they were playing music by a band I had never heard of, called The Grateful Dead. I knew about dead people and I didn't think they were grateful about it. But I liked the music.

We arrived in Byron, Georgia, the next day.

The only road going to the campground, which was in the middle of a pecan orchard, was two-lane and both lanes were going in one direction: in. As we slowly crept past people walking or sitting on the side of the road, I gazed out at the sights. One guy sat on top of a car and held up a sign that said: "Welcome to Byron. Population: 350,000 freaks!" We passed people carrying backpacks, and then as we slowed to a crawl in the traffic jam, they passed us. We opened the side door of the van. Sassy and I and another girl hung our legs out the door and looked at all the people. A shirtless guy walking next to the van handed Sassy a lit joint.

"Just getting here?" he asked.

"Yeah."

"Far out," he said with a grin.

We crawled in a long line of cars for what seemed like miles, and then we were in a camping area of tall pines trees, and the driver parked the van in a spot that would be our home for the next few days.

Sassy jumped out of the van. I followed her.

"Where do we get tickets for the festival?" she asked a passing couple.

"No tickets, man," the guy said. "The concerts are all free."

That sounded like good news to me as I had about seventy-five cents to my name.

Sassy looked a little confused.

"What's wrong?" I asked.

"I was supposed to meet someone at the ticket booth," she said.

I followed Sassy around the camping area as she got a feel for the area. The red Georgia clay was dry and dusty, and soon my feet and legs were orange. It was hard for me not to stare at the people as they set up their camps and mingled with each other. It seemed like they all knew each other. Sassy smiled and waved at people. She struck up conversations with anyone who walked by as if they were old friends. After a while I realized that this was simply the customary behavior of the tribe. They were friendly. Everyone was a brother or a sister. It was like Washington Square Park to the tenth power.

These girls with their long, stringy hair, their halter tops, their bikinis and blue jeans, their clean faces devoid of make up shone with a sense of themselves as beauties. A sense I did not have. I was intimidated by their saucy smiles and their loud laughter, and as I watched them walking languidly down the road or smoking pot or even tending to the occasional little kid, I wanted desperately to be just like them.

If the girls were interesting, the guys were magnificent, walking around shirtless with their long hair and their mustaches. Not all of them were such beauties, but a lot of them could have passed for gods. I loved hearing them laugh and feeling the occasional brush of their eyes on my body.

"There's a lot of people here," Sassy said. "I don't know how I'm gonna find my friend." Then she turned and looked at me thoughtfully. It made me uneasy. Not to mention that I was starving. A girl so skinny she looked like she was made of twigs sat over an open pit fire roasting corn on the cob. She saw me staring at the corn.

"You can have one for a quarter," the girl said.

I took one of the three quarters I had in my pocket and gave it to her. That was the most delicious corn I'd ever had.

The stages were across the road from the camping area, but Sassy and I weren't in a hurry to get to them. There was so much to see right in the camp and there was plenty of music from every direction. We went down to the free stage for a while and listened to the jangly rock music, the thudding bass and the hissing of drums. I felt as if I had no identity at all. I was a piece of dust floating through the air and landing wherever I was blown. I wondered about Wolfgang. He wouldn't have enjoyed this very much, I thought. But it would be better than jail. If you could stand the liquid heat. It was like being inside the mouth of a large dog. Even Sassy seemed limp and wavery like a figure from a Dali painting. Sweat and dirt marbled her neck and arms. I didn't want to know what I looked like.

Finally the sun slid down the sky, and a single breeze teased us with the hope of a cooler evening.

"So let's go hear the music," Sassy said.

"Sassy," I said, "all these guys here. How come they're not going to Canada? Why isn't the army after them?"

She shrugged. "Some of them have college deferments. Some

of them got lucky in the draw. And some of them just don't give a damn."

Poor Wolfgang, I thought.

We moved in a herd toward the music. The field was amazing. Freaks and hippies for as far as the eye could see. We found a spot of ground next to a group of guys with shaved heads who had split open a watermelon. They gave us slices, and the smell of watermelon rinds and sweat and beer and mud surrounded us. It was a good smell. I didn't care that I was hot and dirty. It took my grief away. I was too busy observing this brave new world to remember the pain of losing Wolfgang and Mattie.

Sassy and I stayed at this spot for a while. A group called The Allman Brothers played and left, and the sky dimmed. I couldn't tell who was playing after that. It wasn't like I knew the music very well. But whoever it was played a mean guitar and it sounded like a black man singing. Pretty soon people were up and dancing. I had only had two years of tap dancing lessons so I didn't think I knew how to dance, but I saw that you just had to move any way that you wanted to move. You could sway and wave your hands in the air.

Remember this, I told myself. Remember this for the rest of your life. Finally, the music ended for the night. The field was blanketed in smoke and bodies like the aftermath of a delirious battle. Sassy and I picked our way over the people lying on blankets or sitting on the grass. I passed a couple kissing and felt sad, wishing Wolfgang were with me. Though if he were, we wouldn't be here and probably wouldn't be kissing. Maybe Wolfgang had cared for me, but something—caution?—kept him from showing it. Or maybe I was just a pest.

"We've got to get back to the van," Sassy said. All night she had been distracted, even during the music. I was worried that the friend she wanted to find was some guy she liked and then I'd be dumped again and on my own out here.

Lots of people had gone back to the campground. You could smell campfires and stoves and hear a raucous party, music and laughter and shouts into the hot night. I thought of Mattie's parties when I would fall asleep under the piano. My feet hurt and I wanted to curl up on the ground and sleep like the dead.

We reached the edge of the campground and had to pass the Hell's Angels' camp, their hogs haphazardly making a barricade. An enormous biker stood up as we approached.

"You gotta pay a toll," he said.

Sassy in her ever-friendly way answered him. "Not now, okay? We're just looking for somebody."

"Well, you found him, darlin'," he said, with a cold grin from under a droopy mustache.

"Yeah, that's really cool, but really you need to let me pass," she said.

"I will. I'm just asking for a toll," and then his eyes locked onto me and lingered on my halter top. "Just leave her with me."

Sassy shook her head vehemently. She was starting to lose some of her niceness. But the biker didn't pay attention. He grabbed my wrist and pulled me close to him. The heat and smell of his body engulfed me, and I was too startled to react.

"Let her go," Sassy insisted.

"No way, chick. This is my toll. You go on," he said.

I suddenly felt I might wet my pants in terror.

"I'm not going anywhere," Sassy said. "We have to find her father."

My head whipped around. I looked at her in shock.

"And she's way underage, so unless you want a statutory rape charge, I suggest you back the fuck off," Sassy said, her face just inches away from his.

"My father?" I asked. "Willie?"

Sassy didn't answer me. She just grabbed me by the other wrist and pulled me away. The biker didn't follow.

"Were you telling the truth back there?" I asked.

"Yes," Sassy admitted. "Some old lady in Rochester managed to somehow find your old man, who by the way has been frantic trying to find you."

Now, I realized that Sassy wasn't my great friend after all. She was just trying to return to my dad.

"So you just snitched me out?"

Sassy turned on me, her face inches from mine, her long hair swaying as she spoke: "You did not tell me that your dad was Will Burnes. He's a hero of mine. His speech in Chicago in '68 probably saved a thousand lives."

"What are you talking about?"

"Will Burnes has been against the war since the mid-60s. He helped organize SDS in the Midwest. He's a good guy. Not part of the Establishment. How could you have run away from him?" Her hands were on her hips and her head was tilted. I could smell a musky sweat from her flesh.

"I hardly know him, Sassy," I said. "He was never around. Never."

Her lips tightened and her dark eyes looked into mine.

"Well, he's here for you now, kiddo."

We trudged through the campgrounds without speaking. And then standing beside a beat up old pick up truck tucked between some pine trees, a familiar figure turned toward us.

"That's him," I said with a sigh.

"Thank God," Sassy said.

We walked up to the truck. Willie's face lit up with recognition.

"Sassy?" he said, stepping into the lane.

"Will Burnes?" Sassy asked.

"Yep," he answered.

"It was kinda hard to find you," she said. "I walked around a lot, hoping you'd recognize your kid."

I stood back, but Willie grabbed me and hugged me hard and whispered in my ear, "You shouldn't have done that, Eli."

Life was full of things I shouldn't have done.

"How did you find me?" I asked.

"A very kind and concerned lady called down to Augusta and found someone who knew Mattie, who then gave her my number. She said you were in Rochester, so I started calling everyone I knew and someone directed me to Sassy."

"I told you I was a messenger," Sassy said, suddenly friendly again. "You're the message this time. Don't be pissed off, okay? Your dad is a cool guy. I'm pleased to meet you, Will Burnes. You've done some amazing shit."

"That was a while back," Willie said. "I haven't been that involved lately. You know, marriage . . . kids."

I was too tired to make sense of what they were saying. But here I was with my dad at the Atlanta Pop Festival. Maybe it would be okay. I wondered if he would want to stay to hear Jimi Hendrix play the next night.

15

The next day the heat came down on us like a busted bag of cement. People were saying it was 106 degrees in the shade so I hated to think how hot it was not in the shade. Willie's campsite was two rows away from Sassy and her friends. We had a sheet tied to some pine trees for shade and a couple blankets on the ground. It was weird to suddenly be with my dad at a big gathering of freaks, but with his long hair, his faded jeans and his big beard he wasn't anymore out of place than I was. We didn't leave our campsite for the morning but just sat and watched the people walk around. Once a completely naked man walked by, droning the words, "Acid, acid, acid." Fortunately, at that point Willie was lying back on a quilt with his eyes shut. I didn't think I could stand the embarrassment of the two of us observing that tall, skinny man's penis bouncing like a windsock with his every step.

Sassy showed up about eleven that morning, wearing a bikini top and her long Indian-print skirt and carrying a bag. She said that one of the guys among her friends had overdosed and they were leaving early.

"Stay with us," Willie said. "I'm sure you can find a ride back." He turned to look at me with one eyebrow raised to get my approval of the idea. Willie had this way of including a person in any scheme he had, making you feel like you were in on some conspiracy with him.

"Okay," she said and dumped her bag of possessions in the back of Willie's truck.

"I'm going to down to the creek," she said to me. "Want to come?"

"Sure," I said, happy to see her again. I'd forgiven her for her treachery, and in fact, felt a kind of relief that I didn't have to figure out the course of my own life for a while.

When we got to the creek, people were skinny dipping, and Sassy shucked off all her clothes, revealing her pendulous breasts, her pale butt cheeks and all. Hot as hell's furnace, but I was not about to get naked around all these people so I just sank into the water with my clothes on, which probably made me more conspicuous. Sassy smiled but didn't say anything. I looked up at the cloudless blue sky and the water's warm mouth engulfed me.

When we got back to the truck, Willie made us peanut butter and jelly sandwiches on Roman Meal bread. I ate two and could have gone for more but didn't want to look like a pig.

Sassy pulled a strand of hair from her mouth that had gotten caught in the sandwich. She seemed so comfortable with her flesh. Willie's eyes got soft when he looked at her.

"How did a boy from Augusta, Georgia, become a radical?" Sassy wanted to know.

Willie stretched his legs out in front of him. I picked some pine bark off the tree I was leaning against and began breaking it into tiny pieces. Already the cooling off we'd gotten from our dip in the creek was turning hot and steamy again.

"You know," Willie said, stroking his beard and looking sideways at Sassy. "I can remember the precise moment." I wondered why I had never thought to ask this question of Willie. It just seemed to me like he had *always* been different from the rest of the people in Augusta.

Sassy tilted her head, her long dark hair lolling over her breasts in a way that made me wish I were her instead of me.

"I was about eleven years old, and I had some money to go to the movies. But I had to take a bus to get to the movie theater. So I get on the bus and I sit down somewhere in the middle, minding my own business. There's a black man a few seats ahead of me, and he keeps turning around and looking at me with the crazy look on his face. And for some reason the bus wasn't moving. I didn't know what the hell was going on. I saw the bus driver looking in that big mirror over his head at us. And I thought, does he know this man is crazy? Am I in danger?"

Sweat snaked along under my t-shirt and I was wishing I had a bathing suit on.

"Then suddenly the black guy gets up, and I just about wet my britches. I thought he was coming back to kill me. He had this angry, crazy look on my face. But he went right past me and sat down about three rows behind me. Then the bus started moving forward."

Willie stopped for dramatic effect. Sassy shook her head.

"That's when I realized that a grown man had to get up and move seats because of me, a little boy. And I realized that the crazy look on his face was pure and utter humiliation. That was the moment. I knew it was all wrong. Everything they were teaching us in school. Everything my father spouted about the gentility of the South—*The Negroes are happy, son.* It was all bullshit."

"So you became a radical?"

"No. Not till I left. In Missouri and Illinois, I got involved in SDS and went to some communist party meetings. We marched. We had sit-ins. I got tear-gassed and billy clubbed and jailed. Good times," he laughed.

"And what about now? What with the movement in disarray? Did you join Weathermen?"

Willie shook his head. "I help out when I can. But I've got a family now so I'm not exactly active anymore. I mean, I still go to protests if they're local and sometimes I get messages through on the radio for people. Or at least I did."

Sassy reached over and hugged him, which made me feel a little nervous. He did tell her he was married. A couple of times. But he hugged her back and they released each other slowly as if they were somehow glued together but the glue hadn't dried yet.

"I'm kind of tired. Mind if I take a nap in the bed of your truck?" Sassy asked.

"Sure, go ahead. Eli and I will go out and mingle," Willie said, getting up with surprising speed for such a big guy. He turned to me and said, "Ready?"

Willie and I wandered around the enormous campground. Willie would strike up a conversation with anybody, asking about the music, where they were from, how were the drugs. We'd approach a group, and usually some young guy with thick hair that had to be pushed from his face would answer him, a spokesperson, a kind of philosopher. These guys seemed to enjoy talking and knew all sorts of things. They had an amused gentleness about them that made my throat feel tight.

Eventually we sat down in front of the tent of a group of surfers from Florida. The philosopher of this group was a tall blond guy who invited us to have some hotdogs, which we did. From an 8-track player inside the car rock music poured out.

"Mitch Ryder and the Detroit Wheels," my dad said, shaking his head with a smile. "I love the way Badanjek's bass drum kicks off that song."

"You know your music, man," the tall surfer said.

"Hell, I've been in the music biz for twelve years. You ever hear of Wildman Willie?"

The surfer was putting some mustard on another hotdog; he stopped and stared at my dad.

"You're not shitting me. That's you, isn't it? Say it again. Say Wildman Willie."

"You're listening to Wildman Willie on K-rock, AM Radio," Willie said in his radio voice.

The surfer's cohorts were now all ears, laughing and slapping each other.

"Yeah, I heard you before. Late at night you can get radio stations from all over the place. I've even listened to Chicago sometimes. And I'm talking about from Florida."

"Cool, man, very cool."

"So are you still doing that? You work at K-rock?"

Willie finished off his hotdog, wiped his beard and shook his head.

"Naw, man. I got canned," he said. My head swiveled toward Willie. This was news to me.

Another of the surfers leaned forward. "No way, dude."

"Yeah, it's true. I got sick of playing that payola crap day in and day out. Always bubble gum for the boppers. I wanted to spin some Airplane, Dead, Joplin, something decent. Finally, one night I got really pissed off."

Willie leaned forward and everyone else leaned forward, too, including me, since this was the first time I'd heard any of this. "I played 'Revolution' over and over again. It was about midnight. I figured maybe the boss was asleep. But that dog never slept. Phone light started flashing in the studio. I didn't pick up. Just played it again and again. About twenty times maybe before the engineer could shut me down."

"Far out," the tall surfer said with a laugh.

"Yeah, but you got shit-canned the next day," the other one said with a sympathetic expression. A wave of dread overcame me. If Willie didn't have a job, how was he going to feed his family, which now included me? God, he was useless as a father. I began to feel really pissed off. Not just at him, but at Mattie for leaving me and Miz Johnny for not keeping me in Augusta and Wolfgang for getting busted and everyone I could think of just because.

"I don't mind. AM is dead. FM is the wave of the future. Album rock. Free-form broadcasting. I'm digging it. You can do whatever you want on FM. I'm doing a little underground station from my basement right now, but pretty soon I'm going to get one of those FM licenses and then nothing but good music. The best." Willie settled back, and the surfers lit up a pipe, which they started to pass around. When it came to me, I passed it on to Willie.

"This is my kid," he said, smoke billowing from his lung sacks. "She's not into grass."

Now suddenly all the attention was on me, and I wanted to shrink into the earth.

"It's just too hot right now," I said in my defense. Of course, I'd guessed all along that Willie was a pothead, but this was the first time he'd smoked in front of me.

"Your kid? Wild!" The blond guy smiled sweetly and said, "You're a pretty cool chick."

I couldn't find any words that seemed to be an adequate response. A cool chick, I thought. I was a far cry from being a cool chick, but it felt good that he said that. Yes, I could be cool. I wouldn't worry about whether or not Willie had a job. He didn't seem to be worried. I stuffed my fears inside me. Maybe Cleo was working. Anyway, we had some cash from selling those antiques. I didn't know how much money you needed to live on, but surely we'd be all right for a while.

Eventually, we got up and wandered on. I thought of the naked man who had been walking down the lane earlier, calling out "Acid. Acid."

"Willie?" I asked. "Is acid LSD?"

"Yeah," he said. "Lysergic acid diethylamide. It's made from ergot. A grain fungus."

"A fungus?" Someone was cooking corn on the cob on an open fire. It smelled good, but we kept walking.

"Yeah."

"What's it like? Doesn't it make people jump out of windows?"

"Not often. But it's best to stay on the ground if you're tripping."

What would they say back home about this, I wondered, kicking up orange dust. Here I was with a bunch of crazed hippies on drugs. I stuck my hands in my pockets and figured I better stick close to the one person I knew and be thankful there weren't any windows.

That night we went back to the festival and heard Jimi Hendrix play. Sassy came with us. She and Willie walked close together, and I stayed right behind them. Occasionally, they'd brush up against each other. I could see the dance they were doing, and I thought about Cleo back home with their two kids. Willie must not care about them any more than he ever cared about me, I thought. What a shithead was my next thought, but right now I was stuck with him.

We got as close as we could. Up on the stage, this wild head of hair waved back and forth behind a microphone. He was wearing some kind of headband and what looked like a robe. Sometime after midnight Hendrix played "The Star-Spangled Banner" with his teeth. Willie shouted in my ear: "This is it. This is the defining moment of our times." Then the fireworks started and a single word flew up from a half million mouths: "Far out."

Happiness swept under me and seemed to lift me as if I were on the crest of something magnificent, as if I were on a mountain looking out over the world. And all the sorrow and worry that had plaqued me since that night in Augusta when Mattie first pointed out the huge bulge in her abdomen seemed to float away. I felt a weird cramping in my belly but I ignored it. I was probably just hungry again.

That night the three of us fell asleep right there on a blanket on the festival grounds. I woke up the next morning. Sassy's head was on Willie's chest. He was snoring. People were just waking up and moving around. At least Sassy and Willie hadn't been able to sneak off and do anything. I made my way to a porta-jon, which smelled like dead skunk and cherry candy. On my white underpants, I saw a dark stain. It took me a moment to realize that I was having my first period.

Finally, I thought. Far out.

16

Willie and Cleo lived in a small house on a gravel road in a place called Webster Groves, one of the cluster of towns that make up St. Louis County. We had taken Sassy to the bus station. In the bus station bathroom, I'd been able to buy a sanitary pad from a machine with a dime that Sassy gave me.

"Congratulations," she said.

"Thanks," I said, chagrined that she had figured out it was my first time.

Then she got on the bus, and Willie and I drove away. I slept for most of the way home. When we arrived, the boys tumbled out of the house, screaming. Cleo stood in the doorway. She was thin and tall with long red hair, large lips, a snub nose and sleepy, beautiful brown eyes. I had met her only twice before—once when she was six months pregnant and she and Willie had just gotten married and once when all four of them came to Augusta for Christmas. I had not liked her or disliked her. But now I decided I had better try to make her my friend. I wouldn't mention Sassy.

Willie took her in his arms and swung her around while the boys screamed. I stood and watched the family reunion. When Willie set Cleo down, Jake, who was almost five now, climbed onto Willie's back and Turtle jumped into Cleo's arms, pawing at her breasts.

"Sweetie, you're a big boy now," she said. "Big boys don't get num-nums. That's for babies."

"I'm a baby," Turtle cried.

"Baby! Baby!" Jake laughed.

I felt a momentary pang of jealousy for the way Cleo seemed to dote on her children. I felt large and conspicuous, an imposer. But Cleo smiled at me and led me into the small gray house.

Willie disappeared into the bathroom while Cleo and the kids showed me into a room in the basement, which wasn't a bad place though it had no carpet and no telephone and no canopy bed. Cleo showed me a clock radio and an afghan she'd made that I could use. A single bed occupied one corner, and there was a cheap looking dresser with a mirror against the wall. My trunk full of my belongings waited at the foot of my bed.

"You can put posters on the walls and make it look cool," Cleo said brightly. Two of the walls were paneled wood and two were cinderblock. It was a makeshift room, I realized, but it was mine, and she was right. I could decorate it. Maybe get a lava lamp or a black light.

"It's great, Cleo," I said. "I like these windows." They were level with the ground outside. They made me feel somehow secure as if I were nestled away in a little cave and yet if I needed to leave, all I had to do was open a window. I unlatched one and pushed it open. A big furry gray dog came ambling to the window, stuck her face in and licked my cheek.

"That's Heidi," Jake yelled. "Go away, Heidi."

"I like her," I said. I'd never had a dog before. Maybe she would come sleep in my room with me. Ever since I'd read *Wild Fang*, I always wanted a dog that would be at my side.

As I unpacked one of my suitcases that Willie had brought back with him after the funeral, Cleo noticed a pair of gold earrings and said they were pretty. I gave them to her. The boys ransacked my clothes, but it didn't matter until one of them got hold of a bottle of Mattie's perfume. I snatched it out of his grubby little paw and gathered the perfume and tape that Carl had given to me and put them in a drawer along with my copy of *Jane Eyre* and Wolfgang's book.

When Cleo finally herded her kids out of the basement and back upstairs, I took a look around the basement itself. Willie had a workshop on the other side of the stairs. It was cluttered with protest signs, radio equipment, records and tools. He had a long desk made of a door on two wooden sawhorses. Newspaper clippings about the war, about protesters and about music were thumb-tacked to the wall. A big picture of a distraught girl standing over a dead student—the Kent State shootings—hung in the middle.

I continued searching through the basement. A short flight of steps led to a storm door. When I opened it, Heidi wagged her whole body in greeting. I let her in and she followed me around, stopping to lick my toes if I stood still. There were pipes, a hot water heater, storage places and boxes scattered around. A musty smell hung over the place. It was not unpleasant though it was a far cry from my comfortable room at the front of Mattie's house in Augusta. I thought it was funny how I thought of it as Mattie's house and not my own. Maybe as a kid you never had your own house except whatever little den you created in the bushes and trees outside.

That night after a late supper, I went back to my haven and spritzed a shot of perfume on my arm so I could smell it as I slept. It smelled like Mattie and while I slept, a light tickling voice in my head sang, "hush little baby, don't say a word, Papa's gonna buy you a mockingbird."

Mattie had had her "set" and I soon got to know Willie and Cleo's friends and co-conspirators. First and most unforgettable was Jeremiah, a slight man with a scraggly gray beard and long stringy brown hair. He wore a beret most of the time and a pair of baggy corduroy pants that looked like they had once belonged to his grandfather. People who casually saw Jeremiah might think he was a crazy street bum. But as soon as you started talking to him, you realized he was probably the sanest person you ever met. Just looking into his deep brown eyes was mind-altering. It was like looking into raw genius without any of the usual masks. He laughed frequently, and his laughter, a loud "ha-ha-

ha", spread like a contagion. It seemed that most of the other people in the anti-war movement were uniformly pissed off, but Jeremiah had a way of being angry and happy at the same time. I adored him almost instantly and was a little scared of him at the same time.

I met Jeremiah and the others—Bill and Janet, original members of Students for a Democratic Society, which apparently was no longer a functioning organization, JoAnne and her husband, Stump, a Vietnam Veteran, and a few others—sitting on the patio of my dad's house where they had get-togethers nearly every weekend, while it was still warm, to drink beer and bitch about the government and plan "actions" against the war.

They argued a lot, too. Janet and Stump seemed to be in favor of planting bombs in the United States in retaliation "for the terrorizing of Hanoi." Bill, JoAnne and Jeremiah didn't think that violence was the answer. Willie could see both sides of the issue, and Cleo kept her thoughts to herself.

"It's not like they don't warn people before they set off a bomb," Janet said. She had thick curly black hair, a sharp chin and murky eyes behind a pair of granny glasses. "There is always a communiqué. No one has ever been killed or even injured."

"Except for the townhouse in Greenwich Village," JoAnne said. "And that bomb was definitely meant to kill people."

"True," Stump interjected, arguing against his wife. "But that was a mistake. And they learned their lesson the hard way. How else are you gonna make these assholes listen? I've been to Vietnam. I've seen what we're doing to those people. It isn't pretty."

"These actions are against the law, dear heart," Bill said putting his hand on Janet's. "And as a lawyer, you should not be in favor of illegal tactics."

"Weatherman's hearts are in the right place," Willie said, "but you have to be very careful when you turn to violence that you don't lose your soul in the process."

"You will always lose your soul," Jeremiah insisted. "You become violent then you become like the enemy. Nonviolence is the only way. Ghandi proved it."

Janet had tears in her eyes. "But, Jeremiah, they're killing children in our names. Blood is on our hands. My hands."

I would listen to these endless debates, not knowing who or what they were talking about most of the time. But I had nothing else to do with myself—no friends my own age to hang out with, no operas to help put on, no boyfriend to daydream about. Heidi, part Schnauzer and part Shepherd and part something else, would come and put her shaggy head on my knee as if offering herself to my lonely little heart.

Summer in the Midwest was just as muggy and thick as it was back in Georgia. I turned fifteen, uneventfully. Cleo made a cake and the boys put on party hats and opened my presents: a leather purse that Willie made for me with a butterfly stenciled on the front flap and a stack of used record albums. Cleo gave me a shawl she had knitted. The boys had drawn pictures for me and glued macaroni to them.

Cleo and Willie grew tomatoes that were fat and juicy. I had never liked tomatoes before but my mind was changed when Cleo pulled one off the vine and told me to take a bite. As the juice ran down my chin, I shuddered with delight.

On Sundays I was allowed to call Gretchen. Though Cleo kept me busy around the house and Willie's protest work was interesting, I still sometimes felt a hollowness in my chest that only seemed to be alleviated by those phone calls. I missed Gretchen, and at night I worried about Wolfgang. I thought of Miz Johnny's dinners, and I imagined Mattie's voice singing me to sleep.

Labor day weekend I called Gretchen on Sunday afternoon. Gretchen sounded like she had just woken up, but really she had been crying.

"They sent Wolfie home. But he's leaving this week," she said.

"Leaving for where?"

"He's going to bootcamp."

"Shit."

Gretchen was silent for a minute.

"Maybe it's not so bad. He says if he lives through it, then the army will pay for him to go to college. He wants to be a philosopher or maybe a scientist."

I was sitting at Willie's desk in his basement office with the phone clutched to my ear, wishing I could crawl through the wire and hold onto Wolfgang, tie him up, kidnap him, anything to keep him away from the war. Once again, there was nothing I could do. I would have to let him go like I let Mattie go. But while Mattie had lived a full life, Wolfgang's was only beginning.

Gretchen and I hung up. It took me forever to fall asleep. In the morning Jake and Turtle tumbled into my room. They bounced on the bed while Heidi, who had taken to sleeping on my dirty clothes, barked at the three of us.

"Get up, Eli. Mama says we're having a cookout today. You got to help. Get up right now."

I struggled out of bed and shooed the boys out of my room.

Cleo cleaned the house and I mowed the lawn. Then she made beans, macaroni salad and homemade bread while I kept the boys out of her hair. Willie had gone to work the early shift at a radio station where he was substituting as a DJ until he could get a job at an FM station. When he got home, he went outside and lit the grill. People started showing up in the early afternoon. Fortunately, though the house was small, we had a big backyard, and people brought their own chairs.

Jeremiah showed up first with some middle-eastern mixture that he said was for the vegetarians though I think he might have been the only vegetarian there. Janet and Bill brought a cherry pie with a tiny toy soldier stuck on top. Others showed up with beer or wine or cokes. A tall black guy with a mustache and muscular arms in a t-shirt with a big black fist on the front arrived with Stump and JoAnne. He shook hands with Willie in that inverted handshake that hippies gave each other.

"I'm Smoke. Just moved here from the coast. Stump invited me along. I hope that's cool."

"Sure," Willie said. "What's happening out in California these days? Are you from Frisco?"

Smoke stroked his mustache and said, "I am. It's radical, man. Very well organized. We had Jerry Rubin out last month for a demonstration. All the different groups were there. Panthers. Yippies. Socialists. Weatherman. You name it."

"Are you a Panther?" Janet asked, thrusting her sharp chin at him.

"I am. But I don't mind hanging out with white folks sometimes," he said, "as long as you're on the right side."

"*Viva la revolucion*," Jeremiah said and then ha-ha'd in a way that made the rest of us giggle. I could tell having a Black Panther in the midst made everyone feel upbeat.

Bill strolled over and said, "You know, I'm pretty sure I saw an unmarked cop car around the corner when I was driving up. They're hip to you, man."

Willie glanced around. He had a slab of ribs on the grill along with some hotdogs.

"Well, we're not doing anything illegal, man," he said. "Just having a cookout."

"Your phone has to be tapped."

"I don't say anything on the phone," Willie said.

Janet put a hand on Willie's arm. Janet had graduated from Harvard Law at the top of her class, and Willie constantly spoke about how smart she was, which often elicited a jealous smirk from Cleo. I had just recently learned that Cleo had met Willie when he was on the campus of SIU organizing an anti-war rally. It was her first year. She never went back for her second year.

"Willie, they know that you know," Janet said. She had a beer in her hand and reminded me of Fallene when she had one too many.

"Know what?" I asked.

She turned to me with her blinking murky eyes and said, "Willie knows where the safe houses in this area are. He picked them out."

Willie's right eyebrow went up as he looked at Janet.

"Loose lips, Janet," he said.

A nervous shiver passed through me.

Cleo came out of the kitchen, followed by Turtle.

"Has anyone seen Jake?" she asked.

"He's around here somewhere," Willie said.

"Where?" she asked insistently.

"Um," Willie looked around and called out "Jake?"

"I'll find him," I said, rising from the chair where I'd been sitting. I couldn't believe Willie didn't even seem to give a damn. Then again, he'd left me, hadn't he?

Cleo handed Turtle off to Jeremiah, and we split the search. She took the house and I went to the basement. I checked my room and then under Willie's desk and the nooks and crannies where a mischievous kid might hide. Heidi followed but she was no bloodhound. Then I went out the storm door to the garden, but he wasn't out there. Cleo came back onto the patio.

"He's not in the house," she said, a note of panic in her voice.

A look of annoyance crossed Willie's face.

"Jake?" he called out again. "Jake!"

Most of the guests had stopped talking and were glancing around, unsure what to do. Willie went into the house to check it again. Janet and JoAnne were peering into the surrounding backyards.

"I'll check the front," I said.

Cleo's panic had infiltrated my brain. I hurried down the gravel road, calling Jake's name. I could hear Willie calling for him, too. Maybe Jake went down to the IGA store, I thought. He was an enterprising kid. Maybe he found some change and went to get candy. But everywhere I looked, I saw nothing but houses and trees and cars.

The gravel road was only a block long. I turned at the corner and headed down to the IGA, but the parking lot was empty. It was closed for the holiday.

I headed back to the house, hoping someone else had found him. Sweat trickled along my back and it felt like I was blind, like Jake was standing right in front of me but I couldn't see him. How could a kid just disappear? When I turned back onto the gravel road, I saw Stump at the other end of the street and there beside him was Jake's small form. Relief rushed over me, followed by chagrin that I had been so worried in the first place. Yet still I found myself running toward them. Cleo had spotted them as well and she was dashing across the front yard to get to him. She swept Jake in her arms, and I saw her shoulders shaking from behind as I trotted up to them.

"He's all right," Stump said in a reassuring voice. "He just wandered off."

"A man gave me a truck," Jake said, holding out his fist.

By now Willie, Smoke and Jeremiah, still holding onto Turtle, had joined us. Jake was smiling, all his baby teeth showing, as he reveled in the attention.

"What man?" Willie asked him.

"A man in a car. He came out of the car and said was we having a party? Then he said I could have this truck."

Jake opened his hand and inside was a tiny army truck about the size of a Matchbox car.

"What did the man look like?" Smoke asked.

"He was tall."

Stump said, "Well, anyone would be. To a little kid."

"Never mind," Cleo said. "Jake, you aren't supposed to leave this yard without us. Do you understand?"

Jake nodded soberly. Willie hoisted Jake onto his shoulders and galloped with him back to the backyard. Cleo took Turtle from Jeremiah and followed. I stood with Stump, Smoke and Jeremiah. They were silent. Then Smoke said, "That was the pigs, man. Trying to interrogate the little boy."

Stump nodded. Jeremiah didn't say anything, just bowed his head as if in prayer. I felt a sliver of anxiety cut through my belly. I thought about how the cops had taken James and Val away and then gotten Wolfgang next. Maybe I was a jinx.

The party resumed with Jake's return but Cleo didn't let him or Turtle out of her sight. We sat in chairs eating dinner off paper plates, and people traded stories about marches and demonstrations and going to jail.

"What people don't seem to know about Kent State is that the National Guard were actually using bayonets on people," Janet said in her crisp smartest-girl-in-the-class voice.

"You're not serious," Cleo said.

"I am. They stabbed Bill," she pointed at her husband. Bill shrugged and nodded.

"In the leg," he said.

"Let's see," Smoke said.

Bill rose and unzipped his jeans. "Don't worry. I'm wearing underwear. But you gotta see this."

He lowered his jeans, his t-shirt hanging down past his underwear, and showed us a puckered patch of skin—pink as a rose.

"Bled like a stuck pig," he said with a laugh. I looked down at the rib I had been chewing and felt my appetite disappear. He pulled up his jeans and sat down, having silenced the group.

During the momentary silence I spoke up. I had never said much more than hi or bye at these gatherings, but now I couldn't stop the words from coming from my mouth.

"I saw a black man get shot by the police in Augusta."

Willie leaned back and turned to me with a puzzled look on his face.

"You never told me about that."

"It was during the riots last May. Wolfgang and Gretchen and I went to see what was happening. We got trapped between the rioters and the fires so we went to hide at Miz Johnny's, but on the way we saw the police shoot down one of the rioters. It was awful. Another man was screaming because it was his brother. And there wasn't anything we could do."

Everyone was quiet as I spoke. I felt Jeremiah's soft eyes watching me. Janet shook her head. Smoke crossed his arms and his face took on a masked expression.

"Now Wolfgang's been drafted into the army and he's going to Vietnam, and I'm scared for him." They didn't know who Wolfgang was, but I knew that they would understand. Stump reached over and patted me on the shoulder. Jeremiah stood up and came close to me. Then he squatted in front of me and took my hands. He didn't say anything, but just looked at me with moist brown eyes full of kindness.

To be honest, I had mixed feelings about this war that my father and his friends hated. I knew I was supposed to agree with them, but it was hard to believe that the president of our country didn't know what he was doing. Why would he and the Congress would send Americans to die unless it was important? I mean, this was America. We had stopped the Nazis, and the communists were just as bad, weren't they? What about Stalin? But as I sat there in the cooling twilight with Jeremiah's warm damp hands on my own, I was convinced that whatever the reason, it was not good enough for Wolfgang to lose his life.

Then Smoke spoke up.

"I was overseas. It's pretty bad there, but I'd go back if I could," he said.

Janet looked shocked.

"Why?"

Smoke reached around and pulled his wallet from his back pocket. He opened it up and with his thumb and finger pulled out a picture and showed it to us. A beautiful Asian woman with her hair pulled back into a bun smiled in the photo.

"That's Lin Si," he said. "I left her behind. I don't know how to get her out of there. That's one reason why I want this war over. I want my girlfriend with me. I want to marry her."

We all felt sorry then for Smoke and Lin Si. I was the last to look at the photo. When I handed it back to him, he looked at my hands.

"Do you play piano?" he asked.

A small jolt rippled through my body.

"I used to," I said. "Back in Augusta. We had a Steinway."

"Wow," he said. "Well, you've got piano-playing fingers. Very strong looking."

I looked at my hands. They didn't look like much to me, but I had enjoyed playing. It might be nice to do it again but not much chance of that here.

Then Stump started asking where in Vietnam Smoke had been and what division he had served in and all that, and the attention was safely off of me and my hands.

17

My first day at Webster Groves High School. What the hell was wrong with me? I was living with my long-haired war-protesting hippie dad and my 24-year-old hippie stepmom, but I was still dressing like the bookworm girl from Augusta. Well, actually I was trying to dress like the cute popular girls at my old junior high. I had on a gray dress with white polka dots that flattered my budding figure and a pair of strappy black shoes with a slender two-inch heel. I thought, this is high school. I need to dress like I'm grown up now.

So there I sat in my homeroom class surrounded by kids in jeans and t-shirts, sneakers and flip-flops and Candies. I was like a Martian. No, that planet is too close to Earth. I was like someone from Uranus, yeah, the butthole of the solar system.

Each class was steadily more painful. Everyone was friends with everyone else. At least back home I had Gretchen and a few others I could sit with at lunch. But here no one. During lunch period I traveled to different bathrooms from the third floor to the first. I spent about ten minutes in each until thank god classes started again.

Finally it was over. The day was not eternal after all. The buzzer rang and I made my way through the jostling kids in the halls and out the nearest exit. Too late I looked around. Perched on the stone rail and sprawled over the steps were a strange breed of teenaged adults. They stared at me.

"This entrance is for seniors only," a voice informed me as I hurried down the steps. And then on the last step, the heel of my right shoe broke off. I hobbled to Cleo's station wagon amidst a roar of laughter.

"How was your day?" Cleo asked.

I wiped away a tear and said, "It was really cool."

That weekend I took all my old clothes to a Goodwill and traded them in on used jeans. Then I went into Willie's workshop and Cleo showed me how to make roach clip earrings.

I didn't immediately start winning friends and being a bad influence on people, but at least no one laughed when I walked past. In fact, it was as if I'd become invisible.

"I'm going to a consciousness-raising meeting tonight," Cleo said, wiping off Turtle's dirty hands with a washcloth. The boys and I were sitting at the table waiting to eat the grilled cheese sandwiches that Cleo had fixed for dinner. Willie did that thing with his eyes and eyebrows, looking at me with a sly look that managed to say Cleo was up to something he thought was silly but he wasn't saying anything.

"What's a consciousness-raising meeting?" I asked.

Cleo poured some milk for all of us and then put the milk carton away. I loved milk, but she never let me have more than a glass with dinner. Milk was expensive.

"It's where a bunch of chicks get together and talk about how bad men are," Willie said.

"That is not true," Cleo said. "You of all people should understand women's desire for equality."

"I do understand it, darling. I do. It's just that I think the war and racism are more important issues right now," he said. Cleo deposited the sandwiches on our plates with a spatula and then walked briskly back into the bedroom. She came out draping a shawl over her shoulders.

"If women were truly equal, there would be no war," she said.

"Can I come?" I asked with a mouthful of grilled cheese.

"Really?" she said. "You want to?"

"Yeah," I answered.

Willie's lips were pursed as if he was about to say something but then changed his mind. Instead he abruptly changed the subject.

"The problem with the Judeo-Christian model," he said, pouring some Lay's potato chips into a bowl, "is that there's no room for paradox. Zen Buddhism on the other hand embraces paradox."

"What's paradox?" Jake asked, except that he pronounced it "paracots."

"It's when two things don't seem possible at the same time but really are. You dig?"

"I dig," Jake said and Turtle started singing "Old MacDonald" at the top of his powerful little lungs.

"You'll have a great career in opera," I told Turtle, which made Jake laugh and spit milk all over the table. Jake found everything funny even though he didn't understand a fraction of it.

"Are you ready?" Cleo asked me. "JoAnne is picking us up."

I bolted down the rest of my grilled cheese and the milk, wiped my face and got up. Cleo kissed the boys and Willie.

"We won't be late," she said.

"Don't run off with a lesbo," Willie said.

Cleo's eyes narrowed. "Why do men equate feminism with lesbianism?"

"Because you got to admit a lot of them are man haters."

"With good reason," Cleo said and turned her back on him. We walked outside and waited for JoAnne.

We rode with three other women in a station wagon. I sat in the back between Cleo and a big-breasted woman named Nancy. Everyone was talking all at once it seemed, and the conversation revolved around one topic—sex. I didn't have anything to add, but I sure did listen.

"We balled for three days straight," Nancy said, laughing, her peppermint breath wafting across my face. "God, I was so sore I swear I couldn't walk."

"Use K-Y jelly," Cleo advised. "Your labia skin is very tender,

Nancy. You need to keep it lubricated."

The blond in the front seat turned around and said, "Is it true that men like their balls licked?"

Nancy started cracking up, and I thought I would choke I started coughing so hard.

"Are you a virgin?" the blond woman asked me.

I hesitated. I was so embarrassed already I wanted to wither to the floor, but I finally said, "Yes."

JoAnne, who was driving, interrupted the conversation. "Why is it that we're talking about sex? Why can't women get together and have an intellectual discussion?"

"Because we've been repressed for too long, JoAnne," Nancy said and tapped her finger on the back of JoAnne's head. "Men talk about sex all the time. Men sleep with whoever they want to. They're admired for their prowess, but if a woman wants to have sex with different men, then she's a slut."

Cleo put her two cents in: "We need to stop being ashamed of our bodies. We need to be able to talk about anything and everything, including sex."

"Yes," JoAnne said, "but how about not limiting it to sex. How about talking about equal pay, equal opportunities, exploitation, rape, domestic violence."

"We'll talk about those things at the meeting," the blond woman said.

"Well, all I can tell you, Daphne," Nancy said, addressing the woman in the front, "is who cares if men like their balls licked. It's time for them to do the licking."

I looked over at Cleo with wide eyes. She shrugged sheepishly.

The meeting was held in the living room of a nicely furnished house, which was owned by two women. I figured they were the "lesbos" that Willie was worried about. Their house was filled with books, all kinds of pictures hung on the walls, and it smelled clean and childless. They definitely weren't hippies.

The talk at the meeting was about the fact that there were no "women's studies" courses at the local universities, about whether the issues they were concerned about were also issues that black women had, and about various stories of injustices that each of the women had experienced.

"It's worse in the movement," JoAnne complained. "Women's opinions are discounted and devalued. These men are supposed to be progressive, but only when it comes to their causes."

Suddenly I piped up, which surprised everyone including me.

"Where is Janet?" I asked.

Cleo turned to me. "She thinks that the war is more important."

"That's fine. Let her work on ending the war. We'll work on the war here at home," someone else said.

JoAnne turned to Cleo and asked, "Honey, why don't you go back to college? I know that you want to."

Cleo pulled herself up and said, "Well, I will when the boys are a little older."

"That's right. You as the mother have to stay home, don't you?" Nancy asked.

Cleo stammered.

"But Willie has a job."

"So what?" JoAnne said. "His schedule is flexible. Cleo, don't wait too long. Don't put your life on hold forever."

I was stunned by the turn of the conversation. I never dreamed that Cleo might want to go back and finish college. She seemed so happy being a mom and a wife. She looked down at her sandals and didn't say anything. I suddenly felt very sad for her, and I wanted to join the others in telling her she should do it.

"I can babysit more often," I said.

The rest of the women erupted in cheers and one of the "lesbos" kissed me on the cheek, which made me feel wonderful, and I was glad I had come to this meeting and met these women. For a second I wondered about my real mother. Was she somewhere in a meeting like this? Talking to other women about equality? Maybe she was telling them to just abandon their children. And maybe that had been the right thing for her. Cleo was laughing now. She seemed unbearably young.

18

That Monday during lunch period at school, a girl named Cherisse came up to me as I sat on the brick wall in the courtyard where the kids were allowed to smoke. It was the earrings that attracted her to me, that and she was also a new kid. I had seen her before. She was small boned with dark wavy hair and very pale skin. I thought she had sneered at me before but now I realized it was just the way her lips looked.

"I'm Cherisse," she said in a husky voice. "I'm new here."

She sat next to me and fingered the earrings.

"You want a pair?" I asked. Cleo had suggested I sell the earrings to make some money, but I couldn't bring myself to sell them. I pulled a pair from the big leather purse my dad had given me for my birthday and handed them over.

"Thanks," she said. She had a sharp little chin and tiny teeth. "Cool purse. Say, where are you from? You have a funny accent."

"I was born in England," I said. "Moved to Georgia with my governess when I was four."

"Really?" she asked.

"Mmm, hmmm," I said. Why not, I thought.

She pulled some Marlboros from her purse and handed me one. I didn't like smoking, but figured I had to if I wanted to keep the conversation going. She pulled out a lighter and lit both our cigarettes.

"So, are you a virgin?" she asked.

I wondered why everyone was so curious about the state of my hymen, but I decided to answer truthfully, since my ignorance would be difficult to hide.

"Yes," I said and blew a plume of smoke into the air.

Cherisse looked furtively around and then said, "Don't tell anyone that you're a virgin. I mean, anyone!"

"Okay," I said and then she went into a long story about how she was in a girl's home because she'd tried to kill herself and about her boyfriend and how great sex was.

"He calls me the swamp," she said with a laugh. I didn't get it. We spent the rest of lunch time talking and smoking. At my school in Augusta, you would get suspended for smoking, but Webster Groves was a more lenient sort of place. That day after school we walked together for several blocks before our ways split. Cleo had stopped picking me up from school, but I didn't mind the walk.

Since Cherisse lived at a girl's home, she couldn't get out much, and I spent a lot of my time outside of school in my basement room, listening to songs and Willie's voice on the clock radio. He'd finally gotten a fulltime radio gig at an FM station, and his show was definitely the best one on the air. While I listened to the music, a black-winged butterfly—like one of those black swallowtails that used to dance on the Queen Anne's Lace in our backyard—beat madly against my ribcage. I was still a girl, but I was becoming something else, too.

The weather changed. Mornings were brisk, afternoons balmy and nights downright chilly. Willie and his friends were planning a big demonstration against the war. Several of the ringleaders congregated over at the house one Saturday night: Jeremiah, of course; Bill and Janet, Smoke, Stump and JoAnne. Stump had lost his left leg below the knee in Vietnam. It seemed in major bad taste to call him "Stump" but he wouldn't let us call him anything else. Stump spoke in a quiet voice. He was not a tall guy, less than six feet, I guess, with long blond hair that he kept in a braid. He looked like he had been cute once, but the war had scrubbed all the cute out of him.

I was sitting in the kitchen, eating a piece of chocolate cake that Cleo had made. I loved food and couldn't get enough sweets. I would have eaten the whole cake if she'd let me, but Cleo kept a close watch on the food consumption in that house, and I was always just a little bit hungry. Stump came in on his crutches and looked in the refrigerator for a beer.

"How ya' doin'?" he asked. "You coming to the protest?"

I shrugged my shoulders. "I don't know. Probably not." After my experiences in the Augusta riot, I wasn't that interested in mob scenes.

Stump maneuvered himself into the chair across from me and opened the can of beer, throwing the poptop on the table. I broke off the tab and slipped the ring on my finger.

"Now, we're married," Stump said with a laugh. I laughed, too.

Then I asked him a question that I'd been wanting to ask ever since I met him.

"What was it like? In Vietnam, I mean?"

Stump took a long slug from the beer and then wiped his mouth with his hand.

"Here's a tip for how to make your own luck, kid. When your government comes to you singing 'My Country Tis of Thee' and waving those pretty stars and stripes in your face and tells you to come be a hero, saying you gotta go halfway across the planet—9,000 miles—and kill people you don't even know, you tell them to kiss your ass. 'Cause even if your ass winds up in jail for a few years, you will still have more luck than those sumbitches over there. I'm here to tell you, if you listen to them, then the rest of your life you'll have the stink of blood on you. And that stink is a magnetic draw for bad luck. Don't go. No matter what. No matter how bad they say it will be if you don't go, it will be worse if you do. If you go, then it's always with you, always. Ever wonder why guys don't talk about the war. Even the guys been back a few years like me? They can't even make their tongues do that trick. The tongue is too thick in the mouth, swells up with blood. Think about that." He closed his eyes and took another swig of beer.

I didn't say anything. Stump wasn't that much of a talker and yet he had damn near delivered a Shakespearean monologue. Then JoAnne's voice called from the living room, "Stump, honey, come on and help us get this thing figured out."

Stump winked at me and pulled himself up on his crutches.

"Duty calls. Remember what I told you."

"I will," I said. "I won't ever forget it. Thank you."

I thought about Wolfgang, surrounded by the stink of blood, and I wanted to scream.

Every day at lunch I listened to Cherisse tell me about her boyfriend and how much she hated living in the group home. I went home with her after school one day and realized I would hate it, too. She had a room that she shared with another girl, who stared at us the whole time I was there and annoyed us both with her cloying little comments. Other girls seemed to swarm around the place. They said everything in a yelling voice, and the woman who ran the place wasn't a drill sergeant but she wasn't any kind of mother-figure either.

Cherisse smoked cigarettes and sat on her bed, blowing the smoke out the window. I liked her but I felt sorry for her, too. Her parents didn't want her, and I knew how that felt, but at least I had my crazy dad and Cleo and the boys. It was almost like having a family.

One afternoon Cherisse said she was going to audition for the school play. She wanted to know if I'd come with her for moral support.

"Sure," I said. I had nothing else to do. We sat at the back of the auditorium. Cherisse had pulled her dark hair into a high ponytail. Her cheeks were pink with blush and she'd loaded on the mascara. When it was her turn to audition, she strode to the stage with her head held high. I admired her confidence. She had something special, I thought, and I should know. I'd seen enough performers to know talent when I saw it.

Cherisse commanded the stage. The play was *Our Town* and I thought she was a shoe-in for the girl who dies and comes back to look at the town where she grew up. The rest of the girls seemed like robots next to Cherisse.

"You were fantastic," I told her as we left the auditorium.

"You really think so?"

"Absolutely, man."

But the next day when the parts were posted, Cherisse's name wasn't on the list. It seemed that newcomers like us weren't wanted for school activities. She bit her lip and said it was no big deal.

"Hey, why don't you come spend the night at my house sometime," I said. "Maybe Friday night." I thought it would be a lot more fun to be at my house than in that weird prison where she lived.

She said okay, and then she went through all kinds of rigamarole to get permission. I had to get Cleo to sign some form, and Cherisse had to find other girls who would do her chores. Finally we were all set.

When Friday came, Cherisse wasn't at school.

Cleo picked me up that day. Both of the boys were in the car.

"Where's your friend?" Cleo asked.

"I don't know."

Turtle was jumping up and down in the back seat and Jake was blowing spit bubbles. I turned around and squeezed his knee.

"Mule munching corn," I said.

"Stop," he said, laughing.

"Me. Do me," Turtle said, sticking out his knee.

When we got home, I called the group home to find out what happened to Cherisse.

"She isn't here no more," the woman who ran the place said. "She tried to kill herself last night so we sent her to an institution."

"Oh," I said. I hung up the phone and stared at it.

"Something wrong?" Cleo asked.

"No, she went back home," I said. "To live with her folks."

"Well, that's a good thing," Cleo said, bending down to wipe some peanut butter off the floor.

"Yeah," I answered.

I no longer had a friend. But at least she was still alive. I wondered why she wanted to die. True, life was sad, but there was something nice about its sadness, something good enough to make you want to wake up and be sad for a little more.

I went into the living room where Willie kept the little stereo and a stack of records. I put on Jefferson Airplane and lay down on the carpet, looking up at the ceiling. As I listened to the music, I thought, yes, yes, I do, I do want somebody to love.

19

I sat in the courtyard of the school where the long-haired guys and the girls who liked them came to smoke during lunch time. Since I had no one to eat with, I did not ever go to the cafeteria. Rather, I brought an apple every day and that was my lunch. I'd been at the school for more than a month and the only friend I'd made had been Cherisse, and she hadn't lasted long. So I just sort of sat on the wall by myself, eating my apple. I observed the cool kids. I didn't know how to approach them and they were so wrapped up in each other that they didn't even know I was there breathing in the smoky air. I suppose I could have bummed a cigarette from someone but then what do you say?

The door to the school opened and a guy came out that I had seen before. Everyone always talked to him. I guess you could say he was "stocky" but that implies muscles and this guy was kind of soft looking. Girls would say he was teddy bear shaped. He had thick curly hair that hung in his eyes and a sheepish, mischievous smile. The other kids seemed to like him. I took a bite of my apple and looked away.

"Nice earrings. Smoke much?" I looked up and there he was. The teddy bear guy, looking at me with large, bulbous brown eyes. I thought he meant cigarettes and so I played it off, saying, "I'm trying to quit."

He tilted his head and looked perplexed.

"Why?" he asked.

I scratched my ankle and tried to think of an answer. Then I realized he didn't mean cigarettes. He had noticed the earrings. The roach clip earrings that Cleo had taught me how to make.

"Oh, you mean . . ." I was embarrassed suddenly, but he just grinned.

"Yeah, now you get my drift," he said.

"Oh, well, sometimes. Not a lot," I stammered.

"My buddy Tod's got a doobie. Want to come out to the tree with us and enjoy the pause that refreshes?"

I giggled. Something about him made even less than hilarious things seem really funny.

"Sure," I said. I hadn't taken even one toke while I was at the biggest drug fest in America, but that was over. It was time for me to start acting like every other American kid who had the tiniest shred of cool. After all, what was wrong with it? Even my own dad smoked pot. I'd seen a few alkies in my day. Pot was a much mellower high. It was the love grass that Steppenwolf extolled, the green-leaf symbol of freedom, defiance, nonconformity and independence of mind.

In addition to his curls and teddy bear shape, my newfound friend had puppy dog eyes and thick lips that sidled into a near constant grin. I hitched my leather purse over my shoulder and walked with him out of the courtyard and along the back of the building. I felt the other kids glance over at us as if seeing me for the first time.

"Where's your buddy?" I asked.

"He'll be here," he said. Then he stuck out his hand and said, "I'm Dave."

"Eli," I said. "Eli Burnes."

"Cool name."

"Thanks."

"Hey," a voice called out. Dave and I turned around. A thin red-haired boy came loping toward us.

"Hey," he said to me.

"Hey," I answered.

"You're the new chick," he said. "I'm Tod."

"Her name is Eli," Dave leaned forward and said.

"Oh," Tod nodded. "You know, all the guys have been asking who the cute new chick is. No one knows you."

No one had ever called me "cute" before. I was stunned, but managed to stammer out, "I'm from Georgia." I didn't add, *where everyone thinks I'm flat chested and ugly.*

"Damn. All the way from Georgia?" Dave said in a pseudo-southern accent. "Hotlanta?"

"Augusta. But I was born in England."

"Really?" Tod asked.

Suddenly I couldn't lie.

"No," I said. "I just say that sometimes because my grandmother was British. Actually, my step-grandmother. It makes me sound more interesting."

Dave looked down at me with mock concern, "Don't worry, you're plenty interesting."

"Why are you living here now?" Tod asked.

"Came to live with my dad. She died. My step-grandmother, that is."

"Bummer," Dave said. "But we're glad you're here."

We had started walking again. An autumny glaze shined in the air as we climbed a small hill up to a bright green playing field. An enormous elm tree threw a shadow over the closest corner. That, I gathered, was "the tree."

We glanced around and saw that no one was spying on us. So we headed toward the tree where we positioned ourselves so we could be half hidden in order to smoke the joint and watch the school at the same time. It wasn't really that I wanted to get high. But I did want to become friends with these two guys, who seemed to have fun oozing out of them. I took a hit off the joint, and for the first time since Mattie's death, I felt like I was no longer alone.

When I got home that afternoon, I was not surprised to see an unfamiliar Volkswagen Beetle in the yard. People were always coming over to hang out with Willie and Cleo. I came inside the living room and found the boys on their bellies in front of the TV set, watching *Sesame Street*. Turtle looked like a miniature version of Jake.

"Hey, dudes," I said. Their brains were locked by some kind of tractor beam emanating from the television and they were unable to respond.

I heard voices in the kitchen, so I headed that way, hoping for an after-school snack that sometimes was waiting for me, if the boys hadn't scarfed everything like locusts. If there was nothing to eat, I'd have to go down to the IGA and get a Three Musketeers Bar, which I'd been able to eat again after my illustrious New York boosting career.

Cleo was leaning against the kitchen sink with her arms crossed. Willie sat at the table and there was Sassy and some guy with his back to me. When I came in, Sassy jumped up and hugged me.

"Hi," she said and smiled enormously at me. "Hi, hi. hi."

"Hi yourself," I said, hugging her back. "What are you doing here?"

"I'm on my way to the coast. Did you see my car? Isn't it cute? Frank's gonna stay here in the midwest. Lots of people need to go underground right now."

"Frank?" I said.

Sure enough, the guy at the table with his back to me was Frank with short hair and wearing a button down white shirt.

"Hey, Frank," I said.

"Hey there, kid," Frank smiled at me. "I'm *incognito*."

"*In cognito*? What's that?"

"In disguise. He has to look all straight these days."

Smoke was also sitting at the table with his jet black skin and his half-hooded eyes. Seeing him reminded me of James and Val and David. I asked Frank what had happened to them.

Frank shook his head.

"James got 25 years in the penitentiary," he said with a shrug.

"They pinned some bank robberies on him."

"Oh," I said, stunned.

"But Val's okay. She's running a day care center. No one knows what happened to David."

I tried to fit this information about James with what I had seen in New York. Granted I hadn't known him long, but he just didn't seem like the type of person to go out and rob a bank.

Willie reached over and shook my shoulder.

"Smoke brought something over for you," Willie said. "Go downstairs and look."

"For me?"

I went to the basement door and looked down the steps. I couldn't see anything but the same old mess. So I walked down the steps and looked into the big room by Willie's workshop. I saw a keyboard on a metal stand. I went over to it. It was already plugged in and turned on, so I hit a note. Twang. It sounded like, like rock and roll. Like "96 Tears" or "House of the Rising Sun."

"Cool," I whispered.

"You like it?" Smoke was standing on the steps looking at me. His face was in shadow so I couldn't see his expression.

"I love it," I said.

"I don't play it anymore. Thought you might want it," he said.

"It's great. Thanks."

"Don't mention it," he said. He turned around and went back upstairs.

I looked back at the keyboard. Now, I'd have to learn some more songs. I was excited thinking about it. Now music could come back in my life as more than just the songs that my dad played on the radio.

When I came back upstairs, our guests were getting ready to leave. Cleo had her arm around Willie as if she instinctively knew a threat. But there was something else going on with Cleo. Her smile, her voice, none of it was quite real.

"So Frank, you've got a place to stay?" Willie asked. "You can always crash on the couch."

"Smoke here knows a place," Frank said. Then he leaned in confidentially to Willie and said in a lower voice, "I know how important you are to the leadership, man. They speak highly of you."

"Well, we were good friends from way back," Willie said.

There was something in Frank's eyes and Willie's set of his mouth that told me things were being unsaid. Then Sassy hugged me once again and hugged Willie and then even hugged Cleo. She was soon in her Bug and on the road. Smoke and Frank walked down to the main road to catch a bus into town.

"I don't like it," Cleo said after they were gone.

"No need for you to worry, darling."

"He's Weatherman, isn't he? I wish you wouldn't help those people, Willie," she said. "It's dangerous. And I know that you help them. You can't hide it from me."

"Yes," Willie said. "I do help them. But that's because I have no other involvement. And so I can help them. I help them get new identities. I help them find places to hide. They'd get killed, Cleo."

"The white ones wouldn't," she said. "They have rich parents. They might serve a few months in jail. That's all."

"You don't know that," Willie said.

"Yes, I do," she said. She went into the living room and turned the television off. "Go outside and play," she told the boys. "Eli, take them outside please. I have a headache."

I took the boys outside. Heidi came along. We played with their matchbox cars in the dirt and pretended we were fugitives on the lam.

20

I was walking home from school down the main thoroughfare to the road that led down the steep hill to the next road and then the next and the next before I would finally be able to get out of my boots and sprawl on the floor by the stereo with a glass of chocolate milk and listen to King Crimson. It had been three weeks since Cherisse had been shipped off. She'd written me a letter telling me that she wasn't coming back to the group home. Her mom and stepdad had taken her back. Now she could be with her boyfriend as much as she wanted. I mean, that was all she ever talked about anyway, so maybe she'd be happy and wouldn't go playing with razor blades anymore.

It was the beginning of November. I was afraid I would be unbearably wretched this month. Mattie's birthday was in November and though she had pretended to ignore it, it generally turned into a month-long celebration every year. I never saw her as pleased as the birthday when I threw her a surprise party.

I was nine years old but already I knew the elements of a good party. I asked Miz Johnny to prepare a mess of "ordurves" and put Carl in charge of booze acquisition and called up all her friends—Fallene, Max, Louise, Lawrence, all of them till I had a guest list of thirty people. Then I got her to go out for dinner. When we came home, the house was dark as a cave. I ran in and said, "Come in the living room, Mattie. I got a present for you." She followed me, saying, "Dear, you didn't need to get me . . ." Just then we flicked on the lights and Carl's fingers went crazy playing a boogie woogie happy birthday song and all her friends yelled "surprise!" and then sang the Happy Birthday song. Imagine a room full of opera singers belting out "Happy birthday!" Mattie clapped her hands over her mouth and looked like she might faint. Even Mattie couldn't have acted that well. For a moment she was stupefied and then she looked at me, her eyes bright and wet. But only for a moment because no one could answer the challenge of a party like Mattie, and the rest of the night was a whirl of laughter, clinking glasses, singing, and eating.

I was lost in this happy memory, walking along the street by myself, shuffling through the brown leaves when I glanced up and noticed a girl walking on the other side of the street. She was as skinny as a praying mantis with a long sheath of platinum blond hair hanging halfway down her back. She wore light blue jeans and a jean jacket. I stopped and stared at her, she was such an unusual looking thing. At that moment Martha Lyons, one of the popular athletic-looking girls, came walking alongside me.

"That girl is a skank," she said and kept walking.

Martha Lyons seemed to be the type of person whose life was scripted out for her. She would never have to adlib a moment of it. If she thought the platinum-blond girl was a skank, then probably the platinum-blond girl was a fascinating and worthy companion. But I had never seen her before so she probably didn't even go to our school.

Friday, Dave and Tod and four or five of the long-hairs from school decided to play a game of football.

"You wanna play?" Dave asked me.

I shook my head. My tackle-loco days were over. Besides I was starting to get good on the keyboard and I didn't want to break a finger playing some stupid game.

"I'll come and be the cheerleader," I said. We all got a good laugh out of that.

"You can wave a joint and be like *Don't hurt 'em, team. Don't hurt 'em.*" Tod said. So then we started making up stoner cheers and amused ourselves all the way to the field.

"W-E-E-D! What's that spell? Weed! What's that spell? . . . Uh, I forget."

Or

"Two, four, six, eight. Why the hell am I doing math?"

We thought we were funny enough to be on Johnny Carson's Tonight Show.

Through my association with Dave and Tod, I had gained some acceptance into the cool kids' crowd. They were pretty nice overall. Not like some of the snotty girls in my gym class like Martha Lyons, who were always talking about someone behind their back. *She fucks like a fish,* they said about one chick and I had wondered if fish were especially promiscuous.

I sat on the bleachers enjoying the chilly air, my arms wrapped in a big sweater, Dave's jacket over my knees, when a girl came loping up and sat down beside me. I looked over at her matchstick legs and the white-blond blanket of hair. It was the girl I had seen walking down the street a few days earlier.

"What's happening, Toots?" she said.

"Not much, Jellybean," I answered.

And that pretty much settled the whole matter.

Jellybean went to a private school, but she didn't like the kids there, so we started hanging out after school and on weekends. Dave and Tod knew her and liked her so she was a comfortable addition to our group.

One Sunday afternoon Jellybean and I thumbed out to Forest Park. Hippies still flocked there to gather and flaunt their freedom. The guys with their bushy hair wandered around shirtless, flinging Frisbees into the sky, and the women lounged on the grasses or danced, their long hair flouncing about like so many silk scarves. And everyone shared~their blankets, their pot, their music and laughter. Jellybean and I strolled among the tribe, breathing in the fragile moments, sweet as maple syrup. Jellybean ran into a guy she liked, and we got involved in a Frisbee game with him and some of his friends. After the game Jellybean sat down in the grass with the guys, and I wandered around by myself. I grew thirsty and headed toward the stone pavilion to find a water fountain. I ascended the long granite steps of a Parthenon-like building, feeling like the Goddess Athena, and saw the water fountain across the court. I walked toward it. A thin, tall figure leaned against the wall. His head was turned the other way but as I got closer, he looked over and we saw each other.

We stared. I felt a smile pushing its way across my lips. A floppy suede hat topped his six-foot frame, and under it he had a bushy afro. He had caramel-brown skin and deep thoughtful eyes. As I got to the water fountain, he reached over and turned the handle for me. I leaned forward, holding my hair back with my hand and gazing into his eyes for a moment before I looked down at the clear fluid rising toward my lips. It twisted and reflected and caught the contours of the chrome spout like a Dali painting. I bent my face closer and closer until the cool water splashed against my lips and rushed over my tongue, gathering in my mouth before I swallowed. I could smell patchouli oil on his hand. I stood up, drops of water clinging to my lips, and said, "Thanks."

He smiled. I turned and walked away.

St. Louis is a pretty big place, but when you're destined to fall really in love, it doesn't matter what kind of odds are against you. The next time we saw each other was at a Moody Blues Concert. Jellybean and I had the worst possible seats in the house, nosebleed section, and what's even more traumatic—no drugs.

I was walking through the throngs trying to find a bathroom when I saw him again.

"Hi," he said with a smile. I said hi back.

"Where you sittin'?" he wanted to know.

"Nowhere," I said, which was stupid but I didn't want to admit that we were in the worst seats possible.

"Come sit with me," he said. Then he took my hand and led me down to the seats in the second row. About five of his friends were sitting there, and they all watched me silently.

"Where will I sit?" I asked.

"Right here," he said, sitting down and patting his legs. I lowered myself onto his lap and I knew I would never hear "Nights in White Satin" like that again for as long as I lived. The music rolled across us like ocean waves.

"So where do you live?" he asked after the concert. We were standing in the refreshment zone, waiting for one of his friends to come out of the bathroom. I needed to find Jellybean.

"Webster Groves."

"Hey, that's where our shop is. Come by and see me."

"What shop?"

"The headshop where I work. All of us work there," he said, nodding to the group of guys behind him. "Have you seen it? We just opened a couple weeks ago. It's called Illuminations. How do you think we got second-row seats?"

"Oh. I know the place you mean. It's on Old Orchard, right? I haven't been in yet." I had heard talk about the headshop at school. The "heads" at the school were in awe of the water pipe collection.

"Well, come and see me. Okay?"

"Okay," I said, just as Jellybean came storming up to me.

"Where have you been?" she said in an exasperated voice. The guy from the headshop was already walking off.

"Wait a minute," I called. "What's your name?"

"I'm Zen," he said.

"I'm Eli," I answered.

He smiled. Then the crowd pushed between us and he was gone.

"I'm in love," I said to Jellybean.

"You do know he's black, right?" Jellybean asked.

"Uh, yeah," I said. I had noticed the color of his skin, it was true, but it hadn't mattered.

"He's cute though," Jellybean admitted.

"He's beautiful," I said.

When I walked into the headshop, a little bell tinkled. The aroma of incense spread over every inch of the place. I glanced around. It was a fantastic place, with posters and black lights on the walls, glass cases filled with various styles of water pipes and beaded necklaces and earrings and clothes and everything the aspiring hippie could ever desire.

Zen leaned his elbows on the counter and smiled at me. I felt like Dorothy seeing color for the first time.

"Eli," he said.

I floated over to him. I don't remember what we said. It was nonsense, but I gave him my phone number and he said he would call. Then he gave me a pair of earrings and wouldn't take any money for them.

"They're a present for you," he said.

I put them on and he said they matched my eyes. Our hands touched. It was magical. It was first love. I'd had a crush on Wolfgang, but that was a little kid thing compared to this.

Zen started calling every night before eight because Cleo said I couldn't talk on the phone after eight. I didn't mind. There hadn't been any rules with Mattie, but having a few rules made me feel like I was a regular kid. Zen went to a different school from me. He told me that Jimi Hendrix was his idol, and he was dumbstruck when I mentioned that I'd actually seen Hendrix play. Hendrix had OD'ed in September, and Zen couldn't get over the fact he would never get to hear him play live. Zen told me he had an older brother who had a green '57 Chevy that Zen could borrow, which meant we could go out.

"Like on a date?" I asked. I'd never been on a date.

"Yeah."

The headshop sponsored most of the rock acts that came through town, and so Zen got to go to every concert for free. The next weekend Joe Cocker was coming to town. When I told Willie and Cleo that I was going to the concert with a boy, Willie looked at Cleo for guidance. He had no idea what to say.

"Okay," Cleo said, trying to be an authority figure, "but you need to come home right after the concert."

I said I would.

I went to Illuminations after school to tell Zen I could come to the concert with him. He went to the clothing rack and pulled off a slinky black shirt with tiny buttons going about halfway down the front.

"Wear this," he said. "You'll look foxy. I mean, you're foxy anyway, but this will look really good on you."

My face prickled in embarrassment. I was so ravenous for this guy I thought my heart would erupt from my chest. He'd said I was foxy!

I stood in the bathroom trying to hold my hand steady as I applied a black line to my eyelids. Jake stood on the toilet seat, watching me. I could smell his milky breath. Turtle sat on the floor and hummed.

Cleo suddenly appeared at the door.

"He's here, Eli," she said in a whisper. "He's a black guy."

I glanced over at her, holding the eyeliner brush in my hand.

"I know that," I said.

She grinned and said, "Power to the people."

I grinned back. I thought how lucky I was. In Augusta, the color of his skin would have meant everything. But in the world of Willie and Cleo, it was a trivial, but interesting, detail.

Zen was 17, but his friends were all older. I stayed mute around them, relying on my instincts to hide my ignorance. I wasn't sure how I had gone from a homely flat-chested girl trapped in a jungle gym to being with the most awesome male alive. I didn't have the faintest clue how to act. They seemed to regard me with amused tolerance, but Zen was crazy about me. That much I could tell. Oh, and Joe Cocker was amazing. Star boots, spastic hand motions and all.

Zen wanted to go out again the next Friday night but I had to babysit.

"I'll come over there," he said.

"Well, okay."

I didn't mention to Cleo and Willie that Zen was coming over. They might not have even cared, but I couldn't take the chance that they would say no. So about a half hour after I got the boys in bed, Zen showed up at the door.

My dad had this very strange paisley couch. He had sawed the legs off it and so it was a long drop down. Zen's lanky body folded up like a grasshopper as he sat. I went to the kitchen and brought out a couple of milkshakes and sat next to him. It was the first time we were actually alone.

"So," he said, licking chocolate ice cream from his lips, "what was it like living in Georgia?"

"Weird, I guess," I said. "But, you know, not bad."

Then for some reason, nervousness maybe, I began to tell him all about Mattie and Miz Johnny and the operas and even the riots. Memories were thronging through me, each one leading to another when suddenly Zen leaned over and planted a kiss on my lips. I was so startled I knocked over the chocolate milkshake. But the kiss continued and drained every memory down, down and away. Then a small but insistent voice broke through the spell, and I looked up. Jake stood there with his feet in the chocolate milkshake, telling me he had gone pee-pee in his bed. Zen peeled himself off me.

"I guess I better go," he said. We said good-bye about 37 times and then finally he was gone, and there was milkshake all over the floor and I didn't even mind changing the sheets and I promised Jake I wouldn't tell his mother ever. And he promised he wouldn't tell on me either.

21

After the Deep Purple concert the next weekend, Zen and I drove to the park by my house. I still had a half hour before I had to get home. It was cold out, but I jumped out of his car and began to run across the field. I felt alive, alive, alive—air licking me, the sky stretching blue-black overhead. A shock of white moon dangled above us.

And then Zen caught me. I sank to the ground. He lay on top of me, the sides of his fringed suede jacket hanging to either side like the wings of a hawk. My bones sang; my blood rushed through my veins like neon. The sky stretched limitless and black and unknowable above us. I felt the velvet taste of his neck against my lips. Our bodies were pulled together by a force stronger than gravity.

But it was getting late, and Cleo already had her eye on the clock in the kitchen.

"I have to go home," I whispered. We walked to his car slowly and got in. But he didn't start up the car right away.

"Will you be my girlfriend?" he asked.

"Yeah. Who else's girlfriend would I be?" I asked with a laugh.

"So it's official," he said.

"It's official."

Then my boyfriend kissed me again and I kissed him back for a long time.

When we were done, he turned the key and gunned the engine.

At school word got around that I was going out with one of the guys who worked at Illuminations. My status among the kids in the courtyard rocketed. I was still best friends with Dave and Tod, but now the others made a point of including me in their conversations and asking if I wanted to get high after school. Usually I didn't.

But not everyone admired my new situation. In the locker room after P.E. Martha Lyons and her flock began to eye me curiously. Finally, walking between the lockers in her white bra and her gym shorts, Martha Lyons approached me.

"So, I hear you're going out with a black guy," she said.

I shrugged. I didn't think of Zen as "a black guy." He was just Zen. Hippies, freaks, whatever you wanted to call us—we were our own race. Not black, not white. I had grown up in the deep South. In Augusta there was a line, a barrier, a brick wall between whites and blacks that would have taken a stronger heart than mine to scale. But I wasn't in Augusta anymore.

"What's it like? I mean, do you kiss him? Aren't his lips really big?"

I turned to Martha with my hands on my hips. I didn't dislike her, but she was definitely showing her ignorance.

"Yes, I kiss him," I said. "It's amazing. His kiss is like drinking a really fine wine. You know, a beaujolais say from 1959."

I was completely bluffing, recalling conversations from Mattie's dinner table, but since Martha Lyons had never had a fine wine, I knew the right superior tone to invoke, the way to toss it out as if I knew what I was saying, as if it were I who had traveled the world and sung in Italy and Brazil.

"Oh, my," Martha Lyons said, pretending to make fun of me, but she didn't have much else to say after that, and she and her minions went about their business. They were harmless enough. Of course, it's never the ones you suspect who wind up hurting you.

22

As usual Jellybean met me, Tod and Dave at the Squeeze where we jammed ourselves into a pink-cushioned booth, pictures of cows and heaping bowls of ice cream painted on the wall. Dave bent over his root beer float and slurped. Jellybean twirled a strand of her long platinum blond hair while Tod tried not to stare at her. Tod may have been the most normal of the four of us, but his crush on Jellybean had nearly debilitated him.

The real name of the Squeeze was the Velvet Freeze. Dave dubbed it the Squeeze. All the cool kids went there after school. I had eyed them enviously for the first couple of months of my non-existence at Webster Groves High School, and now here I was with my three best friends, doing something so mid-western—hanging out in an ice cream parlor—so unlike my strange sequestered life with Mattie back home in Augusta.

After we'd sat there and methodically tortured and killed the afternoon, Jellybean and I walked to the corner separating rich from poor Webster Groves. I went one way. She went the other.

"See ya, Toots," she called after me. "Don't call me tonight because I'll be busy studying." Then she laughed like a lunatic because Jellybean never studied.

On weekends, I would practice on my keyboard in the morning, then wander down to the main street where I'd stick out my thumb and catch a ride to Jellybean's house—a big brick two-story that reminded me of the house where I had lived with Mattie back in Augusta. If Jellybean was one of the skinniest girls I'd ever known, her mother was one of the fattest women. Her mother would waddle from the front door and call upstairs to Jellybean that I had arrived. Jellybean's mother couldn't say anything, not even one word, without Jellybean rolling her eyes and sucking her teeth and muttering something like, "shut up, stupid."

Her mother ignored the muttering or maybe she couldn't hear it, maybe her head was packed with fat, but she always offered me something to eat—something sweet and unhealthy and, unlike her own daughter who never ate anything from her mother's table, I was a willing recipient of Twinkies and ding dongs and homemade chocolate chip cookies because God knows Cleo wasn't feeding me much.

My friends couldn't get over the fact that my dad was Wild Willie or that we lived in a tiny house on a gravel street.

"I thought you'd be millionaires," Dave said the first time he saw the house, peering out of the car window at the gray wood house, one of its white shutters hanging forlornly by one hinge.

"He got fired from that AM station and didn't work for almost a year," I said. I didn't mention that although they might be famous, radio DJs didn't make all that much money, and Willie was currently supporting a wife and three kids. "Also, he hates money. He's always giving it away. To his causes."

"Is he really a commie, Eli?" Tod asked.

I shook my head.

"Just because he hates the war and doesn't want to see guys like you get your faces blown off doesn't mean he's a commie," I said, annoyed. Sometimes I was so angry with my dad just for being who he was, but on the other hand, I had come to believe that he was right about the war, about social justice, about all those causes he so fervently believed in.

Tod and Dave had the accessories of the hippies, but the 60s were over in their minds. They didn't get what the movement was really all about. They were still a couple of years from being draftable and they probably didn't get lectures at their dinner table about the evils of McNamara, Kissinger and Tricky Dick. They probably hadn't heard about LBJ's treachery, didn't know that the Gulf of Tonkin crisis was a big lie and didn't realize that American tire companies were salivating over Vietnam's rubber crops.

But I knew more than I'd ever wanted to know and the more I learned, the more I felt that it was hopeless to care.

I usually hung out down in Willie's workshop at night while Cleo bathed the boys and tucked them into bed. Ostensibly I was doing homework but really I was sitting there after my allotted 30 minutes on the phone with Zen or Jellybean, looking through my dad's stuff, reading his science fiction books while I rocked to and fro in the big office chair he'd gotten at some garage sale.

There were plenty of interesting things to look at—*National Geographics*, old records, protest flyers, posters of rock and roll bands from the early 60s—The Beatles, The Shondelles, The Supremes. Before things went psychedelic. There were also books of all kinds, including a book called *Siddhartha* that I read, and halfway through I remembered the guy in the turban in Rochester who had mentioned it to me. That book made me miss my river back home.

Willie's workshop is where he came to get away from Cleo and the kids when he wasn't working. I would come in sometimes, and we'd talk. Well, he talked and I listened. Willie would rant about Tricky Dick Nixon and J. Edgar Hoover. He hated all the rich and powerful men who ruled the world and who could send young men to their deaths whenever they felt like it, whenever they couldn't have a bowel movement or their mistresses were mad at them.

"Don't you know Ho Chi Min is a great leader for his people, like Lincoln or Washington was for us? If we would let them have elections, he would win by a landslide, but we don't want democracy for anyone in the world but us."

Zen was seventeen and when he came to pick me up on dates, he would stop and listen to my dad for a while and I could tell he was wondering what he would do if his draft number was low and from his occasional comment, it was obvious he was wondering about career opportunities for headshop clerks in Canada. College deferments were no longer an option.

It was late on a Monday morning. Willie squeezed his fists on the table. His July-green eyes looked like shut doors.

"I'm going, Cleo. We won't lose the damn truck."

"I hope not," she said. "It's not like we can afford to lose it, you know."

Willie and I left the house. We got into his rusty blue pick up truck. A row of rainbow peace symbols lined the bumper and probably held it on to the truck. He had bumper stickers on the gate from the '68 election that Hubert Humphrey lost—probably because his first name was Hubert, which is, I'm sorry to say, even worse than Dick.

Willie flipped his hair into a ponytail and grinned at me. He was excited about this demonstration, and I had finally agreed to come along. I was missing school, but this was not the kind of demonstration that could be undertaken on the weekend. About two hundred people were going to park their cars in front of some major corporation that built weapons for the U.S. military. We were going to block off the exit from the freeway so the workers couldn't get in.

When we got there, already there must have been fifty cars parked, building a metal blockade.

"It's like in the Civil War," Jeremiah said. "When the North blockaded the ports of the South." Jeremiah wore jeans with two long Indian-bead lanyards dangling from his belt loops. He wore a thick red sweater and carried a back pack in his arms. Instead of his beret, he wore a baseball cap over his stringy gray hair.

Frank was there.

"Have you heard from Sassy?" I asked.

"Yeah, she's in the Haight right now. I think she's getting into the music scene there," he said, chewing his Juicy Fruit. His hands were jammed in the pockets of his jeans. His hair had grown longer and he was starting to look like his old self. He glanced over me and while Willie was off passing out protest signs, Frank said, "You're growing up, aren't you?"

I could feel myself blush and realized his eyes were lingering on my breasts. I didn't know what to say. Thank god, Smoke came up at that moment. Smoke always seemed partial to me, but I didn't think it had anything to do with my growing boobs.

"Yo, how's the budding musician?" he asked me. "Learned any good songs yet?"

Willie had come up. He draped an arm over my shoulder, "She plays a mean 'Satisfaction.' "

Frank laughed, which embarrassed me even further. Then he grew serious and stroked his mustache.

"So you ready to go to jail for the cause?" he asked me.

"If I have to," I answered. Which I really hoped wouldn't happen because Zen and I were going to a Jethro Tull concert that weekend.

"She doesn't know any secrets, does she?" Frank asked Willie.

"What kind of secrets?" Willie said. Frank laughed knowingly.

The demonstration felt more like a big party than anything else. Our side was happy. No one was building weapons at this particular plant today. The cops who showed up were friendly. Willie said they were called the Red Squad because they had to be at all the demonstrations. It was as much protection for the demonstrators as anything else, Willie explained to me. He even stopped to talk to them. By now the regular demonstrators and the Red Squad knew each other by name.

"Not all cops are pigs," he said as we drove home. "They've got families, too."

"Since when was that so important to you?" I asked.

"What's that mean, Eli?" he asked. The hurt in his voice surprised me.

"Nothing, Willie," I said. "I didn't mean anything at all."

I decided to change the subject.

"What did Frank mean about secrets?"

Willie sighed. "The way it works is this. I may know something and you may know something, but if I don't know what you know and you don't know what I know then whatever it is we know is safer than if we both know everything. Like say I know half the combination to a safe and you know the other half, then no one can get the full combination from either of us."

"Okay," I said, "so what does that have to do with you?"

"I used to be in the movement. I made friends, bonded with people. Those are bonds you don't break easily. The leadership knows they can trust me. So there are some things that I know and that only I know. But because I'm just a D.J. with a family no one thinks I know anything."

"Except Frank."

"Yeah, except Frank."

"And Cleo."

"And Cleo."

Later that night I heard voices upstairs. I should have been asleep but I wasn't. I opened the door of my basement room and heard a low murmuring upstairs in the kitchen. Out of curiosity, I sat on the steps and listened.

"No, man, what the government is doing is illegal. Those fuckin' pigs are the enemy."

"Smoke, the only way to change things is through the system. You gotta vote. It's a democracy."

"I don't know"—someone else's voice. "He might be onto something. The pigs are in power and they've got the sheep brainwashed."

Then Cleo's voice: "I wish you wouldn't call them that, Will. They're people."

"People who lie, who murder, who commit atrocities."—was that Janet's voice? It sounded like something she would say. "The movement is fighting back. By any means necessary. Do you understand?"

"Kidnapping heiresses and making them rob banks?" Cleo's voice.

Willie said: "That was SLA, not Weatherman."

Cleo said, "I don't care. Willie can't help anymore. He is a father."

"Do you want to see your boys grow up to be sent to another senseless war? As long as these people are in power, we will continue to have wars that are fueled by greed and a sick ideology," Janet said.

I wasn't even sure what ideology meant. But I did know that I was tired and I had school the next day. And it was hard to have all this stuff in my head about the government and the war. I crept down the stairs and went to bed.

23

The Grateful Dead were coming to Kiel Auditorium. Illuminations, the headshop where Zen worked, had tickets for sale and that meant that Zen and I would be in some primo seats. Cleo let me borrow her white lace peasant blouse and a pair of dangling turquoise earrings.

She looked at me wistfully as I gazed in the full-length mirror hanging on her closet door.

"God, what I wouldn't give to be young again," she said.

I stared at her in shock because she was only 24 years old, which was only nine years older than I was. But just then Jake jumped onto her back from the bed and yelled, "Let's go, pony!" and Turtle let loose with an ear-piercing shriek that could split atoms. So I understood what she meant.

Zen came to pick me up and he had never looked so beautiful, his smooth coffee with cream skin and his fro like a fluffy halo around his head. He wore a purple shirt, blue jean bell bottoms that covered his feet and a single silver chain around his neck.

When he smiled his large white teeth flashed, and made you want to swoon. Cleo practically did somersaults as she offered everything in our kitchen—soda, beer, animal crackers, cereal—anything to get him to stay, but I slid a hand around his silky waist and tugged on him and in a moment we were out the door and riding to the concert in the back seat of his boss's VW. His boss was a guy named Gordon. He was short and Jewish and scared the hell out of me because he was so much older than we were, and I was often scared of people in general. And he tended not to smile much but always examined me with a caustic eye.

"Don't drink the Kool-Aid," Zen advised me as we walked through the chandeliered lobby. The glamorous old building made me think of Mattie and how she would have liked to sing Aida in a place like this and probably did back when she was young. We walked across the red carpeted floors. I gazed up at the enormous dome of the gilt-trimmed ceiling. Then I asked in a perplexed voice, "What Kool-Aid?"

"The Kool-Aid that's gonna be passed around the auditorium tonight."

"Why not?" I asked.

"It's electric," Gordon wheeled around to inform me.

"Electric?"

"That means, little chick, that you'll be tripping your brains out approximately twenty minutes after your first sip."

"They put acid in it?" I asked, incredulous. "Far out."

Zen gave me a razor glance. He was strictly against alcohol and not fond of drug use either, which I thought was odd since Jimi Hendrix was his idol. Zen was like his name, sort of Jesus-like. I didn't know why I kept getting involved with these guys who didn't like to get high. But Zen was different in a thousand ways. Sometimes when we were alone he would read snippets of the *Tao Te Ching* to me. But other times we would devote to my favorite activity: kissing. I could lock lips with Zen for hours, panting in between kisses in the back seat of his brother's enormous 1957 Chevy, our bodies pressed against each other so hard it was as if we were welded together. Zen said the worst thing that could happen to either of us would be for me to get pregnant and looking at Cleo's life I concurred, so we kept our clothes on. But sometimes I felt they'd burn off our bodies from the friction.

We sat in the ninth row and after what seemed like hours of some other band playing and then Frisbees being tossed and lighters being flicked and the hazy aroma of reefer settling over the entire auditorium, the band emerged. They had long hair, beards, tie-dyed t-shirts and guitars. A motley looking group until the crowd grew quiet and then suddenly the guitarists like pied pipers struck their chords and a voice sang, "Come hear Uncle John's band, by the riverside." We were mesmerized.

Then they sang "Sugar Magnolia" and my heart reeled back to Augusta, to the thick magnolia trees I climbed, drunk on the color green as I hid behind the hard oval leaves that clicked like castanets in the southern breeze. I remembered how I lost myself, how I became self-less with no sense of fear or failure or all the things I was just beginning to sense were part of the landscape of my approaching adulthood.

As luck would have it, Zen was talking to his boss when a plastic carton of grape Kool-Aid was passed to me by a laughing barefoot hippie girl. I didn't stop to think. I just raised it to my lips and drank.

That night was a school night so I would have to go home as soon as the concert was over. Gordon let Zen take the bug, and he stayed to party with the band, which as the proprietor of the coolest headshop in town was his perogative.

As we drove home, snow began to fall. It rarely snowed back where I was from, but this was a full-bodied Midwestern snowstorm. I was amazed at how quiet it was. I could hear the earth thrumming. This night my mind opened like a starfish as the universe flowed freely in and out of my head. I sat in the front seat hypnotized by the enormous snow flakes flying at the windshield in the white glow of street lights.

"You sure are tripping on this snow, Eli," Zen said. I felt my heart go cold as I wondered what he meant by that. I glanced at him but realized he was just talking. He had no idea that everything was turning oddly purple and that when he moved his hand, five thousand hands followed. But he didn't know. When we got to the house, I kissed him quickly and said I'd see him later. He seemed surprised that I didn't want to grope in the dark just a bit, but he shrugged it off.

Cleo had fallen asleep in front of the Johnny Carson show. The Smothers Brothers were on, and the laughter followed me like a clanking skeleton. The kitchen appliances were breathing as I tiptoed past them to the basement door. Slowly I maneuvered my way down the flight of steps, which seemed to go on as far as the Grand Canyon. My legs stretched down for miles to reach each step. Finally I was down on the bottom, and there was my dad reading an R. Crumb comic. A stick of sandalwood incense burned in a brass incense burner that I had given him.

"Hey, Darlin', how was Jerry Garcia and crew?" he asked.

"They were great, man. It was totally far out. They sang 'Sugar Magnolia' and 'Truckin' ' and I drank some Kool-aid and now everything is all weird."

Willie looked at me with a grin. His face was soft and doughy and his voice echoey and strange.

"Groovy," he said. "Wait right here."

I stood there like a statue while Heidi's fur grew longer and longer in a very disconcerting way. Willie returned and plopped down a bean bag chair and opened up an old turntable. He put on the Beatles' *Sgt. Pepper's* album and handed me the cover.

"Sit down," he said. I sat. "Now look at the cover. You'll be amazed at what you can find in that thing."

So for several hours I sat in the bean bag chair as the secrets of the cosmos, which had somehow been hidden in the cover of *Sgt. Pepper's Lonely Hearts Club Band* revealed themselves to me in an exotic foreign language that amazingly I understood. And my dad sat in the room with me reading comic books as reality wobbled and dissolved and took shape again. When I woke up, it was almost noon and I was in my bed, still wearing my clothes. I staggered upstairs and found a note from Cleo that said, "Eli, hope you're feeling better. Your dad said he thought you had a stomach flu or something and that you shouldn't go to school today. I'm at the store. Back soon. C."

I dropped the note back on the table and sank into one of the cushioned metal chairs. Willie had taken care of me last night. I had been able to trust him. Suddenly the anger that I had kept stored in a box in my chest was nothing but ashes. I felt an enormous sense of relief as tears slid down my face. I hadn't even realized how angry I had been with him for not being around all those years. Sunlight shone on the stones of the patio and a red cardinal with a black mask over his eyes nibbled at some seeds on the ground.

24

Sometimes on the weekends Zen and I would go to the midnight flicks. I didn't know at first that "flicks" was another word for movies.

"It's because the movies in the old days used to flicker," my dad explained to me. Willie never graduated from college, but he was the smartest person I knew besides Jeremiah.

If I didn't go out with Zen, I'd usually go riding with Tod and Dave in Tod's old Rambler and we'd cruise through the Steak N Shake and Dave would pretend to be all tough and might yell out the window to someone he knew, "You cruisin' for a bruisin', boy? Packin' for a smackin'?" Then he'd laugh and you'd have to laugh with him because though Dave was stocky he'd never been in a fight in his life.

That Saturday night Zen said he had to do something with his family, so I called Jellybean.

"I can't go out," she whined. "I got a D in biology and I'm on restriction for the weekend."

But Tod and Dave were available so Dave thought we should go to Larson Park and have a bottle rocket battle. In spite of the fact that they were major potheads, Tod and Dave were terminally wholesome. So we drove to Larson Park and spread out each with a dozen rockets and we created our own version of the Mekong Delta, puncturing the cold night air with sparks of light and the loud cracks of our fireworks. We took off running across the fields, shooting at each other and diving on to the brittle brown grass as we dodged the incoming missiles. I had just reached the shelter of a tree and fired when Tod suddenly yelled, "Shit!"

I ran toward him. The sleeve of his jacket was sparking in a variety of bright colors and Dave was weeping with laughter.

"It's not funny," Tod said, beating his jacket. When I got up to him, I could smell the charred leather. "My dad is going to be so pissed."

"Uh oh," Dave said, glancing toward the parking lot. Just then we heard a whoop, whoop and a voice came over a speaker: "This is the Webster Groves Police. You are violating the law. Come over here immediately." All three of us charged across the field like scared rats before he had even gotten to the word Police.

"Over here," Dave said, pointing to a little knoll. We dove behind it and peered over the edge into the dark. "Oh man, we're going to jail," Dave said, wiping the sweat from his forehead.

He glanced into my eyes and we both started giggling so hard it was almost painful.

Tod was breathing hard and looked like a hunted animal, his thin face pale and freckled.

"My car," he whimpered. "They'll impound my car."

We digested that thought and all its implications. Finally, Dave heaved a sigh and said, "All right. Let's surrender to the pigs. We can't let you get in trouble by yourself."

So we stood up, brushed the wet grass from our jeans and walked back to the gravel lot where Tod's rambler waited alone. We could see the tail lights of the cop car as it drove away.

Dave puffed himself up and yelled, "And don't come back either, suckers."

Tod got on his knees and kissed the door handle of his beloved old beater. We squeezed into the front seat, me between the two of them on the bench seat with my feet up on the hump. Dave had his window open, gulping the cold air.

"Roll that up, moron," Tod said.

"I'm sorry but your jacket stinks," Dave said, but he rolled up the window. It soon got steamy inside from our breaths. But I felt great and was secretly glad that I was out with my friends and not out with Zen that night. I was more able to act like a kid, to be myself with Tod and Dave than with anybody else.

"Eli, can you sing?" Dave asked.

"What? Why?" I asked, perplexed.

"I was thinking we should form a band," he said. "I can play lead guitar. Tod plays drums. Maybe you could sing. You know, a little Grace Slick action there. Maybe some Janis Joplin."

I thought about it for a moment. "No, I don't sing," I said. "But I have a keyboard, and I can read and write music."

"We need someone to play bass guitar," Tod said.

"Maybe Jellybean can learn to play," I suggested. Then we all burst out laughing at the idea of Jellybean ever putting energy into anything whatsoever. That was the most lethargic girl on the planet.

"Well, we can find someone to play bass. That shouldn't be too hard. Eli, maybe you could write some songs. We could play cover songs and then you know, slip in some original material. We could become famous."

Yeah, I thought. And I remembered the way Mattie always had musicians over at the house, the parties filled with piano music as they sang and drank their high balls and martinis. I had loved those nights, the warm laughter that seemed to evaporate my inherent loneliness. I could hear Mattie's voice, telling me, "You can do anything you want to do, darling."

"Okay," I said. "I'm in. What'll we call ourselves?"

Tod looked down at the ruined sleeve of his jacket and said, "The Bottle Rockets."

I got home fairly early because Tod's dad wouldn't let him stay out past midnight with the car. I joined Cleo on the couch to watch a

Tammy movie on TV: *Tammy and the Doctor*. I always loved the Tammy movies though it's not something you'd admit to anyone. But for me it was nice to watch someone even more naïve than I was. The doctor had finally fallen in love with Tammy when the phone rang. Most people knew I was not allowed to have phone calls after 9 p.m. so I was surprised when Cleo handed me the phone. It was Jellybean's mom.

"Eli, do you know where Sarah is?" she asked in a worried voice. Sarah was Jellybean's real name.

"No, why should I know where she is?" I asked.

"Well, Zen came and picked her up about 7. I thought they were coming to pick you up," she said.

"Oh," I said. "No, I wasn't with them. Sorry." The phone felt like a hunk of lead in my hand. Zen. And Jellybean.

I didn't cry. In my life, pain was a given. After all that had happened, this betrayal was a tiny pebble like the kind that came at you from a sling shot. It only stung. It couldn't damage me. No, I wouldn't cry. I hadn't even cried at Mattie's funeral. She said, never cry real tears, darling, it will ruin your mascara.

I went to my bedroom in the basement, the fake paneled walls covered with psychedelic posters that Zen had given me, the large banner of Jimi Hendrix's face hanging over my bed. My mind drifted back home, back to Mattie and the Southern Opera Guild.

"Why would an Italian write about an American man and a Japanese woman?" I asked Mattie as we drove to the airport to pick up Gary Kingman, the tenor she had brought in from New York to play Pinkerton, the man who breaks Butterfly's heart.

"It was originally a play," Mattie said, "by David Belasco, produced in New York at the turn of the century. It was an immediate hit, and they took it to the Duke of York's theatre in London . . ."

I interrupted her, "The same cast?"

"I don't know. Anyway, the stage manager in London loved the show and

sent word to Puccini that he had to come and see it. That stage manager just knew it would be a fantastic opera. Hardly anyone even remembers the play anymore. But the opera, the opera is unforgettable."

"I'm glad you're performing. I like to watch you," I said.

"I like it, too. Directing is fun sometimes, but hard work. I shouldn't complain though. It's one of the reasons I started the company. Otherwise a woman can almost never get a directing job. Certainly not in New York."

"Why do you want to direct?" I asked.

"Because the male directors can be such beasts. Did I ever tell you about the time Toscanini cupped his hands over a singer's breasts and said, 'If only these were brains.' She should have slapped him. But she didn't. I would have."

"He would know better than to do that to you," I said.

"Maybe," she said. She pulled in front of our small airport and we got out. A short red-headed man with thinning hair threw open his arms when he saw Mattie and exclaimed, "God, you are the sexiest woman alive."

Mattie laughed. "And you are the biggest flatterer alive, Gary, darling. Come and meet my granddaughter, Eli."

When Gary turned to me and smiled, his eyes fixed on mine, I realized that audiences would have no trouble believing that Butterfly would fall in love with this man. He was not beautiful, but something about him seemed more alive than most people. Electricity crackled about him as if he were beckoning you to get on a roller coaster ride with him, a roller coaster without any straps holding you in.

"I met you when you were five years old and Mattie's company brought me down for Figaro. You were an adorable little sprite and now you're a brilliant young lady, aren't you?"

"Yes," I said with a laugh.

We'd already had rehearsals for the chorus members and the rest of the cast, and the last two weeks were devoted to working Gary's scenes and then putting the whole show together. I was the assistant to the stage manager and also helped out the director, who had come from Atlanta to do the show. I furiously took notes during rehearsals, ran to the Coke machine for the director, helped the costumer create headpieces and kimonos, and even sometimes ran the spotlight. On weekends, I painted sets and hammered together the little paper house where Butterfly and Suzuki (Fallene) lived during Pinkerton's three-year absence.

There was not a moment to think of anything other than the show. Underneath all the activity, Butterfly's passion ran like hot lava. It fueled us all, and I watched Mattie fall in love with Gary Kingman, knowing that when the show was over he would be nothing more than an old friend, but for the course of the show we would all love and despise him. We would feel Butterfly's ache as if it were our own. We would want him in spite of his terrible treatment of us.

I had been working every night on the show, going to school during the day and then helping out on the weekends. Toward the end of the second week, I had to stay up all night to finish a project for school that had slipped my mind, so at rehearsal the next night I was stumbling through the motions from lack of sleep. My eyelids were as heavy as velvet curtains.

"Go take a nap, darling," Mattie insisted.

The rehearsal room was up a flight of steps. It was a huge room with a concrete floor; one end was converted to a loft where the extra "blacks"—thin side and back curtains for the stage area—were stored along with stacks of fabric, and piles of old costumes. Long fluorescent lights hung above the room, and big windows made of glass brick showed black against the walls. I climbed up the wooden ladder to the loft and created a nest for myself in the mounds of fabric. I had brought a book with me in case I needed help falling asleep. The book I had was called Madame Bovary, which I found on Mattie's shelves after I'd learned it was banned from the school library. I was surprised no one had set it to music since it was about love and betrayal just like every opera I'd ever seen. A speaker in the far corner of the room was connected to the stage so that anyone who was waiting in the rehearsal room would know when they needed to get downstairs.

I held the book but had only read a few pages when I felt myself drifting to sleep. At first when I heard the laughter I thought that Emma Bovary had come to life and was standing in the doorway of her parlor laughing at something Leon had said. But within seconds I realized the laughter came from the rehearsal room below me.

"Well, you are my wife, aren't you?" a man's voice asked.

"Yours and my husband's." More laughter.

"You're two-timing me? I'm shocked."

"Not yet you aren't."

"Is that a threat or a promise?"

"Maybe both."

"Shouldn't we rehearse our love making scene?"

"We don't have one." More laughter.

"Are you sure?"

Then the laughter ceased and all that could be heard was Mattie's and Fallene's voices through the tinny speaker in the corner singing, "Gettiamo a mani piene mammole e tuberose" as they scattered violets and white roses in the paper house in preparation for the faithless Pinkerton who was now married to an American woman.

I sat up slowly and looked below. Gary Kingman kissed the mezzo-soprano who played Kate Pinkerton, the American wife. In real life, she was the wife of the orchestra conductor. Gary's hands roved over her backside and around to her front where I couldn't really see what he was doing because her back was to me. She made a strange low moan.

"Here?" she asked in a husky whisper.

Gary Kingman's hands had reached around and were gathering up her long skirts when he chanced to look up. His hands became still as the two of us stared at each other. Then he slowly let the skirt drop.

"Later," he said. "We should get back."

"Really? Is something wrong?"

"No, it's fine. I just got carried away," he said smiling at her. I sank back down behind a pile of red velvet and heard their footsteps as they left the room.

A knocking on the window woke me up. I glanced up. Zen's face loomed in the glass. Heidi was trying to nuzzle his hand. The light behind him was pink and gray. Dawn light.

For a moment I just lay in the bed watching him. He wore an old navy P-coat and his eyes seemed to be pleading. I finally pushed off the covers, knelt on my bed, pulled the latch and swung the window open.

"What do you want?" I asked. He didn't say anything for a moment. The cold air seeped into my warm little room.

"Lemme come in," he whispered.

I hesitated, but in the end I moved aside and he wiggled down through the window onto my bed. I shut the window. We leaned back against the cinderblock wall. Jimi watched us from above my headboard. The smell of winter pawed at the window above us. My pale bare legs stretched out next to his long, jeaned legs and I felt the denim against my skin. I could see my pulse beating in my wrists.

He took my hand in his. His hand was brown, the fingers long and gentle. Mine were white and small.

"I'm sorry," he said.

"Do you like her?" I asked.

"No," he said.

"Does she like you?"

"I think she hates me," he said.

"Then why?"

"Just stupid, I guess."

I sighed. His hand brushed against my cheek. The room seemed filled with his remorse and with something else, as if something inside me were awakening like the moment a flame catches and decides to ignite rather than burn out. Our breaths were synchronous.

"Can I stay for a while?" he asked.

I nodded, a damn tear snuck out of the corner of my eye but I wiped it away. He pushed his shoes off with his feet and peeled off the coat, dropping it on the little rag rug on the floor. Then he put his arms around me. He smelled like wool and sweat and something else, something sort of like licorice. I was rigid in his arms.

"It was stupid," he said. "We didn't do anything. It didn't feel right."

"It wasn't right," I answered. "But it's too bad you didn't have fun. I had a great time with Dave and Tod."

I wanted him to know I didn't need him, to make him feel hurt and alone, but I also realized that I was speaking the truth. I'd had so much fun with Tod and Dave, laughing as the bottle rockets whizzed past us and flashed through the gray-blue night. Zen pulled me tighter to him, his warm mouth against my ear, but my body was stiff and unyielding so he stretched his lanky body along the length of my bed, resting his head on my pillow and I slowly collapsed beside him. It was Sunday and it would be hours before anyone else would awaken.

We lay there like a couple of wooden spoons tossed into a drawer. I thought about how it would be when my band The Bottle Rockets was famous and how I'd be able to sing about heartbreak like Janis Joplin and love like Grace Slick. I pulled the soft yellow blanket over our bodies.

25

I was washing the dishes after supper, and Willie sat at the table, reading a manuscript called *Steal This Book*. Willie chuckled and read aloud: "Free speech is the right to shout 'theater' in a crowded fire."

"Huh?" I said.

"It's backwards, don't you see. The Supreme Court debated whether shouting fire in a crowded theater was considered free speech. But the yippies take those ideas and turn them around completely. They want you to reconsider all ideas. What's right? What's wrong? I mean, we're fed a line of bullshit constantly, so you have to learn to question everything. The publishing establishment pigs won't publish this book, so Abbie Hoffman raised his own money to print it. This copy is hot off the press."

"Oh," I said.

I could hear Cleo in the boys' room reading "Peter Rabbit." Another revolutionary, I thought, Peter Rabbit stealing from the man.

A knock-knock rattled the window of the back door. I turned and looked at Willie who seemed as perplexed as I was. Who would be coming over on a Wednesday night and why would they come to the back door?

I walked across the kitchen and opened the door. Janet stood on the concrete stoop. She stepped inside. She was wearing a pair of black jeans and a yellow turtleneck with a white lace vest. She was a bony woman with an always serious expression on her stern face.

"Janet, hi," Willie said. "Dropping by for dessert?"

Janet sat down at the table across from Willie. I sat down at the end between the two of them. The dishes could wait.

"Could I have some coffee?" she asked me.

"Sure." I got up and put the coffee pot on the gas flame.

"There's a problem," she said to Willie.

Willie had put down the book and leaned his elbows on the table.

"What kind of problem?"

She didn't answer right away. She seemed to be thinking, worrying. I poured the coffee into a chipped St. Louis Cardinals mug and placed it on the table in front of her and sat down.

"Is it all right to talk in front of her?" Janet said, indicating me.

I gave Willie a look that said I wasn't going anywhere.

"Yeah, it's okay," he said.

"I've heard that you helped a couple of people last year find safe houses," she said.

"It's possible," Willie said.

"Remember 'days of rage'?" she asked.

"Wasn't there for that one," Willie said.

"Wait a minute," I interrupted. "What is 'days of rage'?"

"It was the first serious action by Weatherman," Janet said. "Took place in Chicago in 1969. It was really important. You know how Bill talks about peace and nonviolence all the time? It's bullshit. He was in Chicago. He helped with the planning and the organizing and everything. I would have been there, too, but I had the flu. How fucking ironic is that?"

"Bill was involved?" Willie asked.

"Yeah, but when he got busted he had fake i.d. on him so he never went to trial. Somehow the pigs have found out who he is. Someone snitched. Anyway, Bill's gone underground."

"When?" Willie's voice sounded tight and frightened.

"Last night. Willie, he needs help, and I can't give it to him. The police watch my every move. It took me hours to lose them and make it over here. I think someone is giving them information, Willie. That's why I came in the back. I climbed over your back fence."

"You're lucky someone didn't shoot you," Willie said. "What can I do?"

She drank some coffee and set the mug down, staring into the black liquid. "Jeremiah is the only who knows how to reach him. Even I don't know. Especially I don't know. Can you get a message to Jeremiah, telling Bill where he can get help. He needs a safe house. He needs some contacts. Can you get out a message through your radio show tomorrow?"

"Not something this complicated," Willie said. "Besides, I'm pretty sure the feds are monitoring everything I say."

I looked from Willie to Janet. Janet's sharp chin pointed toward the table while Willie grimaced helplessly.

"I can do it," I said.

They both turned toward me in surprise.

"No," Willie said. "You can't get mixed up in this."

"Why not? You want me to care about the war. You want me to care about the movement. And I won't be doing anything dangerous. I'll skip some classes tomorrow and take a bus to Jeremiah's. It'll be easy."

Janet looked at me hopefully. Her face was one of studied composure but her eyes were bright.

"No one would suspect you," she said. "You're perfect."

"I can do this, Willie," I said to him.

He sighed. He knew we were right.

"All right, I'll write him a message and we'll give it to Jeremiah."

"Trust no one," she said to me. "No one but Jeremiah."

"How do you know you can trust him?" I asked.

"There are a few people—a very few people in the world whose moral center is so firm that it permeates every aspect of their lives. Jeremiah is one of those people," she said, standing up. She shook

Willie's hand and then shocked me by reaching out and hugging me.

"Little soldier," she said with a dry laugh and slipped out the back door.

I left school after first period history class. I hoped I would make it back in time for geometry. It was the one class I really liked. I had been to Jeremiah's place enough times with Willie that I knew the roads to get there and though I said I would take the bus, it seemed more efficient to thumb over there. Within 45 minutes I was on the corner next to Jeremiah's print shop. I went to the front door, but it was locked and a closed sign hung in the window. I walked around the back of the store to the alleyway where the fire escape led to his apartment. I didn't see his car, but he could have loaned it to someone. Jeremiah had a very loose sense of property.

The potholes in the street were filled with puddles from an early morning shower. The windows at the backs of the buildings were barred and the trash cans were full. A tabby cat skulked between the cans. It was a cool spring morning with a tang in the air. I climbed up the fire escape and knocked on the door. Someone stirred on the other side, and I was relieved that I hadn't made the trip for nothing. The curtain was pushed aside, and a pair of eyes glanced out at me. Then the door swung open.

Frank stood in the doorway.

"Hey, kid," he said.

"Hey."

He opened the door wide and I entered Jeremiah's kitchen.

"Is Jeremiah around?" I asked.

"Nah, he's gone out for a few hours. I was just over here, hanging out, listening to some music." He walked into the living room where some jazz was playing on the stereo.

The blinds were down in the living room; it was dim and comfortably warm. I saw records and piles of books on the tables and in the corners. One wall was covered by shelves. Framed black and white photos hung on the other walls. The floors were wood with a few throw rugs here and there. I sat down on a worn-looking couch. Frank sat down about a foot away from me.

"What brings you over here?" he asked.

"Skipping school. Didn't have anything else to do. I thought I'd see if I could help Jeremiah print up flyers or something."

"Skipping school. Won't you get in trouble?"

"No. My grades are pretty good," I said.

He reached over and lifted a strand of hair that had fallen to my face.

"Pretty girl," he said.

"Thanks," I said.

"Do you have a boyfriend these days?" he asked.

"Well, sort of," I said. "He went out with my best friend the other night. But then he came over and said he was sorry and would I please please forgive him."

Frank touched my hair again and said, "Well, did you?"

"Yes and no. I'm still mad, and I don't trust him anymore," I crossed my arms and sunk lower into the soft cushions of the couch.

The record ended, and Frank got up and turned it over. I recognized the music as a Stan Kenton record that Carl had liked to play at parties when they weren't making their own music. The music had a seductive quality, and I could see that Frank's intentions were not exactly honorable. I could have left, but something inside me didn't want to budge. I guess I was thinking about Zen taking Jellybean out, and that made me wonder what difference it made what I did.

"Are you and your boyfriend having sex?" he asked.

I shook my head. "I don't want to get pregnant."

He chuckled.

"There's lots of ways you can please each other without getting pregnant," he said.

I was silent. Technically I knew what he meant, but it was one thing to read a book about things like that and another to know how to do them.

"What do you think when you see a guy with a lump in his Levis?"

"What?" I asked. It had never even occurred to me to look at a guy's Levis.

Frank's mouth was curved up on one side of his face in a look of amusement.

"How about a lesson in sex education? Jeremiah won't be back for another hour at least," he said.

"No thanks," I said.

"I won't hurt you. I won't even touch you. You need to learn a few things about the male anatomy," he said.

I took a deep breath as an almost unbearable feeling of curiosity took hold of me.

"Okay," I said.

Frank went into the bathroom. I wondered what in the hell I had gotten myself into when he walked back out wearing his t-shirt and underwear. There was no one here but the two of us. He pulled out his penis and began stroking it slowly. He knelt down a few feet in front of me. He had a towel draped over his shoulder.

"Unbutton your shirt," he said.

I opened my mouth to say no, but then I found my fingers were already at the buttons. I unbuttoned the shirt.

"Push it open. Let me see your bra," he said. "Men get turned on by visuals. Why do you think we like those magazines?"

I let my shirt fall open.

"What a goddess," he said. "You have so much power and you don't even know it."

He began to stroke himself harder and faster. I watched in horror and fascination and then he grunted and the thing began to shoot out white stuff. He clamped the towel over himself to keep it from getting everywhere and groaned again. Then sank down to the ground breathing heavily.

He blinked up at me. "See, you can do this to a guy. You can use your hands or your tongue or even your legs. Or you can just sit there and let him take care of himself."

I didn't respond. I began to button my blouse. He got up and went into the bathroom. It was weird what had just happened. He hadn't even touched me and yet I felt sordid. At the same time, I did understand a part of the dark mystery that had been hovering around the edges of my consciousness.

When he came out, wearing his jeans again, he grinned and said, "Girls can have orgasms too, you know."

"I think I'll let my boyfriend teach me that lesson," I said, suddenly wishing he would go away.

He leaned over and kissed my forehead and his hand brushed against my thigh.

"He's a lucky guy," he said. "This won't hurt." His hand moved from the outside of my thigh to the inside. I should stop this, I thought. But I didn't. I couldn't tell him to quit. Something was feeling crazy and strange inside me. His hand moved under my skirt and soon he was rubbing his hand against my underwear, his mouth against my neck. I felt absolutely powerless. Something urgent was happening there between my legs, something that required all my concentration.

And then there was the sound of footsteps on the metal stairs outside.

Frank's hand stopped moving. He pulled my skirt down and stood up. I gazed up at him. He'd won something from me, and I was ashamed. I should have made him stop.

"Maybe we'll finish this later?" he said and put his hands in his pockets.

Jeremiah came in and laughed when he saw us. Jeremiah always laughed.

"I need your car," Frank said. "Thought you'd never get back."

"Take it, take it," Jeremiah said. "Are you with him?"

"No," I said. "You promised you'd show me how to print flyers. I need to make some for school."

After Frank left, I gave Jeremiah Willie's message for Bill, and he gave me a peanut butter sandwich and some juice.

"Why are you a vegetarian?" I asked.

"Because I can be," he answered with a gentle smile.

I was feeling extremely guilty for what had happened in his living room and thinking about that soiled towel in his hamper. What would he have thought if he had walked in on that scene, I wondered.

I got back to school, and I had missed geometry. I walked in to Mrs. Martini's classroom. She was just starting to erase the scrawled figures from the blackboard.

"Wait," I said, sitting down in one of the wobbly old desks with curse words gouged over the top and old gum stuck to the bottom. "I want to write down those formulas."

Martini smiled at me. She was the best teacher, maybe the only really good teacher I'd ever had.

"I'll go over the lesson with you."

She was the kindest teacher in that school, and for an hour I lost myself in the properties of triangles and spheres and cubes. And I forgot about the earlier lessons of the day.

Dave had borrowed his mom's woody for kicks and we were out playing suburbies. Tod was explaining how Webster Groves was once known as the Queen of the Suburbs and we thought that was hilarious. We tooled down Lockwood through Old Webster, one of the original communities that made up Webster Groves, more information from the ever-informative Tod. The sky was a thick leaden gray.

A matchstick-legged girl with platinum hair had her thumb out. The wind shook her hair.

"There she is," Dave said and kept driving. I turned back and looked at her forlorn figure.

"Stop," I said.

"Really?" he asked.

"Yeah," I said.

Dave went round the block. She lowered her thumb when she saw us coming back by again. We pulled up along the side of the street. She opened the door and got in, shivering a little.

"Thanks," she said.

Tod, who was sitting in the back, crossed his arms and looked out the window. Dave started driving again.

I turned around and said, "We're going to the Steak 'n' Shake."

"That sounds good," Jellybean said.

Loquacious Tod's motor had turned off. Dave hummed a song innocently, and I leaned back in the front seat, staring out the window. Maybe I shouldn't have told them to pick her up. No, I definitely should have left her out there. Let her scrawny ass freeze to death.

We pulled into the Steak 'n' Shake and Dave drove up to one of the menu-speaker things. He ordered hamburgers all around.

"Hey, there's Markie," he said. "I'm gonna go try to bum a joint off him."

"I'll come with you," Tod said.

Dave and Tod wasted no time leaving the two of us alone. And instantly all the anger I'd been storing suddenly needed to be inventoried. I wheeled around in my seat and asked, "Did you have a good time with my boyfriend?"

Jellybean shook her head. "No," she said.

"So why did you do it?"

"Because he asked me," she said in a weak voice. Her face was so pale, her blue eyes so big. I didn't know what to say or what to feel anymore. The anger was like a flame on a gas stove—poof and it burned bright hot blue, then poof it was gone.

"Well, we're starting a band," I said. "The Bottle Rockets. Tod is playing drums. Dave is on lead guitar. I'm playing keyboard and writing the songs." I was saying this to try to make her jealous, but then like an idiot I said, "And we need someone to play bass. Can you learn how to play a bass guitar?"

"I can try," she said.

"Then you have to buy one. And you have to come to practices. You can't just flake out. And you can't go out with my boyfriend. Ever. Again."

"I won't," she said. "I promise."

I had my arms crossed. I wanted to slap her hand the way Miz Johnny would sometimes slap mine when I had done something bad.

"I don't know why you don't go out with Tod. He's crazy for you," I said, slumping against the door.

"No, he isn't," she said. "He hates me."

"He'll get over it," I said. "Eventually."

There was a long pause. I watched Dave leaning next to the window of a Corvette on the other side of the lot. Tod was standing straight, his hands in the pockets of his jacket, his red hair ruffled by the wind.

"Will you? Get over it?" she asked.

"Yeah," I said. "Eventually."

A girl on roller skates came up to the car with a tray full of burgers and fries. The Midwest still amazed me.

26

It was Friday after school and the boys and I were sitting at the table eating a snack.

"What are you doing tonight?" Willie asked.

I shrugged and took another bite of cinnamon toast. Zen had asked if I wanted to go out, but I wouldn't mind having an excuse to say no. Jellybean was grounded for smarting off to her mother, and so I wasn't worried about a repeat performance from the two of them.

"Want to come to the station with me?"

I shrugged again. Then Jake began to cry.

"I wanna go. Why are you taking her?"

Willie scowled, his big bushy eyebrows twisting ferociously. Jake shut up immediately. Willie never spanked those boys. All he had to do was scowl like that and sometimes add a growl, and they straightened right up. I could see that he was a pretty good father to them. But with me it was too late for him to step into that role. So he tried to be my friend instead.

Willie kissed Cleo, who was busy wrangling the boys, and we left to go to the radio station. We got into his battered blue pick up truck and headed out to the station which was on the outskirts of the city of St. Louis.

"Radio's one of the greatest forces of democracy," he told me.

"Why?" I asked.

"Because it's something everybody listens to. Television is owned by government puppets. The day that radio no longer belongs to the people is the day democracy will die in this country, mark my words." He had the window rolled down and I studied his profile. He had a strong face, a copper beard that framed it like a pirate's beard and a high forehead.

I said, "All you do is play music."

"Yeah, but have you listened to the words? It's not all about my boyfriend's back anymore. These are songs of the revolution. You just have to listen carefully."

"The revolution," I said. I was thinking of that conversation from the other night. I believed Willie was the most honest, committed person alive. I knew that he took the ideals of truth and justice to be unassailable. And I loved him for it. But I wondered about the direction of this revolution and wondered what would happen if he got in too deep.

"You know Cleo said she wants to go to back to college next year," Willie said.

"That sounds like a good idea," I said. "What will she study?"

"She says she wants to do feminist studies or something like that. Whoever heard of going to college for some kind of shit like that? I don't even think they offer classes like that."

"Well, maybe if there are enough women who want to take them, they'll offer them," I said.

"Whatever. It's not like I have the money for her to go to college," he said. "Still I hate for her not to go if that's what she really wants to do."

Willie was on FM radio now—mellow, free-form, playing albums—not 45s with their bubble gum crap. I sat on the floor of the studio while he sat at the control panel, the mic hanging in front of his lips as he cued records and carts for commercials. While he played music, I looked through the thousands of record albums, reading the liner notes. I read the long essay full of praise for Joan Baez by a man named Langston Hughes. I stared at the orangish red cover of Janis Joplin's album. I loved the way her wild hair swirled in a blur. Too bad she had died—just a couple weeks after Hendrix. I wondered why such talent had turned on itself. But then I thought maybe we didn't deserve to have them with us. Maybe they were sacrificial lambs in a society of lies.

I had to be real quiet when Willie flicked on his mic. Then I watched from my position on the floor as the needles bounced with every word he spoke.

"Yeah, that was from *Electric Lady Land* by the late, great Jimi. The times they are a changin', my friends. Ashes to ashes, dust to dust. But we've still got plenty of great music, folks. We've got Procol Harum up next."

Willie's shift was only six hours on Friday nights. So we left about midnight.

"You tired?" he asked me as we got in the truck. I shook my head. The spring air had every cell in my body feeling all tingly. Winter was finally over, thank God.

We had the windows down as we pulled onto the highway. The pick up truck was like an old man. It didn't move fast, but Willie had it up to about 50 miles an hour on that near empty road. After a while I looked in the side mirror and noticed headlights flashing their high beams at us.

"Willie?" I said.

He didn't answer. I saw an arm hanging out of the window, and that wasn't a peace sign they were shooting at us. Then the car came roaring alongside us.

"Filthy hippies!"

I looked over at my dad with his ponytail and his bandana. He was a big guy but there were at least four men in that big car beside us and no one else in sight. Willie slowed up to let them pass us. As they got in front of us, the bright red brake lights seemed to taunt us. Something flew out the window. Glass shattered on the road.

"We've got to get away from these assholes," my dad said.

When they pulled in the other lane, Willie tried to speed past them. One of them waved a bat out the window. A thud sounded against the side of the truck.

Willie stomped on the accelerator, but there was no way our arthritic old truck was going to outrace these guys. They kept right alongside us sometimes veering into our path. Willie opened the truck up to about 70 mph but it couldn't keep that pace for long. I was so scared of those guys I couldn't even swallow my spit.

Just then Willie yelled, "Hang on." He turned the steering wheel sharply to the right so the truck was going the wrong way on the highway and then he punched it down an exit ramp that we had just passed. I looked around and the other car was sailing away. As Willie flew around the curve of the exit ramp I slid off the seat and banged onto the floor. Willie pulled to a stop and helped me up.

"Are you okay, Eli?"

I just looked at him. The fear that had been lying like a cannonball in my gut burst through me, and I started laughing like a crazy girl.

"Wow, Dad. Wow. That was far out. I was scared shitless."

"Me, too," he said, laughing. "Me, too."

My knees were bruised, but I didn't care. I reached over and hugged him. He hugged me back, holding on for a long moment. Then we drove away, making sure no one was behind us until we got home and were safely inside. The world was a dangerous place to admit you believed in peace.

27

Willie was in his workshop in the basement, making a drum out of elk hide. The room had that weedy smell that indicated he'd probably been indulging earlier even though Cleo didn't like him to smoke pot in the house.

"How should we celebrate Bicycle Day?" Willie asked me.

"Bicycle Day?"

"Yeah, that was the day that Albert Hofman discovered acid," Willie said. "April 19, 1943. It was the first time he tripped. He was riding his bicycle and suddenly started seeing colors and trails and all kinds of cool stuff. Remember when you drank the electric Kool-Aid a few months ago?"

"Yeah. It was kind of cool once I got over the scary part where Heidi looked like a wolf."

"Did you ever think that you were seeing the true essence of Heidi? You saw the wolf inside her."

I was sitting in the big papasan chair by his work table. I scratched my ankle and said, "You think so?"

He shrugged. "Maybe. Maybe it's opening up the doors of perception. You know where The Doors' name comes from, don't you?"

He didn't wait for a reply. "From the poet William Frank, who wrote *if the doors of perception were cleansed everything would appear to man as it is, infinite.*"

Often I could not think of a response to my dad's pronouncements.

This was such a moment. He was pulling the hide tight over the drum head while it was wet. It would dry that way and tighten up on the rim.

"Aldous Huxley wrote an essay called 'The Doors of Perception.' And in it, he said something like the man who comes back through the door in the wall will never be the same as the man who went out."

"What does that mean?" I asked. Conversations with my dad made me feel like I was walking through a darkened maze. He answered my question with a question of his own.

"Do you think that the only reality is the one you can pick up with your five senses? What if I told you there were people who could materialize in another place."

"You mean like, 'Beam me up, Scottie'?" I heard Cleo clunking around in the kitchen upstairs. She never allowed the boys to come down the basement steps by themselves—too many death hazards down here, so Dad and I were relatively safe.

"Not like that. On *Star Trek* they're using technology. I'm talking about the technology of the mind."

"Oh," I said. Sometimes I figured he was just plain crazy.

"Are you two coming up for dinner?" Cleo called down.

"In a minute," my dad said, looking over his drum.

I got up to go upstairs. I was always ready for dinner, but my dad was looking at me with a sly expression.

"Cleo is taking the kids to her folks' place this weekend," he said.

"Yeah?"

"A friend of mine just gave me some psilocybin mushrooms."

I was still confused. I had no idea what that was.

"It's like acid only not manmade. Cow-made. Not quite such a drastic experience as regular acid. Interested?"

"You mean, you and me together. Tripping?" I couldn't believe my own dad was offering to trip with me.

"Yes." He tilted his head, one eyebrow cocked, his finger tapping the drumhead.

"Far out," I said and turned to go upstairs for dinner.

Sunday morning, April 19. I slept late till the morning light shoved its fingers under my eyelids and pried them open. Outside the trees were shaking in the spring breeze, vibrating tiny green leaves. It was still chilly in the mornings, and I was grateful for the little throw rug on the concrete floor. I pushed it with my feet over to the corner where I had tossed my jeans the night before. I grabbed them and jammed my legs into their cold corridors, found a sweater and some socks to pad upstairs in.

The Beatles were playing on the living room stereo. Dad was shirtless, wearing a pair of sweat pants as he cooked breakfast on the gas stove, brown egg shells broken in half and lying empty on the kitchen counter.

"Smells good," I said, sitting down at the linoleum table. He had poured orange juice into the jelly glasses, decorated with pictures of Fred Flintstone and Wilma and Dino the dinosaur. The orange juice felt good in my sleep-furred mouth.

Dad slid a plate in front of me and dropped a piece of toast onto it.

"What is it?" I asked.

He sat down across from me with his own plate.

"Omelet," he said. "Cheese and mushroom."

"Yum," I said and took a bite.

"You like?" he asked.

I nodded and then stopped mid-chew.

"Did you say this was a mushroom omelet?"

He grinned and lifted a big cheesy bite on his fork.

"They don't taste so great by themselves," he said and inserted the fork into his mouth.

I swallowed.

He looked like a pirate with his big white grin.

"Bon appetite!" he said.

"Back at ya'," I answered, and we ate our omelets and our toast and drank our orange juice. As we ate, I thought that even though Willie and Mattie were not related by blood, they had in some ways come from the same mold, or else they were aliens to the planet come from the same solar system. I wondered how my ordinary, stuffy old grandfather had managed to have two such unicorns in his life. Maybe there was more to the old man than met the eye.

We had cleaned up after breakfast and gone to sit outside on the back patio when Willie said, "We've got to go somewhere. We must experience the world."

"Where?" I asked. My stomach felt queasy and my skin had started to feel kind of squishy.

"Forest Park."

I realized at this point that my father was a genius. Such a brilliant idea that only the most brilliant mind could have conceived of it. Forest Park. We would lift our bodies from these plastic chairs and advance out, out into wide world.

I nodded and said, "The deep dark Forest Park."

"Yes," he said. "We'll slay dragons, drink gin with ogres and rescue fair princesses." Willie's face folded upwards in a huge grin. He was a big man with a big expansive way of moving his arms and his head as if he needed lots of space just to be.

I discovered by the ache in my cheeks that I was also grinning. Involuntarily. Why, I wondered, did this silly psilocybin open such vats of golden joy inside me? What was wrong with our species that we didn't grin uncontrollably all the time? Instead we frowned at each other and snarled and brandished our weapons. And for what reason? What if we could somehow put this in the water supply of the military? Would the war end then, everyone giggling and admiring the pretty colors?

"It makes no sense," I said to Willie. We had somehow donned our jackets and were walking out the front door. He shut it with a click that sounded like a cannon going off.

"I know," he said. He was, of course, completely able to read my mind.

"Why do we make it so hard when it's all so beautiful?" I had stopped in the road and tilted my head back so that I saw the sky running like water overhead. "Hey, where are we going?" I asked when I realized that we had walked past his truck in the driveway and were now on the gravel road. "Are we walking to Forest Park?"

Willie laughed so hard tears sprung to his eyes, and I caught it, the laughter I mean, though the only thing that was funny was absolutely everything. Willie's golden beard had flecks of purple in it. I wondered how I'd never seen it before.

"We're taking the bus," he said. "Driving would just be too weird."

"I see what you mean," I said.

So we walked through the air as if we were moving through some material that crackled with every motion. I imagined that brittle pieces of plastic were snapping as I pushed down the road. It didn't hurt, but I could definitely feel the air and it wasn't soft like air is supposed to be. Fortunately there wasn't much traffic when we got to the main road or else we would never have gotten across. As it was, we made it over just as the bus rounded the corner and headed toward us.

We were mesmerized by the sight of the bus slowly rolling down the gray stretch of road and amazed when it stopped and opened its maw for us to enter. Willie stepped in first.

"Hi there," he said to the driver in a ridiculous attempt to appear normal. He looked at me and his thoughts entered my brain: *See how well I'm doing. Follow my lead, kid.*

The bus driver kept his eyes straight ahead. He didn't want to see us.

"Exact change only," he said in a monotone voice.

"Oh, yeah, change," Willie said, panicking as he dug into

his pocket. I giggled helplessly. Finally he pulled out a handful of change.

"Is that a quarter?" he asked me. I nodded, not daring to open my mouth, and he just poured the changed into the metal box. The door closed behind us and the bus rocked forward. We lurched down the aisle feeling as if we must be invisible, then tumbled into a seat at the back.

"This time is different than the other time," I said.

"Really?"

"More fun. Not as scary," I said.

"Different stuff. This is what the Indians use to go on vision quests," he said.

"I thought that was peyote from cactus, not mushrooms."

"Yes," he answered. Of course, yes was the one and only answer to everything.

"Yes," I said.

"Yes."

"Yes," I said with a contented sigh.

When I moved my hand across the window, I saw trails—copies of my hand—following it, but they were rainbowy and blurred, not the stuttering film strip effect that the electric kool-aid had produced. When that had happened I thought I was in a painting by that guy who did the picture of the nude chick going down the staircase. I had seen the picture in one of Mattie's art books. So after I saw it myself—my own body and that of others, I figured that the artist must have been doing a few hallucinogens when he came up with that picture.

But this was a gentler journey, a bodily journey as well as a head trip.

We floated off the bus when we got to the Forest Park stop. The blue sky welcomed us. The sun was spilling a warm white light all over the place. The grass of the park looked green and wet.

"Eli," Willie said, motioning toward a strange warping point in the air.

"What is it?" I asked.

"It's a . . . butterfly," he said wonderingly. As if we were pulled by a string, we followed the wavering spot of air. He was right. A bright yellow butterfly beat its wings in front of us.

"Come on," Willie said. We followed the flitting butterfly across the expanse of lawn next to the museum.

"Is it possible to see into other dimensions?" I asked.

"Must be."

We passed people, families with kids, freaks with Frisbees and couples with their hands entwined. Everyone seemed to be enjoying the bright birthing of spring.

"Hey, brother, can you spare some change?" a guy with filthy clothes and a hungry look in his black eyes accosted us. To me he seemed some strange apparition, but Willie smiled and said, "Sure, brother."

Willie pulled out his wallet. All he had in it was a ten dollar bill. He gave it to the man, who was so shocked, he dropped it and the bill floated like a butterfly between the two of them before the guy recovered himself and snatched it out of the air.

"Thanks," he mumbled, stuffing the bill in his pocket and hurrying away.

"What a beautiful man," Willie said. Beautiful had always been his favorite word. Now I understood why.

We sat on a bench near the lake, which rippled under a breeze the way a cat's skin will ripple under your fingers. The museum stood like a Greek temple.

"Willie," I asked. "Is there such a thing as God?"

"What do you think?" He was gazing out at the lake.

"Well, if there is, why can't we see him?"

"What if God isn't a him?"

"Why can't we see her then?"

"What if God isn't a her either? What if you are seeing God all the time, but you don't know it?" He leaned forward as he said this, and the purple words slipped across his lips in strings. Then he leaned back and we were looking into each other's eyes. I saw the gold flecks gleaming in his green eyes, the black pupils large and round like dimes. I thought I heard an engine humming all around me; at that moment infinity shot from his eyes and engulfed me. I shook like a fish on a hook and then it was over. Willie smiled at me.

"I think I just saw God," I said.

"So did I," he said.

Then we laughed, and it seemed we couldn't stop laughing for a long time.

We passed the rest of the day, wandering through the park, enjoying the sensations, seeing figures in trees, patterns in the grass and designs in the sky. It seemed like the years we had been apart were erased.

The afternoon grew chilly. Slowly the colors that had been so bright began to fade.

"How are we going to get home?" I asked.

"I don't know," Willie admitted. He had given away all his money.

We walked across the dulling grass that before had looked like freshly washed emerald. On the museum steps we saw a small bearded man with scraggly gray hair, hands deep in the pockets of baggy corduroy pants. Willie chuckled.

"Is that who I think it is?" I asked.

"Jeremiah!" Willie called out.

Jeremiah turned and saw us. I recognized the smile, the beaming eyes, the ecstatic wave.

Jeremiah gave us a ride home in a big old Buick that his grandmother had left him in her will. Before she died, he had always refused to own a car. But now it was his grandmother's wish that he have a car so he said he would drive it but none other. He was not a good driver. He liked to talk, one hand flying up to emphasize his point as he looked over at my dad. But some angel would always take care of Jeremiah. It was the least God could do for the troubled world.

When we got home, I was tired and yet happy—the way you are when you've gone on a long journey and had innumerable adventures. Cleo and the boys were back, and the boys climbed all over Willie, establishing his body as their territory once again. Cleo offered me some Hamburger Helper, but I shocked her by saying I wasn't hungry.

I went to my room, and as I fell asleep I wondered if that Huxley guy was right about how you're different when you come back through the door in the wall.

28

A few nights later, I was lying in Zen's arms in my little single bed. Zen's legs were draped over mine; his breathing had gotten slow and steady. Zen had taken to sneaking into my room after dropping me at the front door on weekend nights. We still weren't having sex, but we both knew it wouldn't be long before we did. His skin felt like flannel next to mine. I was almost dozing when I heard the door to the kitchen open and footsteps creaking down the wooden basement steps. I shook Zen, and his breath stopped. The footsteps continued down. There was nowhere to hide and no time for Zen to slip on his shirt and get out the window. I waited for the door to swing wide and for us to be officially caught. My dad was cool, but was he that cool?

But the door did not swing open. Instead it sounded as if the storm door on the other side of my thin paneled wall was opening. Then I heard voices. Zen and I held our breaths.

"Man, you don't know how much I appreciate this, man. But it's for a good cause, you know."

"I'm with you, man." That was my dad's voice. "But you've got to get it out by this weekend. I've got kids in the house. It would be way uncool to get busted."

"I can dig it. We're cool. Saturday night. I swear. You won't regret it. And I'll pay you. I know you need the bucks."

"Yeah, I do, but still . . ."

"Look, we gotta do what we gotta do, man."

"Keep it down. My daughter's asleep."

"Oh, sorry."

I thought I recognized the other voice, but I couldn't be sure. It sounded like Frank, and I suddenly felt guilty. The voices moved to the far side of the basement over by the hot water heater and I couldn't hear what they said anymore. I turned and looked at Zen.

"They're stashing something in your basement," he whispered. I pinched him to make him shut up. He pinched me back and I would have slugged him but I didn't want him to make any more noise. A few minutes later the storm door opened again and then shut. I heard my father cough and imagined him standing out there, his big hand rubbing his thick beard. Then his footsteps slowly climbed back up the stairs and the basement door closed.

"I'm scared," I whispered.

Zen didn't answer right away. Then he said, "Don't be. Your dad's smart. He'll be okay."

"He's so crazy about the war," I said.

Zen leaned over and kissed me on the lips. I felt that falling out of orbit sensation that happened sometimes when he kissed me like that, real slow and gentle. His hands drifted over my breasts and I felt a deep thirsty longing for more than kisses.

"I better go."

He stood up. He was so tall and skinny. I had managed to forgive his betrayal of me, but I had learned something important. I had learned that of all the characters I had studied in Mattie's opera, I would never make the mistake that Butterfly made. I would never let betrayal drive me to my own death. There were princes out there who were willing to step in when straying Pinkertons had tried to crush your heart.

The Bottle Rockets were gathered in my basement. Sandalwood incense sticks burned in the corner, smoke curling past us. Tod had brought his drum set over. Dave had his Gibson guitar, and I had the keyboard that Smoke had given me. Jellybean had a bass guitar that she had wheedled out of her parents. She had actually learned how to play a simple bass line, and we figured that was all that was necessary. Most songs have basically the same chords and so if you know a few patterns, you can play a bass guitar—a few bass lines will work for any number of songs.

We had spent the afternoon nailing egg cartons to the walls to try to create some sound-proofing. I had looked around earlier that morning to try to find where Willie and his cohort had stashed whatever they were hiding, but I couldn't find anything. I figured he'd already gotten rid of it, which was good. I didn't want the band to find it while we were creating our practice room. That would certainly derail the practice session.

By that evening we were working on Neil Young's song, "Down by the River."

"Why does everybody shoot their girlfriends?" Jellybean asked.

"Huh?" Dave looked up at her, his lower lip hanging down and a blank look on his face.

"You know. Like in that Hendrix song. Joe shoots his old lady down and in this song, Neil Young shoots his baby."

Tod pushed the hair from his face and said, "Well since you're a girl and you're singing it, it can be a girl shooting her boyfriend, okay?" Then he gave me a sidelong look. And Dave smirked and looked down at his fingers on the frets of his guitar. They couldn't get over the fact that I had forgiven the both of them. Tod, with his crush on Jellybean, tried hard to hide how miffed he was, but I knew. He didn't bother to pretend like he didn't hate Zen, which I thought was unfair. I mean, they both deceived me, both of them cheated. So I figured I could hate both of them and lose them or neither of them and keep them.

We played through "Down by the River" about three times. We continued to be amazed by Jellybean's voice. She was a scrawny girl but her voice had a pure, beautiful quality that made shooting your baby sound like an angelic act. I was having some problems with the chord progression in the middle of the song and knew I'd have to work on it some more.

"You kids want some pop?" Cleo asked, coming halfway down the steps. I was from the south and I thought it was weird that she called cokes "pop," but the others didn't think anything of it. They all turned on their speaking-to-a-mom charm even though Cleo wasn't even ten years older than any of us.

She brought down some drinks, and the boys were laughing and cutting up like they always did when Cleo was around. I think they were smitten by her. A knock on the storm door broke through the revelry. We all jumped, especially me, remembering that strange drop off of a few nights ago.

But it was only Zen.

"Hey, baby," Zen said, leaning down to kiss me. Suddenly Dave and Tod both had somewhere to go. And Jellybean sure wasn't going to be left behind and have to stew in her putrid pool of guilt. I tried to get them to stay, but the moment was seriously awkward. Zen said he was sorry to see them go, but his fingers were already crawling through my hair and I knew he wasn't sorry. He wanted to go out, he said, just for a drive.

Now that the band was gone I didn't have anything else to do. So I told Cleo I was going to bed. I closed the basement door and left through the storm door with my hand in Zen's. We climbed over the fence and strolled through the neighbor's yard in the moonlight.

"Give me a piggy back ride," I said.

He was so tall, I had to leap up to get on his back. I draped my arms over his shoulders and smelled the scent of incense and sweat in his thick hair.

"Have you ever been to the Arch?" Zen asked.

"No," I lied. Once when I first came to live with my dad, he and Cleo had taken me and the boys to the arch. We'd gone up inside it all the way to the top where we could gaze over half the world. I remembered thinking that Mattie with her claustrophobia would have been climbing out of that little elevator like a cat trying to claw its way out of a bath.

"Then let's go," he said.

"Won't it be closed?" I asked.

"Doesn't matter."

He was right. What mattered was that he and I were out together alone in the night, and being with him made me feel happy. I let my fingers crawl across the front seat toward his hand. Our fingers just touched and we left them like that as he drove along the dark, empty streets into downtown St. Louis toward that sluggish dark vein, the Mississippi River.

I think the whole tragic episode with Jellybean must have brought us closer together. As we walked across the park with that totally weird structure looming over us like the metal legs of a giant whose body disappeared into the clouds, Zen started acting the fool, dancing like Fred Astaire and saying, "Ginger, how lovely you look in the moonlight." Pretty soon I was giggling, caught up in the game, twirling and saying, "Oh, Fred, darling, you are simply dashing."

Except for a rumpled bum trying to sleep on a wooden bench and a bored security guard who may or may not have been on duty, we had the place to ourselves.

Once we had stopped dancing and had reverted to our former selves, I asked, "Can you swim in the Mississippi?"

"Hell naw, girl," Zen said, feigning a country accent. "That thing is brown. Water is supposed to be blue, don't you know? You can't swim in brown water. Didn't your momma teach you anything?"

"I don't have a 'momma' to tell me that kind of stuff, Zen," I said, pretending to be hurt, but he knew better, and that's one thing I liked about him. He had no problem translating the language of me.

"Oh, that's right," he said. He pulled me close to him as we walked side by side toward the whispering water. "How about if you let me be your momma? I'll teach you all the things you need to know about life."

"Like what?" I asked with a laugh. We had reached the edge of the park, and I leaned back against the railing that separated us from the wide river, sloshing its way past us. The night sky hung dusty gray-orange over our heads. He pressed close to me. The heat of his body wrapped around me like a cloak.

"First of all, I want you to stay away from boys," he said.

"Then you better get off me," I said.

"I said boys, not men."

I just laughed again and punched his arm, but not hard although he pretended that I had broken it.

"And don't have sex," he said, his voice dropping. "Not until you're at least . . . sixteen."

"You mean, I have to wait . . .?" I asked, letting my fingers rove along his thighs.

Zen looked into my eyes and nodded.

I shivered. I realized if I didn't want to go through with it, I could break up with him before then. And if I didn't break up with him? My arms locked around his waist. I could hear his heart thrumming against his rib cage—a tall, skinny boy. I had not known it was possible to feel like this.

Then the moment broke free like a pigeon suddenly fluttering to the sky.

"I better get you home, Cinderella, before your wicked stepmother turns into a pumpkin."

"Cleo isn't wicked, and that's not the way the story goes anyway."

"I know that," he said. "It's Cinderella who turns into the pumpkin."

"You are crazy," I said. We swung hands as we walked back to the car. On the way back to Webster Groves, I laid my head against his shoulder with his arm draped over me and fell asleep.

Then it happened again. The kaleidoscope turned, all the tiny pieces of colored glass fell and rearranged themselves and this new life with my dad and Cleo, this life that had begun to feel right, almost normal, dissolved into something altogether different.

I had snuck back into my room about two o'clock in the morning and fallen asleep hard, snuggled under my yellow blanket, my giant Jimi Hendrix silk banner watching over me like a guardian angel. I was dreaming of Mattie and in the dream she wore the white pearls and her crimson gown. She sat at her mirror, worried about something, and I stood behind her brushing her thick, golden brown hair, trying to soothe her but she wouldn't be calmed.

Then the noise began. Thudding on the stairs woke me fast, making my heart beat like a racer in the last lap. I heard Cleo yell, "Damn you. We have children here."

My first thought was that we were being robbed. Then I heard someone banging on the storm door. I sat up, clutching the blanket. I heard men's voices, but it was impossible to make out what they were saying. My bedroom door swung open, and a flashlight beam danced across the room until it landed on my face. I squinted.

"Who's this?"

A light came on in the other part of the basement and suddenly I could see the men mingling in there.

"That's my daughter," Willie said. "She's only fifteen. Leave her alone. I'll show you where it is."

"I want to talk to her," the man said.

My father's radio voice took over as he planted himself in front of the flashlight. "No. She's just a kid. She doesn't know anything. Do you want the stuff or not?"

Then Willie shut the door to my room. My throat felt tight like someone had a noose around my neck. I threw off the blanket and slid into my jeans. Pulling on a t-shirt, I went to the door and cracked it. An army of cops converged on the far end of the basement.

"Daddy?" I asked.

He turned and looked at me. His lips were tight, and his eyes glimmered with tears. He shook his head at me.

"Got it," one of the cops said, pulling a garbage bag from behind the paneled wall by the hot water heater. The other cops leaned over the bag so that each one could inspect it.

"William Burnes, you're under arrest for possession of marijuana with intent to distribute," a short man, sweating in a coat and tie, said to my dad. The suited man grinned up at my dad, and he hung his head. I started to shake as they led him up the stairs.

Cleo and I stood on the front lawn under the elm tree in the swirling blue-light night and watched as the police shoved my handcuffed father into the back of the patrol car. He glanced at us just once and then leaned back as the car pulled away. The police ignored us and loaded the two garbage bags of pot into the trunk of another car. Cleo clutched me. I had finally stopped shaking, but my breath was hard to find.

We stood there even after the police were gone in the silence of the cool morning as the sun slowly aimed its rays in our direction. A morning breeze stirred the full branches of the tree. The screen door creaked open and Jake came out onto the front steps.

"Mommy?" he said.

Cleo slowly turned and walked inside the house. She didn't seem so young anymore. I sank to the ground and leaned back against the trunk of the tree. I didn't think I would ever get up. I'd been living with my dad for nearly nine months but I'd never told him that I loved him. It seemed like I was just getting to know him, to understand who he was. I thought of that moment when we were tripping in Forest Park and I saw God in his eyes. Now I was bereft. Mattie was gone. Wolfgang was gone. Willie was going to jail. I was completely alone. I would stay there and melt into the tree, become hard like the wood and forgetful of everything except the way the ground held on to me even when the wind wanted to pull me away.

After a couple of hours, I got up. We would have to do something, something to save my father and bring him back home.

29

Willie's picture appeared on the front page of the newspaper. Cleo sat with her cup of coffee staring at it while I fed the boys and got ready for school. I glanced over her shoulder at the picture. He looked maniacal in the picture like the long lost brother of Charles Manson.

"Where did they get that picture?" I asked.

"That's a publicity shot from a few years back," Cleo said. "They were trying to promote his 'wildman' image. You know, he was supposed to be the next 'Wolfman Jack.' But if you look at his eyes, you see how gentle he is." Cleo started sniffling as I took the boys in their room to get dressed.

When I walked the halls of Webster Groves High School, people pointed at me and whispered behind my back. Martha Lyons pretended to be sympathetic, but she couldn't hide her smirk. Dave and Tod took turns accompanying me between classes and I think that kept anyone from outright saying anything to me. The "heads" of course all raised their fists in the power to the people sign when they saw me as if having a dad go to jail was the ultimate act of revolution. I knew that, in a sense, Willie was a political prisoner. He never would have been targeted if he hadn't been active in every demonstration, protest and hippie bakesale in the county. But conveniently he had gone and broken the law so in another sense he was just another criminal.

Even my teachers paused after calling my name for roll call and glanced up to look at me curiously with their eyebrows raised. Except for Mrs. Martini, my geometry teacher. For Martini nothing existed outside the realm of geometry. Since I had an affinity for the subject, she saw me with an objectivity that no one else did. All my life it seemed that people looked at me and saw something about me, but they never saw me. She was different. She didn't take notice of my clothes or my roach clip earrings or anything else. Sometimes if I came to school early, she and I would go over problems together. She would show me advanced stuff that you learned in calculus and trigonometry and together we would marvel at its beauty.

One day she asked me if I planned to major in mathematics in college. I hadn't even considered college except as a place to have sit ins and protest the war. Dad said that Berkley was the best place for radical action. I turned and looked at her. She had a squarish, pleasant face and wavy dark blond hair cut short. She was ordinary in every way except for her eyes that shined with theorems and proofs and isosceles triangles.

"Yes," I answered, thinking there might be sanctuary in the clean order of shapes and patterns.

Every moment, every conversation, every glance between me and Cleo circled around my absent father. How could we get him back, we wondered. Where would we find a lawyer? Could we raise the money to bail him out? Could he go on the run and get away?

"I don't think it's fair to the boys to raise them in Mexico," Cleo said.

"It would be better for him to go on his own," I said. Cleo and I had both watched *Butch Cassidy and The Sundance Kid*. Getting gunned down in South America didn't seem a pleasant prospect. "I could go with him."

"No, Eli, you can't throw away your whole life to be a fugitive. And he can't spend his life hiding. It won't work." She tugged at the roots of her hair.

"Then we have to get a lawyer," I said.

After school I went out looking for work. But IGA wasn't hiring anyone under 16.

"Don't have any openings no way," the manager said.

I asked Zen to ask Gordon if I could work at the head shop, but he said Gordon had a strict policy against boyfriend-girlfriend relationships at work.

Yeah, I thought, I might be a deterrent to the girls who came in to ogle my dude.

Finally, Cleo and I took the station wagon and drove into downtown St. Louis to find Jeremiah's print shop. When we got there, he shuffled to the door and smiled that big wide open smile of his, his eyes all bright like a squirrel's.

"Come in," he beckoned. The back room behind the print shop was full of stuff—old broken chairs, paintings of wide-eyed children that nobody could ever want, bales of wire, boxes filled with toothpaste and mouthwash. There was even a box of old troll dolls. Jeremiah saw me looking at it and insisted I take a troll. I wasn't a little kid. I was there on business, important business. I grabbed one with long green hair sprouting from its ugly little head and stuck it in my pocket.

Once we got past the junk room, we took the stairs to his apartment. We sat down at a round wooden table.

"Like King Arthur," Jeremiah said. "We're all equal at this table."

Smoke was already sitting there, drinking a mug of coffee. He shook his head and took Cleo's hand.

"Sorry to hear about your old man," he said. That was the first time I ever heard "old man" to mean someone's husband. We sat down at the table.

"They'll most likely try to give him an extremely stiff sentence, make an example of him," Jeremiah said, sorrowfully. "The real criminals, of course, those murderers in Washington, will ride home tonight in their limousines and eat dinner with their spoiled, narcissistic families and sleep the deep sleep of people born without consciences."

Smoke nodded and said, "This is a police state now. The only way is through revolution. Go underground. Bring your guns."

"We need a lawyer," Cleo said. Cleo had become fairly disillusioned about 'the revolution.' She believed in the core values of the peace movement. The other stuff—guns, kidnappings, bank robberies—she said that was "pure testosterone-driven bullshit."

Jeremiah scratched his long, scraggly beard and then the light ignited in his big brown eyes.

"What about Janet?" I asked.

"Too hot herself right now. I know a guy. Allen Schwartz. We went to school together. Brilliant guy. And sympathetic to the movement—for a price."

Smoke again nodded. "Yeah, I heard of him. He's good."

Cleo cleared her throat. She looked so tiny now. "I can sell Willie's truck. Maybe get another three or four hundred dollars."

"If he's that good of a lawyer," I said. "He should be able to figure out how to get my trust money free."

Cleo looked at me with her pink lips open and her brown eyes round.

"You can't!" she said.

"He's my dad," I said.

Cleo bit her lip and drummed on the wooden table with a long fingernail.

"Well, give us his number, Jeremiah. We might as well talk to him," Cleo said.

Jeremiah rummaged through some old papers in a drawer in the kitchen until he found a business card for the lawyer.

"By the way, you know that guy Frank?" Jeremiah said.

"Yeah," Cleo said.

"Well, he's disappeared," Jeremiah said.

"Has something happened to him?" Cleo asked.

Smoke spoke up, "That sucker is either CIA or FBI. He's the one set up your old man. They're hoping they can get your old man to snitch on other people. They figure since he's got a family he'll do anything to get out of serving time."

My jaw dropped. I shook my head violently. It suddenly became so clear. James. David. Val. Wolfgang. Willie. All of them—Frank's victims. What about Sassy, I wondered.

Jeremiah reached over and patted my shoulder.

"Don't worry. Please don't worry," he said. But when I looked up, I could see the couch in the living room where I had let him do that and violence squeezed my intestines. I excused myself to go to the bathroom where I threw up.

I went down to the basement and found a battered leather address book that Willie kept in his office. I studied it, trying to figure out his code. There was no code. Sassy's name was on the last page next to the words "San Fran" and a phone number. I dialed the number.

"Hello?" I asked. "Is Sassy there?"

Sassy came to the phone, full of her usual enthusiasm.

"Hi, chick!" she said, her voice like a wave of love.

"Sassy," I said. For a moment I forgot why I was calling; it was so good to hear her voice. Then I remembered. "Listen. My dad got busted."

"What? What happened?"

"They found some pot in the basement." I figured it didn't matter if the cops were listening. They'd already busted him. "And there's something else. You know our friend, the one who was with us when Wolfgang got busted and James and Val. You know who I'm talking about?" I was trying to be circumspect but if they were listening they wouldn't have much trouble figuring out this conversation. Still the information needed to get across.

"Yeah, I know who you mean," Sassy said.

"He was involved. Like maybe he had something to do with it."

"Oh," Sassy said. "He's supposed to be on his way here. Wow.

Thanks for the tip, Eli. You're a good chick."

"Be careful," I said.

"I will," she said. "I've got friends in Seattle I can go visit."

I knew that was a lie for the benefit of the "party line." I wondered if I'd ever see her again as I hung up. I probably wouldn't.

30

Zen stood in the porchlight with his hands in the pockets of his hiphugging jeans. He had on a Sticky Fingers t-shirt and his hair was braided close to his head. It was dark outside, but he smelled like sandalwood and sunlight.

"We're going to hang out at that chick Sally's house," Zen said. "Remember?"

Sally was a senior at my school, and she was going out with one of the other guys at the head shop.

I didn't bother to say good-bye to anyone. The boys were already in bed. Cleo was holed up in her room.

At Sally's house, Zen and I joined Sally and her boyfriend in the basement. The parents weren't home, and Sally had some music on the stereo. We drank lemonade and the guys talked about the shop for awhile. Sally complained that her parents didn't want her to go to college because they were afraid she'd lose her virginity. Her boyfriend smirked and she giggled.

It wasn't long before they had gone upstairs to one of the bedrooms, and Zen and I were prone on the couch in the dark basement. Was this the night, I wondered. We had said we would wait until I turned sixteen, which wasn't that far away. We had said I should get on the pill first, but here we were alone with Pink Floyd singing behind us. And I didn't want to wait.

Then our jeans were unbuckled, and he was rubbing his slender shaft between my thighs. I was amazed at the velvet softness of it, the way it seemed to be a separate body part. I wanted more. I wanted to feel him inside me, but I wasn't even sure how to go about it. My legs were held together by my jeans and by the way we were slammed next to each other on the tiny couch. I felt like there was something inside me, tearing to get out. I heard sounds coming from my throat. He was pushing at me and pushing me and then he held onto me tightly and I remembered watching Frank with his white exploding penis as I felt a dampness on my thighs. I understood what had happened. The moment was over. We'd had sex—sort of, but I was still a virgin. At least I wouldn't get pregnant, I thought. But I also thought the fire inside me would burn me alive.

Willie was in the county jail. Allen Schwartz had arranged for us to be able to see him in a little room where at least we didn't have to talk through a thick screen, but we could only see him one at a time. So Cleo went in first while I waited outside with Turtle. Jack was at the Montessori preschool.

When Cleo came out, it was my turn to go in. The guard motioned for me to enter the room. Cleo's smile was hard like it was set with plaster of Paris. I went in the little room and saw my dad sitting in a wooden chair by a table. I sat in the other chair. He didn't bother to put a fakey smile on his face. He had blue bags under his eyes and his full lips were pursed tight against whatever he was feeling. There was an obnoxious clanging sound beyond the door.

"Baby, you shouldn't have done that. You shouldn't have spent all your money on me."

"It wasn't all of it," I said, though it was most of it. "Besides, what is money? Look at what it does to people. It makes them greedy and crazy. It causes wars. It makes people mean."

He stared at me.

"You're right," he said. Then he looked even sadder if that was possible. He took my hand and slowly stroked each finger. "Eli, I haven't been much of a dad to you. I was so young when you were born I didn't understand what it meant to be a father. But I love you. I love you more than anything on this planet."

I wasn't sure if he was including Cleo and the boys in that "anything" but it didn't matter. I knew that what he felt for me was unique and good.

"I'm glad you are who you are," he continued. "I'm glad you understand what this has been about it even if it turned out so fucked up. Peace and compassion and love—those are the only things worth believing in."

"I know."

"And for a fraction of a second that's what a whole lot of us believed. But those days are gone."

"No, they aren't."

"Yes, they are. You don't know it yet, but they are. I've seen the signs. Money and power—they're making a big comeback. Mark my words."

"Please don't tell me that. What about the revolution?"

"Eli, there's only one truly revolutionary act," he said, leaning close and speaking in a hoarse voice.

"What?" I asked.

He didn't answer. Instead he smiled, and looking into his summer green eyes I remembered that day, Bicycle Day, and the two of us tripping on psilocybin and the moment our minds seemed to meld and he looked like God to me and I looked like God to him.

"Stay true," he whispered.

I felt his fingers on mine, and I got a feeling like colors swirling. I realized or thought that I realized, I wasn't sure, that those words, "stay true" were being roadmapped into me.

So the weeks passed and interest in me and my father's arrest waned. Zen would come over to help me babysit while Cleo was out meeting with people trying to raise money so we could survive. The rest of my money was unavailable until I turned 21.

The morning of my dad's trial, I didn't go to school. Instead I went with Cleo to the courthouse. Dad didn't have a jury trial. It was actually a fairly quick process. While Cleo and I sat on the hard wooden benches like sinners in church, a bunch of men clustered together and talked in low voices, sometimes laughing and sometimes looking all serious. My dad sat in a suit that one of the radicals had given to Cleo. His beard was shaved and his hair cut. He looked at us and tried to smile as if everything was gonna be okay. Then his lawyer came over and whispered something to him and his smile fell apart.

"Ten years." Apparently, Willie hadn't told the feds anything. And now he was paying the price. Cleo didn't say anything. I didn't say anything. We just sat there like we were statues.

Tod and Dave understood when I explained I didn't want to go to the Squeeze that day. Instead I walked to the headshop to see Zen. I wanted to tell him what happened. I walked along Big Bend to Old Orchard, a little section of Webster Groves that I guess was once an orchard of some kind and now was just a few shops and restaurants. Illuminations was in a brick building on the left hand side of the street. I crossed over and glanced in the window past the display of brass incense burners, posters and black lights. They didn't put the bongs and water pipes in the windows.

I saw Zen leaning over the counter. He was talking to a beautiful girl who looked like she probably went to Webster College. She ran her hand through her black hair and I saw that her breasts were large and the halter top she wore barely concealed them. Zen was smiling at her and she was smiling back at him. It was nothing really. Why shouldn't he smile at her? Was he supposed to ignore a girl if she was pretty? And yet seeing him talking to her I wanted to plunge my head through the plate glass window. And I knew that wasn't good. I knew that wasn't love either. That was something else, something ugly and sad, and I didn't want anyone to know about it.

So I turned around and began the half hour walk home.

I walked back along the main street through town. I passed the

Squeeze as quickly as possible. No one noticed me. I turned at the hill and walked down it, remembering how hard it had been to walk up that hill during the icy winter. A southern girl, I had no idea how to deal with ice until I finally figured out I should hitchhike up the hill. Now summer was emerging from its shell. It was a good long walk and I liked best of all just being by myself. Occasionally some jerk in a car would honk at me but I kept my eyes straight ahead.

There were only a couple days left of school. I wasn't looking forward to summer without Willie around. I passed Larson park, which was drenched in green leaf, then turned right and climbed the hill to the gravel street.

When I walked in, I was astounded to see the living room full of boxes. Cleo was on the phone in the kitchen, opening cabinet doors and pulling pans and Tupperware containers out and placing them in a box.

"Yeah, Ma. . . . Saturday . . . I don't know, Ma. Okay, yes. The boys are fine. I'll talk to you later."

When she hung up, she turned around and her eyes did this funny zigzag before landing on me. She wore pink lipstick and her long hair hung in two braids on either side of her pretty oval face.

"What's going on, Cleo?" I asked.

Her hands held onto her hips as if that was helping her stand. Jake and Turtle came running through the kitchen, Turtle holding a matchbox car and making siren noises as he chased Jake.

"I don't have any money left, Eli. Nothing. I'm going to have to get a job, and I need to get someone to watch the boys. I've got to sell the house. A realtor's coming over tomorrow."

"Well, where are we going to live?" I asked.

Cleo hesitated and shifted her eyes to look out the window.

"The boys and I are going to Springfield to live with my parents until I can get on my feet," she said. Then she finally met my eyes, and her meaning started to sink in. I felt like I was in a long tunnel. I couldn't hear anything but the loud humming of blood in my head.

Everything outside of Cleo's face got blurry. I was wondering how to breathe when Cleo turned and walked out of the room.

"What about me?" I asked the empty space where she had been standing.

She came back in, holding an envelope.

"Your father should have told you about this," she said and handed me the envelope.

"What is it?"

"A letter. From your mother. She's not dead, Eli."

Cleo stepped over to the refrigerator, opened it and started rummaging around while I pulled out the letter. Jake and Turtle ran from room to room screeching like deranged eaglets. The letter was dated October, 1970.

I stood in the bright kitchen and started to read:

Dear Willie,

> *I just found out that Mattie died last summer. I know I promised her I would never try to contact you or Elisa, but I do not think I have to keep that promise now that she is dead. Willie, I have been sober for seven years now. Seven years. Every single day I long for my daughter. I know that what I did was unforgivable. But God has shown mercy on me by giving me a new life. I have a job as a bookkeeper for a good firm here in Miami and I started painting. I have even been able to buy a house.*

> *I just want to be able to write to my daughter, maybe to see her if you think she would want to see me. Does she know what happened? Does she know about the baby? Does she know how sorry I am for everything? I'm not asking for much—well, maybe I am. But even just a letter from her. A picture? Or a phone call? Please.*

Marguerite

My hand dropped, and I looked up at Cleo. I could tell she was tired and had already left this part of her life behind. But she opened her arms for me and I stepped into them.

"When are you leaving?" I asked.

"Saturday," she said. "I'll take you to the bus station."

Turtle came crashing into the room, tripped over the box of pans and started crying. I went downstairs to my room, clutching my mother's letter in my hand. Heidi crawled onto my bed, and I cried into her fur. I wanted to look at that old picture of my mom and dad beside the car, but it had been left behind to be thrown away when I left Augusta. I hadn't thought I would ever want to see it again. Then I remembered something. I went to my dresser and searched through the drawers until I found the square box. I opened it. The long strand of brown magnetic tape was coiled around the plastic spool.

I went into my dad's workshop and found his old reel-to-reel tape player. It wasn't very heavy so I brought it into my room. I placed the tape on one of the spindles and threaded the end of the tape around the empty reel. I brought in a set of small speakers and an amplifier and hooked them up. When I pushed the button, I heard the soft whisk-whisk sound of the tape rolling and then the grave released its hold on Mattie's voice. Mimi was resurrected. As she sang for me once again, I fell asleep on the floor, imagining I was under the piano looking up at its glossy wooden underbelly.

31

If Cleo had been older, less preoccupied by two little savages and less broken up by my father's arrest, she might have waited around to see me actually get on the bus. But the bus wasn't leaving for an hour and Cleo was desperate to get out of town. She wanted to shake Webster Groves off her like a dog getting out of a bath.

The day before, Cleo had asked me if I wanted her to call my mother, but I said no. I lied and told her I had called her. I assured her that everything was fine, that my mother said I was welcome to come live with her. Actually I wasn't sure I wanted to give my mother a chance to tell me no.

I stood by the door of the bus station next to my duffel bag. She handed me the ticket to Miami with one hand. Turtle was in her other arm, and Jake stared up at me with wide eyes. He had just turned six years old and like me he was getting to learn about the kaleidoscope turns early in life.

Cleo squeezed my hand, tears gathering in her pretty, almond-shaped eyes.

"Take care, Eli," she said. I bent down and gave Jake a hug. He smelled like milk and Cheerios and I knew that smell would always remind me of him.

"Bye, Sissie," he said. I kissed the tip of his nose.

Then I tried to give Turtle a kiss but he buried his face in Cleo's shoulder.

"Okay, well then, be good," she said and started to turn away. But then Turtle started screaming with his arms out to me. Cleo brought him close to me so he could plant a sticky kiss on my cheek. That seemed to satisfy him. Then the three of them walked back to her old station wagon, Jake turning to wave goodbye before she put him in the car. I watched as they drove away. Heidi's head hung out the back window, her pink tongue lolling in the wind. I couldn't believe they were leaving me, but it was the pattern of my life, wasn't it? Hello, goodbye.

My mother's letter was jammed into the back pocket of my jeans. In the corner of the envelope was her address in black ink. I looked down at the bus ticket in my hand. I didn't want to go to Miami. I wasn't ready to see this woman. What if she had changed her mind since she wrote the letter? Even if she hadn't, she was a stranger to me. She was some kind of boring bookkeeper. I ignored the fact that I had recently discovered the soothing power of numbers myself.

Where I really wanted to go was home—to Augusta. Mattie wasn't there to spill her perfumed love all over me, but Miz Johnny was still there. And I needed her. She hadn't ever been the gentlest person on the planet. But her stern wisdom had felt like a kind of love, the counterbalance to Mattie's extravagant affection.

I walked back to the ticket window of the grimy bus station, asked for a refund, stuck the money in my other pocket and headed outside. My trunk had already been loaded onto the bus, but there wasn't anything I needed in it. I had Mattie's reel in my duffel bag and enough clothes to get me by. The interstate was only half a mile away. I was going home.

My first ride was with an older couple. You could tell they were religious types who wanted to do a good deed. The woman was a plump, bright-eyed lady with her hair in curls as if she still went to the beauty shop once a week for a shampoo and a set. The man was bald. After a half hour or so, I was scared they were going to try to convert me or adopt me or something.

"Where are your parents?" the woman asked me after a lot of small talk about the weather.

"My dad was in prison. But he escaped," I said. "He murdered some people. Said Satan told him to do it. It could be true. My mom is in a coven."

I figured this would either make them more determined to save me or scare the hell out of them. Fortunately, it was the latter.

"This looks like our exit," the man said, pulling off about five miles down the road. "Guess we better let you out."

"God bless you," the woman said as I stepped out, tugging my duffel bag after me.

"And may Lucifer bless you, too," I said with my sweetest smile. Their car left me in the dust.

I had only hitch-hiked around Webster Groves, and it occurred to me as I stood on the side of the road in the hot sun, observing the cigarette butts, drink bottles and random pieces of paper dotting the landscape, the smell of exhaust roiling around me, that maybe it wasn't such a smart thing to do—thumbing across the country by myself. I realized I hadn't told anyone of this plan, which I had only formulated about the same time that Turtle was screaming to kiss me goodbye.

The night before, Zen and I had sat in his brother's car down in the parking lot of Larson Park. He was morose, and I wasn't exactly dancing an Irish jig. I missed my dad more than I thought possible and couldn't stop thinking of him caged like an animal—all because he didn't want to see people die. Zen and I stared out the window until he finally said, "As soon as I save up some money, I'll come down and visit you, okay?"

"Okay," I answered, but I knew this whole boyfriend-girlfriend thing that had just a few weeks earlier seemed like the most important relationship in the entire universe was now complicated and messy like everything else in my life. Somehow that magnetic urge that made me want to graft myself to his body had dissipated. I mean, I still liked him, still wanted him to hold my hand and tell me that I was a fox, but as for all the rest, well, it felt like whatever creature had possessed me for a while had curled up her wings and was buried inside me.

So he had kissed me goodbye, and I had not invited him to come sneaking down through my windows later, and he hadn't asked for an invitation. It was just as well. Hello, goodbye. As for Jellybean, I had gone to her house early that morning and left her my posters and my blacklight. "See ya, Toots," she said in a quiet voice as I walked out of her nice brick house back to Cleo's station wagon.

Huge semi-trucks passed me at a million miles an hour. And I noticed thunder clouds building up in the east—just the direction I was heading. It was funny to watch the grass bend in the wake of the trucks. It was said that truckers were the best rides because they were lonely and usually going long distances, but I was scared of them. I waited till they passed before sticking out my thumb.

I got a ride from an Asian-looking guy in an old Ford Falcon. He drove ten miles under the speed limit and had the air conditioner running as cold as he could get it. His name, he said, was Michael, but I figured it was really some unpronounceable foreign name. He was a small man with a thick accent and I had to lean close to hear his soft voice as he spoke.

"I from Vietnam," he said. Then he smiled very big. "South Vietnam. Not Viet Cong."

"Oh," I said. "I'm sorry about the war."

"War very bad," he said, nodding his head. "U.S. soldiers save my life."

"Really?" I asked.

"Yes, we very happy to see soldiers. So glad when they come. Communists killed my family. But I was saved. Got papers to come here. This great country."

"Yes," I said. "I guess it is."

All my preconceptions were suddenly shattered. I knew Dad was right. I knew that LBJ had escalated the war, and Tricky Dick was keeping it going for his own purposes. I knew that young men were dying for a lost cause. But if I lived in South Vietnam, I realized that I might feel differently. It was not easy to know what was the right thing to do. We humans were such odd beings, each walking around with our separate version of reality. How could there be such a thing as truth?

Michael pulled off the highway after about an hour. This was his exit, he said, but he needed to get gas first. I went to the gas station so I could pee. When I came out of the bathroom, Michael gave me a 7-Up and a bag of peanuts.

"Good luck getting home," he said. Then he bowed to me. I bowed back. He got in his Ford Falcon and drove off.

As I walked up the entrance ramp, I felt a drop of rain on my head. Then another and another. By the time I got to the top of the ramp, the sky was practically black, and thunder mocked me for the peon I was. I glanced around for shelter, but there was none. Cars sped past me. Then the rain tramped down in a torrent. I couldn't even tell that I was crying.

I stuck out my thumb, not caring who picked me up. I just wanted out from this canopy of pounding rain. But no one stopped, no one wanted a soggy waif in their car. Water seeped through my sneakers. I hoped my duffel bag was keeping my stuff dry. I wished so hard then that Mattie had never died, that I had never left Augusta, that none of this had happened. I just wanted to be home in my big four-poster bed with Mattie downstairs singing Puccini and Carl's long fingers dancing on the keys, Miz Johnny quietly moving around the house, dusting, rearranging the knick-knacks and figurines, maybe some collards and fat back boiling on the big gas range in the kitchen. I thought of all the good food I hadn't tasted since I'd left—cornbread, grits, fried fish.

A car slowed down, and I was just about to pick up my duffel bag and run to it when it picked up speed again and kept going with a spray of water from the back tires.

"Rednecks!" I shouted over the rain, spattering and splashing against the pavement. Another car sped past, and I watched its tail lights disappear in the gray rain.

I felt like falling to the ground and sobbing, but instead I turned back around. I nearly jumped out of my skin. There just a few feet in front of me in the embankment lane was the front of a VW van. The windshield wipers knocked back and forth, and in between their metronome arms I saw the face of Jesus behind the wheel. He seemed to be watching me, waiting to see what I would do. I stood there, the rain sweeping across me, and he beckoned. Shaking myself out of my stupor, I grabbed my duffel bag and hurried over. He reached over and pushed open the passenger side door. Squeezing my duffel bag over the seat into the back, I hopped in, slamming the door behind me.

Water dripped from my hair, my face, my fingers, my clothes. My feet made a sloshing sound on the floor of the van.

Jesus grinned at me and said, "I think there's a towel in the back there."

He shoved the long-handled gear shift into first, and the VW engine chugged as we pulled onto the road.

32

We were silent for a long time. The 8-track tape deck played Leon Russell. He had a case of tapes on the floor that I started looking through for something to do. Zeppelin, Cream, The Doors, Sgt. Pepper's Lonely Hearts Club Band. I knew them all from my dad's collection. What an education I'd gotten in the past year.

I was excited about seeing Gretchen and Miz Johnny again. I remembered the first time I ever met Gretchen. Summer had just gotten its engine warmed up when I met her.

She was riding down the hill on her purple bicycle, her blond hair, no longer in braids, streaming behind her. She was standing on the pedals, careening the bike back and forth on the sidewalk. I was on the road on my bike. I turned my bike around and followed her progress on the sidewalk as she flew down the hill and over the little concrete bridge. When she got to the bottom of the hill, I pedaled up next to her and stared.

"What are you looking at?" she asked.

"Nothing," I said, feeling stupid because I was still staring at her. "What's your name?"

"Gretchen."

"I'm Eli," I said and waited for the inevitable remark: "That's not a girl's name."

But she didn't say the inevitable remark. Instead she said, "Hey, you want to race to the stop sign?"

Just like that we were hauling ass up the street past the brick houses behind the mimosa and magnolia trees. She was pedaling fast, and I could hear her breathing hard. Gretchen was a little plump; she couldn't go as fast as I could, but I let her keep up with me until finally she said, "Stop. It's enough. I cannot catch the breath."

Then we parked our bikes under a tree and stomped on acorns. She told me that she and her family had moved from Germany to Atlanta a year ago, but that her German father wanted to be in a smaller town so they came to Augusta. She had a younger sister, an older sister and an older brother and she knew lots of dirty jokes. She told me that a rubber was something that a man put on his penis and rubbed against a woman's leg. I thought it was just the most horrifying idea and yet fascinating, too.

"What grade are you going into?" I asked.

"Seventh," she said.

"Me, too."

Standing under a sprawling live oak tree, I felt like crowing because I had a feeling that I had finally found a friend my own age. She was so different from the girls who went to my Catholic school or even the public school girls who loved to taunt us when they saw us in our uniforms.

"You want to come over to my house?" I asked. This would be the test, I thought.

Gretchen shrugged and said, "I don't mind."

We biked over to my house. Gretchen's eyes went wide as we dropped our bikes in the front lawn and climbed the steps. A big brick two-story with dormer windows in the attic and white shutters, the house looked rather grand from the outside in spite of the weedy lawn and scraggly azalea bushes; I had never stopped to think what it might look like to someone who didn't live there. I led her into the living room.

Gretchen raked her eyes over the shelves of the Chippendale bookcase, which were filled with curios and knick-knacks Mattie had collected over the years and the blue willow china plates that had belonged to my grandfather's grandmother. She sank down onto the sofa and seemed afraid to touch anything.

"Look at that piano. You must be stinky rich," she said. I didn't know *what to say to that. Grandaddy had been rich once, but he was dead now, and I knew that Mattie worried about money. She didn't let on, but I'd heard her with her business manager at the Southern Opera Guild trying to figure out how to pay for musicians or new sets.*

"You can play it if you want," I offered.

Gretchen stood up, walked over to the piano, a Steinway that Mattie had brought with her from New York when she married Granddaddy, and tentatively touched one of the keys. Above the mantel there hung a big portrait of Mattie when she was 21 years old in a low cut red dress with her pearls encircling her long white neck. Her hair was swept back in something she called a chignon, and she smiled at the painter as if he were an adoring fan.

"Who's that?" Gretchen asked.

"That's me, darling," Mattie answered, walking in. "Can you believe an old woman like me ever looked like that? And who are you?"

Gretchen stood speechless. Mattie didn't look exactly like her portrait anymore but she was still gorgeous. She stood straight as a queen. Her skin looked like silk, and her auburn hair was set in waves around her head. But it was the way she always seemed ready to burst into laughter that made everyone around her go stupid with love.

"This is Gretchen, Mattie," I said.

"You sing?" Gretchen asked Mattie, looking at the music on the piano.

"I still manage to croak a little," Mattie said, and brushed a hand over the sheets of music. Then she sang in an operatic voice, "Why don't you girls go see if Miz Johnny has made any lemonade? I'm sure there are brownies in the kitchen."

"Wow," Gretchen said and then giggled. Maybe she wasn't familiar with opera singing.

We ate brownies, drank lemonade and sat outside in the hammock with a big pile of Supergirl comics. When it started to get dark, Gretchen handed me the comic books and said, "I got to go home. I will see you tomorrow, right?"

"Yeah."

"Meet me at the park where we were today. Tomorrow you can come to

my house."

I walked around front and watched her get on her bike and pedal away. I wondered if I really would see her tomorrow. I'd done all right without friends for most of my life. Mostly I preferred the company of adults, but Gretchen was different or else I was different, changed somehow. I had a queasy feeling in my throat that this was some sort of mean-spirited joke on the part of God to make me think I'd found a friend and then take her away from me. But the next day she was at the park and the day after that, too.

The closer I got, the more real my old life became, the more Zen, Jellybean, Tod and Dave started to shrink into the past. Crazy life. What was the point of meeting these people, making these friendships that felt so intense, so important at the time as if no one else ever mattered and now they were gone from my life just like Mattie was except that somehow Mattie seemed more real to me than ever? Sometimes, I'd swear that I could smell her perfume and it would make me remember the way she smothered me in her plump arms.

I glanced over at the man who looked like Jesus—or at least like all the paintings of Jesus because who the hell knew what Jesus really looked like? It's not like anyone took Polaroids of the guy.

"What do you want to listen to?" he asked. "Got some Airplane down there on the floor."

I leaned over and found the tape. "I love Surrealistic Pillow," I said.

He grinned. "You look like you'd be a Grace Slick fan."

"I look like a drowned cat," I said.

"Cold?" he asked.

"No, I'm warming up."

He took the tape and shoved it into the deck. I noticed he hadn't asked where I was going, and I hadn't volunteered. The rain was still falling, and the windshield wipers were slapping time as Janis would have said. Maybe this guy really was Jesus, and I'd gotten hit by a truck on the highway. Maybe I was dead. I wondered if he would take me to heaven or hell, but since he was Jesus, he must be taking me to heaven. Besides, I hadn't lived long enough to do anything to get to hell, which—if I did happen to be dead—really pissed me off.

"So where you headed?" he asked.

"I don't know," I said.

"Just along for the ride?"

"Well, I'm supposed to be going to Miami to live with my mother," I said, noticing how weird the words 'my mother' felt in my mouth.

"But . . .?"

"But I need to go to Augusta instead. I need to see Miz Johnny and Gretchen and find out if Wolfgang is okay and find out some other stuff too."

"All right," he said.

"All right?"

"I'll take you to Augusta and then on to Miami on one condition."

I looked over at him. Don't tell me Jesus is going to want to have sex with me, I thought, although he was a good-looking god for sure.

"I want to hear your story," he said.

"Oh." He wants some kind of confession from me, I figured, still thinking I might be dead after all. "All right."

"By the way, I'm Jackson Hartman," he said and held his right hand out to me, driving with his left. I shook it. It was definitely a real flesh and blood hand.

"Eli Burnes," I said.

"Do you?" he asked.

"Do I what?"

"Burn?"

I blushed and didn't answer.

33

He turned the tape deck off and I started telling him my story. I didn't leave out much. I told him about Wolfgang and my first kiss, told him how Mattie died without letting anyone know she was sick, told him about my dad getting busted and going to jail. I even told him about Zen and how I had thought he was the love of my life. Then I read him the letter that my mother wrote.

"What baby? What did she do that was so unforgivable?" he asked.

"I don't know. That's why I need to see Miz Johnny. She'll know what happened. Miz Johnny knows everything."

"What makes you think she'll tell you?"

I laughed. "Miz Johnny can't lie. I learned that when I was a little kid. But back then I didn't know what questions to ask. Now I do."

We had finally traveled through and out of the storm. The sky was a deep azure blue. By my Timex it was almost six o'clock and my stomach was starting to growl.

"Hungry?" he asked.

I nodded.

"Looks like there's a truck stop up ahead."

I suddenly got a creepy, scared feeling. There were still lots of places where a long-haired guy and a girl decorated in peace signs might get their heads bashed in. Maybe things were different where Jackson came from. Unfortunately, the peace sign was on a patch sewn to my jeans so I couldn't take it off. And I needed sustenance.

The van chugged off the highway and pulled into the truck stop—a small place, painted pink with a green neon sign: "Truckers welcome." Jackson got out and stretched. He was about six feet tall and had long, lanky arms. The air was warm, and I was just about dry. Jackson smiled at me. I didn't know a damn thing about him, but I felt like I'd known him all my life. He looked like he could defend himself (and me, I hoped) if the need arose so I followed him inside. Booths with plastic seats lined the walls, each one with its own little jukebox. After we sat down, I immediately started flipping through the pages of the juke box. The pages were behind a clear case and you used these metal levers to move the pages to see the titles of the songs. D4, for example, was something by Hank Williams. I had never heard of Hank Williams or Conway Twitty or Loretta Lynn.

"What kind of music is this?" I asked.

"Country and western," Jackson answered.

"Oh. I only know rock music," I said. Then I added, "And opera."

Jackson took out a dime and put it in the jukebox. He pushed D4—Hank Williams and I listened.

"Kinda like opera," I said. "Thematically at least."

He shook his head at my weirdness as a surly waitress with bleached white hair and two-inch black roots dropped some menus in front of us.

Jackson ordered the Brunswick stew and I got a hamburger. When she brought them over to us, she slung the plates on the table with her fleshy red hands.

"Thank you very much, ma'am," Jackson said and smiled that warm smile of his. I was ready to sling the food right back into her porky little face, but when Jackson smiled at her, I saw her grimace falter. She must have thought he looked like Jesus, too.

"You're welcome," she said grudgingly. Then she hesitated and asked, "Can I get you anything else?"

"Not for me, thanks. This looks delicious," he said.

"I would like some catsup," I said. She sneered at me, but reached over to another table, grabbed a bottle and then plopped it in front of me.

After she left, I took a bite of my burger.

"So, you know a lot about me," I said, before I had even swallowed my food. "Tell me about you."

He wasn't being any daintier than I was. Miz Johnny would have been appalled at our lack of manners, talking with food all stuffed in our mouths but we were both famished. Standing in the rain will do that to you. I didn't know what his excuse was.

"What do you want to know?" he asked.

"Where are you from?"

"Michigan. I'm a graduate student at the University of Michigan at Ann Arbor."

"Oh. Good protest school, right? What does that mean? Graduate student?"

"Means I don't have a lot of time for protesting. I've already got one degree and now I'm there to get my master's."

"You mean, you can just go to college forever?" I asked.

He shrugged. "Beats working."

He talked some more as we made quick work of our meal.

As we left our table, a lean trucker in big, brown, shit-kicker boots looked Jackson up and down and then whistled like he was whistling at a girl. Jackson bent close to my ear and whispered loudly, "He must like boys."

I felt the temperature of my blood plummet.

"What the hell did you say, punk?"

"Me?" Jackson said, whirling around. He had that warm friendly smile on his face, but I thought something dangerous flickered in his eyes for the tiniest fraction of a second. Then he seemed to think better of whatever he was going to say.

"I was just asking my sister here if she'd like some toys."

I nodded in agreement.

"Get the hell out of here, scumbag," the booted man said.

"Thank you. I think we will," Jackson said. Just then the waitress came up and glared at the man in the boots. She turned to us and said, "Y'all drive safe now."

"Yes, ma'am," Jackson left, leaving some money on the counter before we skee-daddled out of the door.

"You should have beat his scrawny old truck-driving ass," I said.

"You've got to know which fights to pick and which to walk away from, Eli," he said. "Besides, I'm a peace lovin' hippie freak, don't you know?"

"Well, so am I," I said. "But I'd still like to see that redneck get the shit beat out of him."

As we drove along the highway through the mountains, we saw purple and orange and yellow wildflowers clustered in the median and on the roadside.

"Lady Bird Johnson did that," he said.

"Did what?"

"The wildflowers. That was her big project. At the time it seemed kind of stupid," Jackson said. "I mean, there was so much else going on in the world. The war on poverty. The war in Vietnam."

I gazed out at the vibrating purple and orange blooms.

"It's nice," I said.

"Yeah. Now it doesn't seem like such a bad idea," he admitted. "I mean we've still got poverty and we've still got Vietnam, but at least there's something pretty to look at when you're taking a road trip."

We drove till dark. Jackson saw a sign for a state park and he pulled off the highway. He found a dirt lot near a river.

"This is some kind of boat launch," he said, pulling up close to the water and turning off the engine. "Come on. Grab those pillows in the back and let's look at the stars."

He put a sleeping bag on the roof of the van, and we climbed on top. I placed the pillows down and he shook out a quilt that he said he'd bought at some roadside store. We lay down on top of the quilt and stared up at the scattered stars. I held my hands over my chest and inhaled the night.

"Jackson, where are you going?"

"Key West."

"Why?"

"It was as far from Michigan as I could find when I looked at the map."

"Why do you want to get away from Michigan?"

"I'm running away."

"From what?" I could feel the warmth of his body beside mine.

"A chick."

"A chick?"

"My girlfriend."

"Oh."

"See those three stars in a line? That's Orion's belt. And those stars are his limbs. There's his dog, Sirius. The dog star."

"Dog star?" I asked.

"Yep, Orion is a hunter and all hunters have dogs."

Jackson shook out the quilt and laid it over us. It seemed very weird to be lying on top of a VW van with a guy I had only met that day, an older guy, and I didn't know what I should be doing. Should I get up and insist that one of us sleep in the van. But his breathing was soft and slow like someone about to fall asleep.

"Jackson," I said. "Why are you running away from your girlfriend?"

"She's pregnant," he said. Then he rolled over on his side and fell asleep.

34

I staggered sleepily into the dingy bathroom of the Gulf station. Man, what a grimy place—rust on the sink, muddy puddles on the floor. I peed very carefully, then washed my hands and searched my purse for my toothbrush and toothpaste. I scrubbed my armpits with a soapy paper towel and wondered where my deodorant was. I would have to buy some. Not much I could do for the rest of my body, but maybe I could take a shower at Miz Johnny's or Gretchen's when I got there.

When I came out of the bathroom, I found Jackson leaning against the van, holding a bag.

"Breakfast," he said with that smile that was so sweet it had managed to get a girl pregnant. I wondered what *she* was thinking right about now. Jackson handed me a pecan roll and an RC cola and I knew I was close to home. We got in the van and headed back toward the highway.

"You know what you are?" Jackson asked.

"No, but I wish I did," I said. We were listening to Bob Dylan's raspy voice sing (if you could call it that) about the joker and the thief. Mattie had liked the Beatles, probably because they were British, but I think Dylan's warbling voice would have felt like acid on her ear drums. Not being much of a singer myself, I kind of liked him.

"You're a picara," Jackson said.

"What is that?"

"A picara is a female version of a picaro. We learned this in my 18th century literature class."

"What are you studying at that place?" I asked.

"English," he said. "I'm a poet."

"A poet?" I had never met a real poet. "Do you write songs?"

"No, just poetry."

"Well, that doesn't tell me what a picara is."

"A picara or picaro is someone usually of questionable parentage who goes around having a series of adventures. They aren't bad, but they do manage to stir up trouble. Like Huck Finn."

"Well, that's me," I said, swigging some of the RC Cola and feeling better about life in general than I had in a couple of days.

"Tom Jones is another example."

I sat up, excited. "Tom Jones? You mean, 'What's new pussycat? Whoa-woh-woh-woh-woh-woh-woh.' That guy?"

"No, Tom Jones in the book called *Tom Jones*." Jackson gave me the single-eyebrow lift that said I was weird before pinning his eyes back to the road.

"There's a book about 'what's new, pussycat? Whoa-woh-woh-woh-woh-woh?' " I was laughing and kept singing that one line over and over.

"You really are young, aren't you?" Jackson commented. I just kept singing.

"Thomas Wolfe says you can't go home again," Jackson told me, moving the gear shift as we pulled onto the highway.

"Yeah, he's a good writer, I said. "I loved *Electric Kool-Aid Acid Test*."

Jackson gave me another funny look. "I was talking about a different Thomas Wolfe."

"I drank some electric kool-aid at a Dead concert," I said.

"Pretty far out, huh?" Jackson asked, rubbing his face. "Hey, maybe you should drive for a while."

"I can't drive," I said. "I don't even have my learner's permit."

"Do you really think that's important?"

You would think I had not recently witnessed my father in handcuffs for playing fast and loose with the law.

"Okay," I said. "You'll have to teach me."

We pulled off the highway and stopped at a gas station. I got behind the wheel and Jackson took my place. I moved the seat up closer to the pedals.

"Okay, you gotta let up slowly on the clutch," he said. "Slowly."

We lurched forward about five feet, and the van sputtered and died. I felt like an idiot. Driving always looked so easy.

"Try again. Press the clutch all the way in. Turn the key. Yeah. No, you're all right. It's in neutral. Now, slip it into first gear, ease up on the clutch and give her a little gas."

I made it about ten feet this time before stalling out.

"Shit," I said.

"Once more," Jackson said.

Damn it, I thought, any moron could drive a car. Why couldn't I? This time I let the clutch out really slowly and amazingly we were going forward.

"Okay, you gotta change gears, Eli," Jackson said.

"Why? It's going," I said. The road unfurled in front of me. I was the captain of this ship and the only limit was the Atlantic Ocean.

"I love driving," I said.

"Just don't kill us," Jackson responded, shaking his head.

"I won't. Tell me a story. Or a poem. Let me hear one of your poems," I said.

"First, you gotta push in the clutch and change gears."

I finally figured out how to change gears. We tunneled along a country road, moving up and down hills. I never knew the world could be so green and glorious as it was at that moment. My heart was as open as that engine running beneath us. We had the windows open and the air was pouring in over us like holy water.

"This is a poem," Jackson said. "This moment right here."

And he was right.

35

We reached the outskirts of Augusta in the afternoon. Jackson drove. I began to recognize the landmarks that we passed: the Krispy Kreme donut shop, an old factory, a smattering of stores, a post office. But the knowledge that Mattie was not in the city dribbled like liquid lead into my heart, and I suddenly felt so melancholy I could barely keep from sinking to the floor. I stuck my head out of the window hoping the hot wind would revive me, but it only irritated my eyes, causing them to water. What had driven me to come back here? This wasn't home. Webster Groves was my home now. Or it would be if I still had a house to go to.

"Hey, you okay?" Jackson asked. I brought my head back in and wiped the water from my eyes. I guess the sharp drop in my mood was obvious. I nodded.

"I miss Mattie," I admitted.

Jackson was silent. We were closing in on the town now. I saw a few buildings in the distance. That was our little downtown. Augusta wasn't a big city like St. Louis, and it wasn't a suburban satellite like Webster Groves, but it wasn't a little country town either. For most of my life it had been the royal realm. I felt happy and miserable at the same time, and it was making me feel a little carsick.

"Where to?"

I swallowed. I wanted to go by the opera house. I wanted to go by the house where I had grown up. I wanted to go by the playground where Gretchen and I hung out and where Wolfgang had kissed me by the swing set. But I was afraid I would turn into a blubbering baby.

"I guess we should go to Miz Johnny's house." I scratched my knee through the hole in my jeans.

"Where does she live?" Jackson asked.

"In the colored part of town," I said. Then I remembered what Willie would have said if he heard me say *colored*. "I mean, black part of town. Near the Baptist church."

I always had a good sense of direction. I had to develop one when I was a little kid because Mattie was all the time getting lost.

We rode through the streets of Miz Johnny's neighborhood, causing heads to turn as we passed. Not too many hippie vans came through here, I was pretty sure. A couple of black guys called out to us, but I didn't hear what they said.

"They think we're here looking for drugs," Jackson said.

"Drugs?" I asked.

"Yeah, it's the same up north. The races have finally come together to get high. This is our revolution," he said. It made me feel sad when he said that.

"There's her street," I said. Jackson made a sharp right and there it was: fourth house on the right. I recognized the gray shutters against the red brick and the planters on the porch that were full of pansies and daisies and mums. Miz Johnny's house looked so tidy from the outside. I imagined she was probably enjoying not having to take care of that big old house where Mattie and I had lived.

"Is she home?" Jackson asked. "I don't see a car."

"She doesn't drive," I told him, and it suddenly occurred to me that maybe showing up on her doorstep with a long-haired guy ten years older than me wasn't such a great idea. Sometimes I didn't think things through. But Jackson had already pulled into her driveway and turned off the engine. It was too late to ask him to just drop me off.

I got out and went to the front door with Jackson behind me. When Miz Johnny opened the door, she peered at me for a moment with a confused and frightened look on her face as if we were the Manson family come to call.

"Hey, Miz Johnny. It's me," I said.

"Oh, Lordy. Eli, that you, child?" she cried. She swung the door open and said, "Come in. Come in. You, too, young man. Come let me see you, girl. Lord, you're all grown up. What a pretty thing. Your Mattie would be proud. And who is this?"

"He's a friend," I said. "He offered to bring me here." I wasn't about to tell Miz Johnny that I'd thumbed a ride from a total stranger. She could still swat me and I'd let her.

She led us into her living room, and I was happy to see one of Mattie's brass lamps on the table by the sofa and her settee in the corner. Dad had begged her to take as much as she could so the bank wouldn't get it, but Miz Johnny said her house was too small for all that stuff. I hugged Miz Johnny and she hugged me back hard. Jackson stood with his hands in his pockets till Miz Johnny made him sit down and offered us some ice water, which we both agreed would be nice.

When we were all settled down, she tilted her head and asked me, "What are you doing here, Eli? Where's your daddy?"

"He's in prison, Miz Johnny," I answered her, holding the cold glass of ice water between my hands.

"In prison? Lord, no." Her mouth hung open in shock.

"It wasn't his fault. He thought he was helping to stop the war."

Miz Johnny shook her head.

"My William. The only one of my boys to go bad."

"He wasn't bad, I swear."

"Well, foolish then," she said. "You're right. He was never bad. But he always had bad luck."

Miz Johnny's smooth dark brown face was placid as she stared out over my head at something only she could see.

"Miz Johnny, I've got something to show you. It's a letter from my mother," I said.

"Your mother?" Miz Johnny took the letter from my outstretched hand. "Get my reading glasses for me. They're over there."

I got her glasses and she slowly poured over the contents of the letter, muttering now and then. She read it twice and then took off her glasses and gazed at me with her lips pursed.

"What does that mean about a baby, Miz Johnny? What did she do?" I edged closer to the edge of the hard chair and set the glass of water on a coaster.

Miz Johnny dropped the letter on the coffee table.

"Let's go to the cemetery. I got something to show you," she said.

I looked over at Jackson, who was stroking his chin thoughtfully.

"Sure," he said. "Let's go."

Miz Johnny sat in the front seat of the van, and I'm sure that was a sight: her all proper looking in her blue flowered dress, holding her alligator purse on her lap next to this long-haired Jesus man driving a certifiable freak-mobile. We pulled up to the cemetery, but Miz Johnny directed him around to the other side.

"They didn't used to let black folks and white folks rest together," she said. "Which is fine by me. I always said I had enough of 'em in life. No offense to you, Eli. Or your friend."

"None taken," Jackson said. I was so glad that he was cool. Maybe my dad had lousy luck, but I was a picara, and luck was my only saving grace.

The cemetery was beautiful and peaceful with mighty live oak trees strategically placed to spread wide swaths of shade. It covered several acres; a gorge with a little creek running through it dropped along one edge. A big fat blue jay flitted around branches above us and the thick grass shone a bright green color. It made me think of that psalm that Miz Johnny used to say to me: The Lord maketh me to lie down in green pastures.

We reached a section of the cemetery near the southwest corner. A black wrought-iron fence bordered the side.

"This is where my people are laid to rest," Miz Johnny said. "We bought this plot of land soon as we were freed. There's my grandpa and my mama. My husband Jacob who died in World War II. And this here is my grandbaby, Stephen."

I remembered that Mattie and I regularly brought Miz Johnny to the cemetery so she could tend to the graves of her family. Mattie and I would wander through the cemetery, looking at headstones and giggling over the strange names of olden times. Our favorite was Oramel and his wife who didn't even rate her own name being on the gravestone. Mattie would make up stories about the people and give them strange secrets that she made me promise never to tell. But we never talked about Miz Johnny or why sometimes she was so sad and quiet on the way home. I knelt down in the grass by the headstone for Miz Johnny's grandbaby. It read:

Baby Stephen
Born Oct. 3, 1957
Died Jan. 1, 1958

I wondered why Miz Johnny had brought us here and what this baby had to do with my mother. I gazed up at her, waiting.

"Stephen was my grandchild," Miz Johnny said. "And he was your brother. Your baby brother."

I turned back to the headstone and stared at the sparkling granite. What did she mean? How could her grandchild be my brother? I stood up and tried to catch my breath but it was running away from me fast. The blue jay came screeching past me as shock reverberated through my body. Jackson had politely wandered away, but now he was watching me curiously.

"I don't understand," I said. And yet I was remembering, remembering the tension between Willie and Miz Johnny's son at Mattie's funeral. Remembering how Mattie had said my mother almost got three of them killed.

"Your mama, Marguerite, fell in love with my son Randolph," Miz Johnny said. I couldn't stand up. I sank down on to the grass and stared at the baby's tombstone.

I folded my arms close in to my body. In spite of the heat, I felt chilled.

Miz Johnny continued, "Marguerite was a little wild. Everyone thought that marriage would settle her down some. Of course you were the reason she and William got married in the first place. When she got pregnant again, your grandpa and Miz Mathilda thought she'd gotten used to the idea of motherhood. But then Stephen came out with his milk chocolate skin and curly hair. Your grandaddy almost had a heart attack."

"The baby was Randolph's?" I asked.

"Yes," Miz Johnny said. "I raised him better than that. He shouldn't have been messing with a married woman, but she was beautiful and she swore she was in love with him. It's no excuse, I know."

I took a deep breath and gazed up at the clouds swimming over the blue sky.

"Is that when they went to the courts to try to get me?"

Miz Johnny knelt down next to me.

"Not at first, child. Your daddy said he was going to stay with Marguerite and raise Stephen like his own child, but Marguerite didn't love him any more. She ran him off, say she going to raise y'all without him. I know she wanted Randolph to come live with her, but the KKK already came by the house, threatening to lynch my boy. I sent him up north and told him don't come back. And Randolph didn't love her. He felt sorry for her, but he didn't love her. I'm not saying he was blameless in all this, but Marguerite hounded him something terrible."

I actually started to feel sorry for her, too.

"Your grandaddy sent your daddy off to college. That left your mama here with the two of you children. And her Jack Daniels. That's what she liked to drink. Miz Mattie goes over there one day and finds you 'bout naked and hungry. Marguerite drunk on the couch. The baby was with a sitter."

That part I knew from what Mattie had told me.

"It wasn't no problem then for them to get the judge to let them take you away. The baby, he was still nursing, and they weren't blood relatives to Stephen. I hoped Marguerite would do right by him. I didn't have no money to hire a lawyer and try to get him from her though Miz Mattie promised she'd help me when Stephen was weaned."

Miz Johnny sighed and her shoulders sagged.

"What happened to him?" I asked.

"She got drunk as hell on New Year's Eve. The next day when she was supposed to be giving him a bath, she fell asleep. No one knows what exactly happened. She liked to go crazy when she woke up and found him drowned."

Jackson had come over to us. He put an arm around Miz Johnny's shoulders and she didn't seem to mind, which surprised me.

"So then she left town?" I asked.

Miz Johnny stood up and clutched her purse.

"Hmmph. They was gonna throw her in jail for letting that baby die, but your granddaddy couldn't stand the disgrace. Miz Mattie goes over there and gives her money, makes her swear she'll never come back and says they'll make sure the police don't come after her if she promises never to come back and never to try to see you. So she took the money and left town. No one ever heard from her again."

"Until now," I said.

"Until now."

36

We drove back to Miz Johnny's house.

"Come on in and have something to eat," she said.

I had been hoping she would say that. Cleo was an okay cook, but nothing compared to Miz Johnny. And discovering our deep, dark family secret had done nothing to dull my appetite. To tell you the truth, I wasn't sure yet how I felt about this new information. I had never known what it was like to have a brother close to my age so how could I miss him? I did miss Jake and Turtle, but they were little kids and cute when they weren't terrorizing someone. I tried to imagine what Stephen would look like. He'd be 13 now, two years younger than me.

We sat at a scarred wooden table in the kitchen. Miz Johnny got out some pot roast, mayonnaise, lettuce and bread for sandwiches. She scooped macaroni salad onto plates for us and poured two large glasses of iced tea. I couldn't help feeling happy for that moment. I felt sure I'd have plenty of time for grief later.

Jackson was leaning forward on the table, asking Miz Johnny about her sons.

"Herb owns two barbershops now, and he's doing real well with that. And Randolph started working for an insurance company up north when he left here. He's been one of their top salesmen for years now. Say they going to make him vice president. And he's married to a real nice girl. They got three children."

I remembered one time when Miz Johnny left us to go visit

Randolph.

Mattie and I took Miz Johnny to the train station. Miz Johnny always sat in the back seat when Mattie drove her anywhere. She said that it was the proper way to do things in Augusta and wouldn't sit in the front seat. When Mattie tried to insist, Miz Johnny just gave her a look and Mattie always backed down.

When we got to the train station, Miz Johnny, who had rheumatism in her knees and generally moved at a slow, grand pace, practically hopped up and down in excitement when it was time to board the train.

"Have a good time, darling," Mattie called to her, completely forgetting the rules of protocol. It was 1968, after all, and we were in the heart of the South, and that heart had some rotten pathways in it. But Mattie insisted on hugging Miz Johnny good-bye. She brushed tears from her eyes as Miz Johnny waved before disappearing into the train car.

Miz Johnny was still talking about her sons. She spoke in the old black dialect of the South, so different from the way Zen and his family spoke, which was basically ordinary Midwest white except that Zen was of the hippie class which had a language all its own. Miz Johnny could talk proper when she wanted to, but that meant she probably didn't like or trust whomever she was talking to. I was glad that she didn't do that to Jackson even though he was bonafide Yankee and might not perfectly understand her. Since he was a poet, I figured he could hear the beauty in her speech and appreciate it the way I did.

"Miz Johnny?" I asked after stuffing myself at her delectable table. "Would you mind if I took a shower?"

"Child, go on ahead. I was gonna say you was smelling a little ripe. 'Course you always did." Then she chuckled.

I wanted to sink under the table, but Miz Johnny kept right on, "Your friend can help me out here. I got a loose board on this back porch needs mending. Give him something to do to earn his dinner."

I got some clean clothes from my duffel bag and took a steaming shower, washing my hair with a bar of Ivory soap because I had no shampoo. As I dried off, I could hear Miz Johnny outside, telling Jackson about the trip Randolph had won for her back before Mattie died and how she had been waited on hand and feet by white people. She chuckled again; that was one of her favorite stories.

"The world is changing. Do you know that the two most famous Augustans are both Negro?" she asked.

"No, who are they?" Jackson asked.

"James Brown and Jessye Norman." I remembered once going to the black church with Mattie to hear Miss Norman sing. Miz Johnny asked Mattie if she'd help Jessye become an opera singer. And Mattie had said, "Darling, she doesn't need any help from me. She's a world class talent already. A natural."

Then I heard Jackson say, "I'm black and I'm proud."

I looked out the window to see Miz Johnny's expression. She was staring at him perplexed.

"James Brown's song. I'm black and I'm proud."

Miz Johnny laughed. "I never minded being colored. I guess I don't mind being 'black' either."

I never remembered Miz Johnny laughing and chuckling the way she did now. Maybe working as a maid had been a kind of enslavement and we just hadn't realized it.

Yes, things had changed. I thought about how Zen and I had been together for the past six months. Sure, people looked at us, but no one said anything about it. But my mother had nearly gotten a black man hung by the neck when she fell in love with him. Things had changed, I realized, because people like Jeremiah, Willie, Cleo, Smoke, Janet, Sassy, Val, David and so many others sacrificed to make it that way. They joined those clubs that seemed so crazy to me, they marched, they shouted, they had sit ins. They stood together, black and white in defiance of society. Now my dad was in jail, but as I looked at his life I wasn't sure that his efforts had been wasted. He only wanted to make society better, to make it more caring, to make it more just. Maybe they shouldn't have been selling pot, but Dad wouldn't have been involved if he thought pot hurt anyone.

My mom, I decided as I slipped on my jeans and a fresh t-shirt, had been just as bad as Mattie said to dump my dad like she did. I looked at myself in the mirror. I didn't look much like my dad. I wondered if I looked like her besides in my eyes? She was a cheater and even worse, a baby killer, I thought. Why did she have to be my mother? And where could I go, if not to her?

Miz Johnny insisted that Jackson take advantage of a free shower, too. Miz Johnny didn't like people to be unhygienic. Cleanliness *was* Godliness in her rule book. He didn't take much persuading to get in there with a fresh towel. While he was in the shower, Miz Johnny said she had something to give me.

She led me into her bedroom. On the blue wall next to her closet, I saw some framed black and white pictures of her family—sons and wives and grandchildren—and then I noticed among them a picture of Mattie from *La Boheme*, her eyes thick with eyeliner, her wig hanging seductively over one shoulder—that twinkling in her eyes that seemed to let you in on the joke. I felt like she was looking directly into me, prodding my heart with one of her long fake fingernails.

"She was a good one," Miz Johnny said from behind me. I nodded.

"Now look here, Eli, I got something for you," she said, bending down in front of a mahogany chest of drawers. She opened the bottom drawer of her bureau and pulled out a dark blue velvet bag. She straightened and gave it to me without telling me what was inside.

I opened it and dumped the contents into my hand. There across my pink palm lay Mattie's pearls. They were smooth and lustrous. I couldn't believe I was holding them in my own hand. Mattie's pearls. They hadn't been sold or stolen after all.

"I was scared they was going to sell them off in the auction."

I tried not to go all operatic on Miz Johnny and so I dropped them back into the bag and looked at her. Her eyes were happy, and I smiled.

"Thank you so much, Miz Johnny. Thank you."

Then I thought of something. I went back into the living room and dug through my duffel bag. I found the reel of Mattie's songs still in its little box.

"Would you keep this safe for me, Miz Johnny?" I asked and handed her the reel.

Miz Johnny's brown eyes met mine as we held onto the reel together.

37

"You okay?" Jackson asked as we drove away from Miz Johnny's.

I nodded and then said, "Well, it's kinda weird to find out you have a dead brother."

"Yeah, that's some pretty heavy news," he agreed. He pulled his hair into a ponytail at the stoplight and then asked, "You ready to head down to Miami?"

I stared out at the traffic passing by. I felt uncomfortable asking for another favor. I figured he was going to get tired of dealing with me after a while, but I couldn't leave without seeing Gretchen. And I wasn't entirely convinced that going to my mother was such a good idea. She'd already killed one kid.

"Would you mind if we went by Gretchen's apartment first? I want to see her really bad."

"You sure you're not wanting to see her brother?" he asked with a smile.

"He's in Vietnam. I guess I didn't tell you that part," I said.

"Bummer. Look, how about I drop you off at her place while I go get an oil change and buy some parts for the van?"

"Okay."

I directed him to the apartment building where Gretchen lived. It was about fifteen minutes away and in the meantime I realized I had gotten so caught up in my life with Jellybean, Tod, Dave and Zen that I had forgotten about my old friends. I had not written to Gretchen in months. We passed my old school with its yellow walls and the park and turned the corner by the Minit Market. Everything looked the same though somehow older and dingier. We pulled into the parking lot of the apartment building and I counted up the three stories and saw the balcony where Gretchen and I had sometimes slept on summer nights.

Then someone came out and stood on the balcony. I watched a cigarette tumble from her fingers to the ground. It looked like Lana, Gretchen's older sister. But there was something so odd, so languid about the way she moved I couldn't be sure.

Jackson drove away. I realized as soon as the van was out of sight that my duffel bag was inside. What if he didn't come back? He was probably sick of being a babysitter. That nice-guy routine of his was probably an act. Then I wondered why I acted like such a dipshit around him. I wondered how it was that I felt comfortable with him and totally weird at the same time?

Once inside I bypassed the treacherous elevator and climbed the stairs to Gretchen's floor. There were six apartments on each floor, and hers was near the stairs. I knocked on the door and waited. I had never stopped to think what I would do if she weren't there. I looked around and noticed the walls had been painted but the cheap landlord must have only used one coat of paint because I could still the word "Pussy" faded but still visible halfway down the hallway.

I knocked on the door again and waited some more. I heard a television going—sounded like soap opera music—but still no one answered the door, so I sat down on the steps and waited and thought. I didn't want to think, but the thoughts were like flies buzzing around me and one thought was worse than a fly, much worse. I kept imagining my brother, lying in the bathtub, bloated and tiny.

I sat on the steps, the leftover smell of someone's dinner from the night before lingering overhead. I imagined Marguerite waking up from her drunken dreaming to find her baby boy. The boy in my imagination was Turtle. I knew what something like that would do to Cleo, the utter horror, the howl of pain that would come from some deep region in her gut. And I thought about what it would do to the rest of us: Jake, me and Dad.

We trip along innocently enough through our lives, not imagining what might be waiting for us in the next year, month, day or minute. Miz Johnny had often worried about me, saying I swam in deep waters. And here I was again.

Then the door at the bottom of the steps opened and footsteps came slowly up from the depths. Before she turned the corner into visibility I knew it was Gretchen. When she got to the landing below me, she looked up.

"Holy shit," she said. "What are you doing here?"

I grinned and stood up.

"Came to see you, Kraut-girl. What you think?"

Gretchen laughed a big wide open laugh. She had large lips and large teeth and a warm watery laugh. When she got to the top step of the landing, she looked appraisingly at me.

"Shit, Eli," she said, placing a hand on her hip. "You've got boobs!"

"Yeah, I know," I said, embarrassed, and laughed.

"Why are you waiting out on the steps?"

"I knocked, but no one answered. I thought I saw Lana on the balcony earlier, and the TV is going. Maybe she's asleep."

"That bitch isn't sleeping. She's nodding off," Gretchen said angrily and went and banged on the door.

I had no idea what 'nodding off' meant or why Gretchen was so pissed. Lana had always been a temperamental shrew, but we had learned never to expect anything less.

"Open the door, you junkie bitch!" Gretchen yelled and banged incessantly on the door until it finally swung open and Lana stood there, weighing in at maybe 100 pounds and staring at the two of us with eyes so glassy you could drink from them. Lana scratched her face and gazed at me.

"Hi, Lana," I said.

"Oh, it's you," she said in a voice like sawdust. "Again."

"She hasn't been around here in a year, stupid," Gretchen said, brushing past her older sister. I followed a little sheepishly. Lana had terrorized us in the past, but she didn't appear to be much of a terrorizer these days. She went back to the same plaid yellow and brown couch I remembered from before and sat down in front of a small black and white TV. Her eyelids lowered to half-mast and she seemed to forget we were there. I stared at her while Gretchen went to the bathroom.

A few minutes later Gretchen came out and we naturally drifted out to the balcony. The heat surrounded us like the belly of a whale and we sank down to hang our legs between the bars like we did when we were kids, hoping for a piece of wind to come by.

"What happened to your color TV?" I asked, remember how proud they had been of that thing. I liked coming over to watch with Gretchen considering the fact that Mattie would never buy a TV. She thought it was somehow a sign of the lower classes to own a big TV.

"That junkie bitch sold it for drugs," Gretchen said bitterly.

I glanced through the glass door at Lana. She was bent over so that her head seemed to be resting just a few inches above her knees. I'd never seen a real junkie before. This was turning into an interesting day—interesting in a way I could have lived without.

"What did your parents say?" I asked.

"Nothing. They just went out and bought that cheap piece of shit, figuring she couldn't get any money for it. They're scared of losing her. They've already lost one kid." Gretchen leaned her face into the bars, sniffled and then shook her head. I felt a slowly creeping numbness move through my body. I didn't want to ask what she meant. I didn't want to know. Suddenly the bars that kept us from pitching to the ground didn't seem strong enough to hold me. I moved back and the words came out of my mouth of their own accord.

"What happened to Wolfgang?"

Gretchen shrugged. "They say MIA. Missing in action. So we

don't know. Maybe he's dead. Maybe he's a prisoner. Maybe he's gone AWOL and is shacked up with some Jap chick somewhere. That's what I keep hoping."

I squeezed my hands together tight. It was too much for one day. I felt like I was made of clay and someone was pouring water on me. I didn't tell Gretchen that I had met some veterans back in Webster Groves. I didn't tell her how angry they were, how Stump had said if he could have figured out any possible way to desert he would have been gone in the first week. But there was nowhere to run and definitely nowhere to hide.

"I'm sorry," I said. "Wolfgang means a lot to me."

"Yeah, me too," Gretchen said. "I wish he would have made it to Canada."

"I brought something of his with me," I said and reached into my purse.

"What is it?"

"A book." I handed her Wolfgang's beat up old copy of Nietzsche. "Keep it here for him. For when he gets home."

"Thanks," she said.

I looked down in the parking lot below. Some kids were chasing another kid down, probably to beat the crap out of him. It was the nature of the beast.

"Let's talk about something else," Gretchen said. "This shit makes me sad."

"Okay. My mom wrote me a letter," I told her.

"Your mom? I thought your mom was dead."

"Apparently not," I answered.

Gretchen smiled. "You talk so funny, Eli. I miss you. Do you have a boyfriend?"

I pulled an errant toenail and said, "Yes. His name is Zen."

"What's he look like?"

"Tall. Cute. Lots of hair," I said.

"Sounds nice. I'm going with Marvin again."

"No," I said, unable to hide my disgust.

"He's not so bad. Are you still a virgin?"

I hesitated. Gretchen was always ahead of me in these matters, and once again, I sensed she would already be there.

"Technically, yes," I said. "Zen doesn't want me to get pregnant, but we do other stuff until I can get to a doctor and get on the pill." I intentionally left 'other stuff' to her imagination which I knew would be so much more lurid than the truth.

"I don't care if I get pregnant. Marvin and I fuck a lot," she said and giggled.

I was starting to wish that Jackson would hurry up and get back, at the same time praying he hadn't left me for good and wondering if Fallene or Carl or one of Mattie's other opera singing friends would take me in if he had.

"Remember when Marvin and I got in that fight and Wolfgang showed up and ran him off," I said.

"Yeah. Hey, I got a picture of Wolfgang he sent us from Vietnam."

She went inside and came out with the snapshot. Wolfgang's hair was all cut off and he wasn't smiling in the picture. He stood in front of a tent with his arms crossed and a look on his face that reminded me of Jake when he had a bad toothache and had to go to the dentist. We talked about Wolfgang and about Marvin, and I told her about the band I had formed with Dave, Tod and Jellybean. Then we reminisced about things we did as little kids, and finally I heard a horn beeping. I looked down and saw Jackson get out of his van and wave up at me.

"Is dat your boyfriend?" Gretchen asked, reverting to her German accent.

"Yeah," I said.

"Damn. He's old," she said.

"Twenty-five," I said.

"Damn," she repeated. "Way to go, bitch."

38

I had been to Florida once with Mattie when I was little. She had wanted to hear the London Philharmonic and didn't realize it was Spring Break, so all the motels were full. We drove around the city completely lost and wondering where we would sleep when we saw this big white house with a veranda and white rockers and there was a sign out front that said, "The Magnolia." We went inside and asked for a room for the night. The old guy behind the desk looked at us very strangely, but then with this mysterious smile he gave us a key to a room and told us the pool was available to use until eight p.m. I hadn't seen a pool from the street, but we went to our rooms and put on our bathing suits and followed his directions to the pool. When we found it, we were amazed. It was a huge blue rectangle and no one else was using it. The day was hot and bright and we couldn't believe we had this big pool all to ourselves. Mattie and I swam around. We played lifeguard and she let me save her from downing several times. Occasionally some old person walked by and smiled at us. We knew lots of old people came to Florida and lots of teenagers for spring break. We were the odd ones—a middle aged lady and a kid. Some of them thought Mattie was my mother, which made her happy.

After a while we got dressed and went to the concert. It wasn't till the next day as we sat in a dining room full of white-haired women and bald old men that we realized we had strayed into some sort of old folks home. The old people kept smiling at us and coming over to our table to visit with us as if we were celebrities or long-lost family.

"Life was like that with Mattie—whatever happened to us always seemed to be an adventure."

Jackson seemed to like that story a lot. I asked him if he would put it in a poem and he said, maybe.

We crossed the line into Florida and were traveling along highway 90 when we came to the Suwannee River.

"Let's stop," I begged. I didn't even know the Suwannee was a real river. I thought it was just some song we learned in school.

Jackson didn't mind stopping. We found a spot off the highway and I got in the back of the van and changed into my shorts. Jackson put on a pair of cut-offs. It was summer so there was still plenty of light. All the strange sorrows of the day just lifted off me, blown into the sky by the evening breezes.

Jackson and I waded into the water. It was a deep brown color and I could see a current in the middle. I loved rivers. Jackson splashed me and I splashed him back. For someone in his 20s he was more like a big kid. The laughter felt so good. I wasn't thinking about Wolfgang or Miz Johnny or the impending meeting with my mother. I felt something inside me lurching up from the grave. Like the way a plant suddenly gets green and perky when you finally get around to watering it.

A mockingbird in a tree was chirping away, and Jackson suddenly started spouting poetry at it: "Hail to thee, blithe spirit! Bird thou never wert, that from heaven or near it, pourest thy full heart in profuse strains of unpremeditated art."

"Did you write that?" I asked.

"No, a poet named Percy Shelley wrote it in the 1800s."

"Oh, I like it."

"He was a romantic." Jackson grinned at me. I dug my feet into the wet sand.

"Aren't all poets?" I asked. "I thought that was what romance was all about—poetry and flowers and stuff."

"No," he said. "Allen Ginsburg writes about how screwed up America is. He's one of the beat poets."

"My dad would like him, I'm sure."

"Are you happy to finally be meeting your mother?" Jackson asked, as we sat on the sand. I scooted closer to him, trying to capture his body warmth. I liked being close to him. I wasn't falling in love or anything stupid like that. But he was strong and looked like Jesus and was so nice. I was learning that bodies wanted to be close to other bodies. I wanted to touch him, to run my hand along the length of his hairy leg. And I wanted him to touch me. This kind of wanting seemed wrong. This kind of wanting belonged to boyfriends and girlfriends, but there it was like the water gently lapping the banks of the river or the sand scratching the back of my legs or the sunlight bleeding from the sky. He put an arm around me, and I wondered if he felt the same way.

"Jackson," I said. "I don't want to go to my mother's."

"What do you want to do?"

"Why can't I just travel around with you?"

"Aw, man," he said, his arm slipping off my shoulder as he leaned back. "No way, Eli."

"Why not?" I pleaded.

"Because you're underage. It's bad enough I'm even driving you down to Miami. If I kept you, I'd be like a kidnapper or something. They'd put me in the cell next to your old man."

I didn't like that he used the information I had told him about my father that way, but I wasn't ready to give up either.

"But I wouldn't tell anyone. Please? Come on, we have fun together," I said.

"No. It's not possible. I don't even know what I'm going to do next. I mean, I've been thinking a lot about Chris."

"Chris?" I asked. Who was Chris?

"And the baby."

"Oh."

"I just—I don't know what to do, but I think . . ." he didn't finish the statement. He didn't have to. He was going to go back to his pregnant girlfriend. He tried to act like some kind of free spirit, but he wasn't. He was just another working man in hippie disguise. For a moment, I hated him.

He pushed a strand of hair from my face and said, "Are you hungry?"

I was starving but I shook my head and stared at the passing clouds.

"Well, I am. Come on. Let's go get some dinner. My treat. We can spend the night in that campground we passed by the highway."

39

After we ate, I went to the bathroom and changed back into my jeans. Then I walked out of the restaurant and headed toward the van. Jackson wasn't inside the van. I glanced around the parking lot and saw a tall figure leaning into a pay phone intently as if he were trying to reach through the phone. Jackson was talking to *her*. He was definitely going back to her. Well, good for him, I thought. It's bad when a guy abandons his pregnant girlfriend, free spirit or no free spirit. And yet I didn't know why she couldn't just go somewhere and have an abortion. They were legal in New York, weren't they? Or Puerto Rico? But who was I to stand in the way of true love? What was he to me anyway? He was just some stranger who picked me up and gave me a ride. He'd been useful but there were plenty of cars and plenty of drivers. I could travel all over the country if I wanted to, never staying in one place very long. I had my thumb. What else did I need besides my duffel bag? I opened the sliding side door on the VW bus and pulled my bag out. I felt strong and determined. I was getting away from this phony Jesus right now.

I glanced over at the pay phone. His back was to me. Maybe the conversation wasn't going his way. Too bad, so sad. I hitched the duffel bag handles over my shoulder and strode purposefully toward the road. Before I even got to the pavement, a car slowed down. It was a big yellow Cadillac, looked like a Fleetwood and since I liked Fleetwood Mac, I figured this was a good sign. The passenger window opened automatically which was pretty cool, and a man in his 30s or maybe 40s with short sandy brown hair and round, almost circular eyes leaned over and asked if I needed a ride.

I hesitated. I was pretty sure this straight-arrow dude wouldn't have much to offer in the way of scintillating conversations. He wasn't going to have a lot of information on Allen Ginsburg or any of those other dudes that Jackson had expounded upon. He looked like a salesman with a wife and 2.5 kids at home, waiting for him. He looked as interesting as a Twinkie.

Then I heard Jackson call out my name: "Eli!"

I opened the door to the Caddy and got in.

"So where you headed?" old round eyes asked.

"South," I answered, thinking that seemed a reasonable answer.

"Well, I'm going as far as Orlando. Will that work for you?"

"That's fine," I said. I wasn't all that hip on geography but I knew it was somewhere in Florida.

The man asked me my name. I lied and said, "Tina." I didn't owe anyone the truth. Maybe I'd never be Eli Burnes again. I could have a different name for every ride I got, a different history for every driver.

"Hello, Tina. I'm Rick," he said.

We were on the interstate, flying south. Maybe because I had just lied, it seemed as if he did too, as if his name couldn't possibly be Rick. He looked like a Simon or a Howard. But in this brave new world, all lies were the truth.

"Why are you hitch-hiking? Don't you know it's dangerous?" he asked.

"It's been okay, so far," I said.

He seemed to get the message that I didn't feel like telling him my whole life story. So he started rambling on about his work selling automobile parts. He was the distributor for some national manufacturer and blah, blah, blah. Eventually he found a radio station playing easy listening music.

"Do you like this music?" he asked.

"It's egregious," I answered, echoing Mattie's sentiments about anything she didn't like.

"Yeah," he smiled. "I like it, too."

I began to desperately miss Jackson's 8-track tape player with its funny clicking noises as it changed tracks, even the way songs were interrupted from one track to another. I thought that I could be listening to the Doors right about now—"when you're stra-ange." But Jackson was probably already headed north back to Chris and her belly full of baby. She would probably be a good mother, probably wouldn't get drunk and fall asleep while the baby was in the bathtub.

I couldn't say why I was feeling so huffy. It's not like Jackson treated me any other way than a friend. That's when I started feeling sick to my stomach. He had treated me like a friend, a good friend. He had driven me from one place to another without complaining and I had snuck off without even saying good-bye.

Tears began to trickle from my eyes. They were tears for baby Stephen, tears for Wolfgang and even tears for Lana. I stared out the window so he wouldn't see me crying. I reached into my pocket to find Mattie's pearls for comfort. But my pocket was empty. My heart lurched. I reached into my other pocket. It was empty, too.

"Looking for something?" Rick asked.

"I thought I had some gum," I said. "Guess not." I squelched the panic rising in my chest. I knew exactly what had happened. I had put my money and the pearls in the glove compartment of Jackson's van. And yes, I had left them there in my hot-headed haste, which I had to admit was driven by a stupid, juvenile case of jealousy.

I leaned my head back. The pearls were gone. My money was gone. Even if I got out now and started hitching back, how would I ever find him? It had been at least two hours since I left him at the restaurant. How could this day get any worse? I had found out I had a dead brother; Wolfgang, my first love, was lost and maybe dead in the jungles of Vietnam and my best friend was probably going to wind up pregnant while her sister committed a slow suicide with drugs, and I had lost Mattie's precious pearls. I couldn't bring myself to care what happened next. We rode silently through the blackening night. Rain began to fall, drumming the roof of the car and sliding like glassy snakes along the windows. Mercifully, we'd driven out of range of the easy listening station. I shut my eyes and listened to the metronome beat of the windshield wipers and for a brief moment I was a little girl again, falling to sleep under the grand piano while Carl played and Mattie and Fallene sang.

I startled awake. I sat up quickly, trying to get my bearings.

"You fell asleep," he said. What was his name?

I rubbed my eyes. The car was stopped at a stop sign at the end of an exit ramp.

"Where are we?"

"Near Orlando. I can't drive any farther in this rain. I was hoping you'd keep me company but you went and fell asleep."

"It's been a long day," I said.

I saw a gas station up head and a sign for a Budget Motel just beyond the gas station. The rain was falling hard, slapping the ground, drops bouncing off the hood of the car.

"Tina, I can't drive any more tonight. I'm going to get a motel room. If I keep driving, I'm likely to fall asleep, drive off the road and kill us both. Do you want me to let you out at this gas station and maybe you can find another ride?"

I looked out at the pouring rain and at the dark gas station.

"It's closed," I said.

"Oh, you're right. Well, if you want to, you can stay with me and I'll take you as far as Orlando, bright and early in the morning. We can get a room with two beds. I need to call my wife and let her know where I am. Boy, I'm tired."

I was tired, too, more tired than I could ever remember feeling. I did not want to stay in a motel room with this man. That was an awful idea, but it was raining so hard, like the rain pellets were stabbing the earth. And it was so dark and I had no idea where I was.

"I'm not used to staying in a motel room with a total stranger," he said. "You're not carrying a knife or a gun or anything, are you?"

"Of course not," I said. Wasn't it obvious? I was a hippie. We didn't believe in guns and violence. I was wearing a peace sign, for crying out loud.

"Well, how about we get a few hours of shut eye and then get back on the road?"

"Okay," I said. If you're going to live on the road, I realized, you have to be willing to accept what the road brings you. Besides, what choice did I have?

Rick went into the office of the motel and came back a few minutes later. If I'd had my money I could have gotten my own room. What an idiot I had been. He drove the car down to the end of the row of motel rooms.

"I got us the room on the end. It'll be nice and quiet that way," he said.

He went in ahead of me while I got out my duffel bag. The rain had let up some and I thought about offering to drive us the rest of the way while he slept. If I could drive Jackson's van, surely I could drive that Cadillac. When I came in the room, he was on the telephone. On the table was a big ugly ceramic lamp.

"Yes, honey, I love you, too. Give a big hug to Ronnie for me," he said. The room was awful. It smelled like mold and I wondered why a man who drove a Cadillac couldn't afford better than this. I set down my duffel bag and went in to use the bathroom.

This, I realized, as I sat down to pee, was a huge mistake. Something just didn't feel right. Maybe I should just walk back to the highway. Or I could ask him if I could sleep in the car. Maybe there was some shelter behind the gas station? He might be insulted but so what? I washed my hands and splashed water on my face and then dried off using a measly threadbare towel. They weren't kidding when they called this the budget motel.

I came out of the bathroom. A blow to the side of my head sent me sprawling to the floor. He rolled me over on my back and sat down on my hips. I tried to shove him off me, but he grasped my throat with one hand and started pawing at my t-shirt with the other. I tried to grab him and then he hit me hard.

"Don't move and I won't hurt you, Tina," he said in a breathless voice. "Tina. I won't hurt you, Tina. I promise."

Sweat dribbled down his face, and his clammy fingers had pulled up my shirt. He was pulling at my bra, pulling and tugging and then touching me, grabbing me, squeezing. I didn't care if he hit me again, I hauled off and punched his nose.

"Damn it," he screamed and he started choking me. Everything that I had come to believe about the inherent goodness in the world dissolved. He slid off me but kept his hand on my throat as he tried pulling my pants down. "I said I won't hurt you. I'm not going to hurt you," he whispered, blood trickling down his chin. And all along I knew without the tiniest dust mote of doubt that he was going to kill me.

40

His face had transformed from the bland salesman into something alien, eyes with no more depth than a dime, skin like jelly and lips that alternated between grinning and grimacing. Some part of me seemed to have left the building and was merely watching events unfold on a movie screen far away. But another part of me was sick with grief and guilt that I had been so stupid, so gullible, such a fool. He was trying to yank my jeans off my hips but it's not so easy to strip someone with one hand. I resisted as much as possible, all the while waiting for his hand to ease up on my throat.

Then he let loose of my neck and I started screaming, but at the same time he was shoving something—a handkerchief?—in my mouth. The scream became stifled, stuck in my hollow throat. I grunted and bucked. Don't give up, I thought. Don't give up.

But he was stronger than I was, and soon he had hold of both of my hands. He slipped his belt over them and bound them together as if in prayer.

He smiled briefly.

"Gotcha now," he said. "Hog-tied."

He stood up and pulled me up by the belt and by the hair. Tears sprang to my eyes from the pain. He threw me on to the bed and rolled me on my back. I tried to yank the handkerchief from my mouth and he slapped me hard. Bastard, I thought. I would kill him before this was over.

He pulled my jeans and my underwear off, exposing my body. For a moment he just stared. Then I kicked at him. He shoved me back down on the bed and held his fist above my face.

"Tommy, get over here right now!" a voice called from the walkway outside.

There was a thud against the door. The monster's eyes grew wide as he looked at the door. Then he said to me, "Move and I'll beat the living shit out of you."

He quickly bounded over to the TV set and turned it on loud. Then he sidled over to the door and looked out the peephole.

I glanced up at the curtains. Just beyond the window there were people. Bad things were always hidden from view. Then my body acted on its own. I flung myself toward the window and with my fingers I grasped the cheap cloth and pulled with all my body weight. The salesman turned to me in shock as I fell, ripping the curtains from the rod above. Then I yanked the cloth from my mouth.

But there was no one on the walkway. It was empty. I sat up and screamed, and then he was on me again with his hand over my mouth. As I fell back toward the bed, I saw a boy about ten years old rise up from the ground and stare into the window. A moment later a man and a woman were next to him. The salesman looked up and saw them. We all stared at each other.

Then the man outside began banging on the window angrily. The woman was trying to cover the boy's eyes. The salesman shoved himself off my body. He threw open the door.

"Mind your own business," he said. "This is my girlfriend."

And I screamed. Piercingly. My scream was a living thing that clawed at the walls and stung the air.

The next thing I knew he was grabbing his keys. The man from outside was yelling at him, something about police and telling him to get the hell away from me. I just lay on the bed, nearly naked, whispering, "Thank you, thank you, thank you."

They were a couple on their way home from visiting a

grandmother. The boy, Tommy, had been bent over tying his shoe when I pulled the curtain down. The woman came in and undid the belt knotted around my hands and helped me get dressed while the man tried to get through to someone on the motel phone.

"The office is closed now," he said. "This phone doesn't even work."

"Please don't call the police," I said.

"You're just going to let that guy go?" the woman asked.

"If the police come, they'll take me away. I need to get to Miami. I need to find my mother."

"Honey, we're heading north," the woman said. "We're not going to Miami."

"Could you take me north then?" I asked. "My friend was going to spend the night in a campground a little ways north of here. He can take me. I was stupid and got mad at him."

"We were planning on spending the night here," the man said.

"The office is closed anyway, John," his wife said. "Why not take her and we'll stay at another motel after we drop her off."

I looked at John. His long face had an expression that was confused and annoyed. Tommy was still staring at me. I finally looked at him. A good-looking boy. Hell, he looked like an angel to me.

"Thank you for saving me," I said.

He didn't answer but looked down at the ground. Then he said, "She can ride in the back seat with me."

We pulled into the campground near the highway that Jackson had mentioned earlier. I held my breath, praying he hadn't decided to turn around and drive home already. There was his van. Off in the corner.

I thanked my good samaritans, and promised them I would be all right. They looked doubtful, but they had done enough for me.

"Bye, girl," Tommy said.

"Bye, Tommy."

I shut the door. They pulled down the gravel drive and out of the campground. I turned and knocked on the van door.

"I'm gonna take you to a hospital," Jackson said as we started driving south. He'd said he couldn't sleep now, and I didn't want to sleep either.

"No," I croaked. "I'll be okay." I knew that if the two of us showed up at a hospital in the middle of the night, we would probably wind up in jail. I was an under-aged girl, he was a hippie man, and who would believe that a nice salesman in a Cadillac had tried to rape me.

"Why did you leave me?" he asked.

I shook my head. I couldn't answer. I couldn't apologize. We rode in silence for a long time. I didn't even ask where we were going. I was like someone made of rubber. I felt thick with fear and something I couldn't name, some sense of deserving the worst, some awareness of loss, and as we rode silently through the night I seemed to remember crying for someone who wasn't there, someone I wanted with a crazed, desperate yearning. I leaned my head against the window and let the steady hum of the wheels against the road lull me to sleep.

"Where are we?" I asked, waking as the van came to a stop and the engine shut off.

"A parking lot at the beach," Jackson answered. "Come on."

We got out of the van. I had no idea what time it was. Jackson brought the sleeping bag and we walked down the sandy beach, the ocean mumbling beside us. I'd never heard the ocean before. I had only seen it through Mattie's car window that time when we came to see the London Philharmonic.

"Want to go for a swim?" Jackson asked.

The idea came as a complete surprise, but just as swiftly it seemed like the most right and perfect thing to do. We were away from any hotels and Jackson was already stripping down to his underwear. I dug through my duffel bag and found an old one piece bathing suit and changed awkwardly under my t-shirt while he turned his back to me. I had decided to put what little faith I had left on the line. I did not think Jackson had saved me only to hurt me. He was in the water ahead of me; the water was surprisingly warm, not quite like bath water but almost irresistible. The waves were mild and white foam spilled out of the inky black water. All around us tiny neon green flecks swirled.

"What is this?" I asked.

"I think it's called phosphorescence," he said. "I've never seen it before."

Then he splashed me, and I splashed him back. And incredibly, I was laughing. I dove under the water and felt it scrubbing the salesman's fingerprints off me. I realized I was thrilled to be alive. He hadn't killed me. He wanted to, I was sure of it, but I had prevailed like a comic book hero. He couldn't touch me. He couldn't touch me. I had found myself worth fighting for.

Jackson and I laughed and swam around for a while. I remembered how I had thought he was Jesus at first, and now I was seeing Jesus in his underwear in the Atlantic Ocean and I laughed even harder. And I loved him. Not like a girlfriend or a daughter or a sister. I just loved him, and I realized it was myself I loved.

After we got out and put on our clothes over our wet bodies, we huddled together on the sleeping bag. Jackson kept his arms around me and asked more than once, "You okay now?"

"Yes," I told him.

We lay down together, him still holding onto me.

"Thank you," I said.

"Shh. You don't have anything to thank me for."

So I didn't say anything else, and I dozed off, feeling his strong arms holding me.

When Jackson nudged me awake, a pink glow glistened on the horizon.

"Sunrise," Jackson whispered as if talking loud might make the sun change its mind. Orange ribbons streamed across the sky while lavender strips of clouds mottled the far edge. Then the tiniest red crescent appeared directly in front of us. Jackson looked into my eyes. His lips were parted. I thought that it would be so easy. I could give to him what that poor sick fool in the Cadillac had wanted to take from me, and maybe I should—at least it would be my choice. It would be the story I would have for the rest of my life, the loss of my virginity at sunrise to a man who looked like Jesus. And I could tell by the pained expression on his face that he would succumb if I wanted him to. I had worn him down.

My fingers stroked his leg.

"Do you want to go to the van?" he asked, his voice like sandpaper.

I looked up at him and nodded. We stood up and left the sleeping bag on the ground. He seemed to loom over me. Yes, I would do it. I would get this over once and for all. As we walked toward the van, I heard an old song switch on the radio inside my head. Gary Puckett and the Union Gap: "Girl, You'll be a Woman Soon." Gretchen and I had loved that song, dreaming of the day we would give up our girlness and become womaned by some hunk of a guy. But as I crossed the lot bumping into Jackson's lanky body and got close to the van, a thought occurred to me. I was going to meet my mother soon. It didn't seem fair that she would meet me as a woman. It didn't seem right to deprive her of the chance to meet her little girl.

"Jackson," I said. "I don't want to do it."

He didn't say anything for a moment. I wasn't sure if he was mad, disappointed or relieved.

"That's okay," he said finally with a shrug. We turned around and went back to the beach where the sun was creeping up the morning ladder. We sat back down on the sleeping bag, not touching each other this time. Maybe I had just been too scared or maybe this just wasn't the right day.

The sunrise happened too quickly. I wanted to hang on to every moment, wanted to revel in the psychedelic colors and savor them. But in a short while the sun pulled back its orange and pink tentacles; it was a red ball rapidly on its way to becoming the familiar yellow-white orb it always was.

"Ready?" Jackson asked.

I nodded.

"How far is it to Miami?" I asked.

"About two or three hours, I guess."

We pulled up the sleeping bag and shook off the sand. I was sticky from the salt water but figured we could stop at a gas station and I could wash off. We trudged through the soft sand to the parking lot and then both of us stopped short. A cop car was pulled next to the van and an officer was peering into the front window. The words on the cop car were: Melbourne City Police. So that's where we were. Some little beach town in Florida that I had never heard of before. I was suddenly so grateful for my change of heart, and I was pretty sure that Jackson was thanking his stars, too.

"What do we do?" I asked.

"We play it cool," Jackson said quietly.

He walked toward the van with me reluctantly following. So close, I thought, and now I was going to wind up in some Florida juvenile facility. I thought about turning and running like mad. I had to trust that Jackson knew what he was doing. But I didn't. The only thing that would save me now was luck, and I figured I had run out of luck when I got in that Cadillac.

"Morning, Officer," Jackson said.

The cop looked at him and then looked me up and down.

"This your van?" the cop asked.

"Yes, sir," Jackson said.

"Got a registration for it?"

Jackson opened the van and started digging through the glove box for the registration. The cop stared at me.

"How old are you?" he asked.

"Eighteen," I said.

The cop looked at Jackson's registration and looked at me.

"You don't look eighteen," he said.

"Well, I am," I said and gazed at my reflection in his sunglasses.

He handed Jackson the registration taking a few extra moments to peer into the van. Then he checked his watch and said, "You're lucky. My shift ends in ten minutes and I want to go home. But I'm gonna tell the fellas back at the station to come by here, and if you're still here they're gonna haul your asses back to the station and find out a little bit more about the both of you."

Then the cop got in his cruiser and drove away.

Jackson wasted no time finding the highway and leaving Melbourne behind.

41

We stopped at a gas station in Miami and bought a map. Jackson studied the map while I went into the bathroom and tried to make myself presentable. There were two purple bruises on my neck, but Jackson had given me his blue bandana and said I could have it. I tied it around my neck and you couldn't see the bruises anymore. I ran cold water through my hair and brushed the salt and sand out of it as well as I could. Would she know me, I wondered.

"I think I found it," Jackson said when I got back in the van. He pointed to a tiny line between the highway and the ocean. Then he started up the van and we drove into the bright day.

Miami was a revelation to me. I'd never seen such trees or flowers. We got off the highway and I marveled at the thick jungly plants in people's yards. There was a scent in the air like some kind of ambrosia.

"This is a weird place," I said.

"Yeah."

We found the street, and Jackson turned down it, slowly looking at addresses. The houses were small and neat. I stared, stunned at the sight of a strange tree that looked like it was several hundred trees all bound up together. In another yard enormous red flowers bobbed in the breeze. The rest of Florida had seemed so grubby compared to this. The houses, which were white or tan plaster houses—not brick or wood, were spruced up with bright green lawns that gleamed under a thick layer of sunlight like new varnish.

Jackson slowed down, peering at the addresses. Then he pulled into the driveway of one of the houses and said, "This is it."

I looked at the house and noticed bright blue shutters on either side of the windows; a ceramic pink flamingo stood on the stoop beside the front door. White stepping stones lead to the door. I put the pearls into my pocket and got out of the van. Jackson followed me, carrying my duffel bag. I looked back at him as I climbed up the steps, holding onto a black wrought iron rail.

Jackson nodded at the door and set the duffel bag down beside me. A green lizard scooted past me. I noticed a tiny brown sparrow pecking in the dirt by the steps.

"This is it," Jackson said. "The end of the road."

Then he kissed me on the cheek and turned to leave.

I rang the doorbell. I couldn't exactly breathe. I looked back at Jackson; he was walking to the van. A sound came from inside, someone coming toward the door.

Jackson got in his van, and the engine whined as it came to life. The dark asphalt of the road lay like a strip of night sky in front of the house. The end of the road? The road never ended as far as I could tell. I waved good-bye to Jackson as he backed the van out of the driveway, but he didn't drive off yet.

I heard the door unlock. In my head I had practiced introducing myself. It had not occurred to me that I would not need to, that Cleo would have called up to find out if I'd made it all right and that Miz Johnny would have followed suit, assuring her that I was on my way. I had not known that if I hadn't shown up when I did that my description would be going out to every police station in the southeast. I did not know that the long arms of love were reaching out from all around me, probably from heaven as well.

I only knew that when the door opened, my mother knew me, and I knew her.

"Hi," I said.

Before I could say anything, she pushed open the screen door and reached for my face and then drew back as if she were afraid I might not be real.

"It's you," she said softly.

"It's me," I answered.

The van's engine shifted gears as Jackson drove away. Then I picked up my duffel bag and went inside.

Acknowledgements

First I want to thank my brother John, a father-figure, a spiritual teacher, a political warrior and friend, and also my brother David for his stories about growing up in the south. Thanks to Camille, John the fourth and Sharen for a wonderful year growing up together in Webster Groves. Thanks to my mother for guidance about singing and operas and for giving me a childhood in the theatre; to my daughter, Celina, for reminding me of the joy of adolescence. Deep gratitude once again to my friend Pamela Ball, whose balance of comments and encouragement made this a much better book. Thanks as well to my friend Vicki Moreland for comments and suggestions and to Tamara Titus for nudging me in the right direction. I would also like to acknowledge Cathy Wilkerson for helping me understand the dynamics of the anti-war movement in a personal interview as well as in her great memoir on the Weather Underground, *Flying Close to the Sun*. Thanks also to Sheila Ortiz Taylor for introducing me to a variety of literary picaras and picaros. Many thanks to Mary Jennings Sluder for sharing her opera stories with me. Much thanks to the angel Sylvia Zusa who helped take care of my mother. Much gratitude to Joe Taylor for giving this one the perfect home. Thanks to everyone involved in the Kaleidoscope Arts Camp at Winthrop University and to the students there (and Annamarie!) who asked every year: "When are you going to finish the book?" Here it is finally—thank you for your enthusiasm, your applause and your inspiration.

Pat MacEnulty is the author three previous novels and a short collection. She lives in Charlotte, North Carolina, where she teaches writing, literature and communications at Johnson & Wales University. She is the recipient of several grants and awards and has provided creative writing workshops around the U.S. and in Mexico. Her website is www.patmacenulty.com.